ALSO BY KATHRYN K. MURPHY

The Secret About Time

Simply A Matter of Time

I0587777

A TOUCH OF HEALING

A SISTERS IN SIRENS NOVEL

KATHRYN K. MURPHY

Caraway Press

ISBN-13: 978-1-7332463-5-4

Cover design by Caroline Johnson

Cover images © Stocksy

For Carson

CHAPTER 1

The call came just before ten in the evening.

Laura Burton ran through the station toward the ambulance as the dispatch squawked again, echoing up to the rafters of the rescue squad's garage. She jumped inside the ambulance and slammed the passenger door shut just as it pulled out of the station into the hot, hazy night. Jordan, the other paramedic on shift, put the pedal to the floor while punching the siren and lights that would wake the dead, not that the sound bothered her anymore after eight years on the job. Her phone buzzed, and she pulled it out to check the name before answering.

She held on as Jordan raced over the hills in the inky black dark. She knew they weren't far. After a few tense minutes of racing through the dark August night, orange light in the Montana sky rose like a dawn of death, above the dense pine trees on the old, winding country road. The flash of blue and red lights flickered on the trees ahead of them as they approached the curve.

Jordan careened around the bend, revealing a towering blaze through shards of tortured guardrail. The brakes squealed in agony as they pulled up next to the fire truck and Sergeant Ashleigh Myers's cruiser. Laura didn't wait. She jumped out, pulling her bag over her shoulder and running toward the valley, down the hill.

Fifty yards away, the blaze lit up the valley like a sun radiating from a crumpled ball of expensive metal at the core of the fire, laughing in the face of whatever the firefighter was trying to douse it with. Laura couldn't tell if it was Megan or not but hoped to God she was there or coming from the truck. Megan was as pink and bubbly as bubble gum, but damn, she was fierce and knew how to do her job.

Laura sprinted toward a figure she recognized as Ash twenty yards away, now crouched above a body fresh from the flames of hell. The rumpled body lay limp.

Laura slid down to kneel, the gravel from the nearby river biting into her knees through the uniform. The wave of heat hit her face, illuminating the man in front of her in an eerie flickering glow. She felt for a pulse and leaned in to listen for signs of breathing. Both were faint. The body reeked of alcohol.

"What do we know?" she asked, ripping open the seal on an oxygen mask.

Sergeant Ashleigh Myers's voice cut to the chase like the cold, precise edge of a knife, short and sharp to compete with the sirens. "Megan got him out. I'm thinking DUI. There were some bottles on the floor. I'll need to come to the hospital and get a blood alcohol. He likely has injuries to limbs and severe burns—the car's electric. Batteries keep catching. Went off the road and rolled down into the valley."

The fire made everything orange. Laura couldn't see Megan but knew her best friend and the station's top firefighter would be right in the thick of the flames.

Laura pulled out a penlight and shined it onto the hands and face to see the damage before applying the mask. A quick glance told her his hands had gotten the worst bit. One side of his face was red and swollen—

Her breath left her in a rush. "Oh my God."

Jordan slid down next to her with the backboard.

"How bad? Third?"

"No, first, maybe second on the hands. But...I know him."

The older paramedic muscled over, ready to jump in as he always had whenever she needed as long as they had worked together. "Here, I'll take over if you can't—"

"No, I got this. Patient has a history of drug and alcohol abuse." She steadied her voice and got a grip.

"Laura, are you sure?" Ash's voice was softer now. They had been tight friends since Laura had become a paramedic.

"No, seriously. I'm okay."

Ash touched her arm until she looked up. Her violet eyes searched Laura's in the dark for a quick second before nodding once. Laura both understood and didn't mind. Friends in their line of work had to look out for each other.

Now was not the time to get all up in her head. Laura rattled off what she knew, while they went into the seamless dance of triage they had trained for. Each pulled out equipment before the other could ask for it. Muscle memory pulled Laura through the movements, as they secured him on the board.

"Stable for transport? Med evac?" Ash asked, her hands on her hips, badge glinting in the firelight.

"Blood pressure looks okay. We're taking him now."

"I'll follow."

Laura didn't turn around to face her friend, but finished securing the head restraints, careful of the burns on his face, and latched onto the handrails of the backboard.

"One, two, three." Jordan counted as they hauled what was left of Carter Price up and marched toward the hill he had rolled his car down. Laura caught a glimpse of the fire Megan and the other firefighters were beating into submission. The flames reached for the stars above with a frantic desperation. For no reason in particular, Laura remembered her mom's wood stove. She had always thought fire looked like hands of the damned in hell reaching for benediction. The light stretched their shadows, unnatural in the dark night, on the mountain prairie.

The weight in her hands brought Laura back to the present. The large body overwhelmed the backboard, his feet reaching the edge of the board. Carter had always been tall, but the years had changed a lot. He wasn't the same wiry kid from high school. Even unconscious and injured, Carter had a powerful presence, no doubt—what was once skin and bones was now muscle. Laura felt her arms start to give when another firefighter came up behind and helped take up the weight. They trudged up the steep climb, stumbling in the dark on the spot where Carter's tires had plowed through grass, carving their own path.

The ambulance looked like a literal heaven with the pure white light pouring out of the back windows. The team loaded Carter inside, and Laura hopped in the back while Jordan slammed the doors shut. Laura heard the driver's door close in the front, and with a lurch, they sped off into the dark.

In the clear light, she rechecked vitals and assessed the damage again. It looked and felt like a fracture, but she couldn't be sure. Heart rate was elevated, but that could be a mix of adrenaline, pain, or whatever else Carter was pumping in his body these days. His face was banged up. Laura pulled out a burn kit and applied the medicine to his hands and face.

He looked familiar enough as the guy from around town back in high school. What had it been? Fifteen years now?

God. Why was he back? He hadn't wanted to see her ever again, and now they were locked in a steel box together. Had he gotten a say, she was probably the last person he'd want to see again after things had finished between them.

"Well, guess what, buddy? Welcome home," she said in a dry voice.

Had he been any other patient, Laura would've done her thing, alone with no witnesses. They were a small town with a small team of paramedics only going out two at a time, which meant she was alone in the back.

She had learned of her ability through pets and skinned knees when she was young. She didn't know how she came by it, but all she needed to do was close her eyes and visualize the wounds healing to make it so. She'd been practicing for years and had helped everyone she'd ever reached on the job, provided they weren't already gone. She knew she couldn't help the deceased. Burns, bones, and gashes, she could kickstart the healing process before carefully wrapping them in bandages. By the time the nurses at the hospital removed all the coverings, the wounds were well on their way and past the point of infection.

It was the same with heart attacks and pneumonia. Laura would remove her gloves, place her arms on the patient, and with her eyes closed, visualize the heart beating and the lungs draining of fluid and filling with sweet air. Some cases were more complicated, but she did what she could in the short drive between the pick-up and the hospital.

So why wasn't she doing it now?

His face was the one she still thought about from high school. Laura bit her lip and pulled off her gloves before placing them on his skin, tacky with sweat from the fire. Even he deserved help and her oath required it, but something about this situation felt different.

She drew in a breath and tried to calm her mind. The

warm glow from within didn't come. She tried to imagine his burns healing, the broken bone knitting together, but nothing happened. Laura tried again, mimicking everything she had done for years. Starting to panic, she placed her hands on his chest and gave it another go with a steadying breath. A faint tinge of warmth came from within, but the reaction wasn't the same. Why wasn't it working?

The ambulance lurched over the speed bump, welcoming them to the hospital parking lot. She felt the ambulance make the turn into the emergency department entrance, right before the squeal of brakes signaled the end of their journey. A team of nurses opened the doors and pulled Carter Price out of her hands. Jordan followed, giving the notes.

Melanie Harrigan, who went by Mel and was Laura's favorite ER nurse, hustled over in her blue scrubs. "This my car crash? Laura?"

What had gone wrong? She sat there, searching his features, trying to think of why this might be happening.

Mel waved her hand in Laura's face. She snapped out of it and nodded. "Sorry. Burns, broken leg, and a few gashes. Patient has a history of drugs and alcohol."

Mel's eyebrows furrowed as she reached up to play with her wedding band, which was strung on a necklace. "You tested him?"

"No, I knew him a long time ago." Mel's eyebrows rose. Laura kept going. "Ash needs blood alcohol; she'll be here soon. Thinks DUI."

"Gotcha. Fire out?"

"Not when I left. Megan was there though."

"It's electric," Ash said, coming up from behind them. "Those fires can go on for days. All those battery cells."

"Damn technology," Mel said with a shake of her head.

"I'll get your test results, but you know I don't like to do a blood draw on my patient when they're unconscious."

"Supreme court authorized it, and I've already called in for a warrant."

"Yeah, well, the warrant would make me feel better, but I still don't have to like it," Mel said over her shoulder as she walked through the sliding doors into the golden light of the emergency waiting room.

"He'll fail," Ash said to Laura. "He reeked of alcohol."

"If he's anything like I knew in high school, yeah, he will. Big time."

"I'll read him his rights when he wakes up. When do you think that'll be?"

"He might wake up tomorrow, but he'll be out of it for a few days."

"Surgery?"

Laura shook her head. "I don't think so. I'm thinking a fracture."

Ash nodded and folded her arms. Her badge glinted in the light from the ambulance behind them. "You okay?"

"Me? Yeah, why?"

Ash's violet eyes stared at her close enough that Laura felt like Ash was looking into her soul. "Tough running a call with someone you knew."

Laura shrugged. "Business as usual. It was a long time ago."

"How'd you know him?"

Laura paused. There was no getting around it. Ash could sniff out a liar, and they had been friends for years. Lying would just piss Ash off. "We dated for a bit."

"Ouch."

"Yeah."

"You sure you're okay?" Ash asked with a pointed look.

"Yeah, rock steady. I mean, come on. Do I look like I'm that type?"

Ash shrugged. "Old feelings—"

"Yeah, no. There's no need to worry about that."

Ash didn't look convinced. "If you're sure."

"Yep. I am."

"Where's Holden? You don't normally run nights."

"Yeah, I got a sitter for tonight. He's good though. All about Elmo right now, and Mickey Mouse."

"Good. I needed ideas for his birthday."

"Yeah, I gotta plan that." Laura pulled her hair into a knot on top of her head. Birthday parties seemed to creep up out of nowhere. Did she need to invite kids? His birthday was just over a week out. Crap.

"Yep. Good luck with that. Let me know if there's anything I can do," Ash said, heading to her cruiser.

"What about that whole hating kids thing?" Laura leaned back against the bumper, still waiting for Jordan to come back.

"Holden's not a kid. He's my lil dude. Totally different," she said, walking backwards. "I'm going to call you later. Check in."

Laura would've told her not to bother, but Ash wasn't going to listen anyway. Instead, Laura waved her off. With a salute, Ash walked back to her cruiser, no doubt to call the cops who had stayed behind at the scene of the crash, leaving Laura to wonder what had gone wrong.

CHAPTER 2

The next morning, Laura handed over the last two bills she had in her wallet to the sitter who was still stretching from waking up on the couch in her two-bedroom apartment.

"Holden slept great after dinner and hasn't moved an inch. Maybe you'll get a chance to lie down," Jessica whispered.

"Here's hoping. Thanks for giving him a bath."

Jessica waved her hand. "No worries. Happy to do it. Let me know when you need me next. I'm going out of town for the next two weeks, so I won't be available for a bit."

"I'll work around it," Laura said before thanking her again and shutting the door into sweet silence.

The apartment wasn't great, but it wasn't the worst thing ever. Located in the basement of another townhome, though the two were disconnected—Laura never would've gone for someone having a door to her space—the apartment's plan was well laid out and felt roomy inside.

Just enough for her and Holden, who thankfully was sleeping in for once.

Laura threw the lock and pulled off her shoes, placing them down without making a sound. She would kill for a shower after her shift, but that wasn't going to happen with how loud the spray was in the bathroom. Holden had the hearing of a bat hunting at night and the ability to go from zero to sixty in the time it took for her to turn on his bedroom light.

There wasn't a true foyer to speak of—the door of the apartment opened right into the living room. A hallway led toward the bathroom and two bedrooms, which were surprisingly large. Through the living room was a dining area and then a standard apartment kitchen complete with a washer and dryer. She had loved the layout so much that she was willing to overlook the thin, worn carpet and the cabinets, which probably weren't real wood and definitely weren't on trend.

Overall, the price had been right, and that's what mattered these days and ever since her husband of a year and a half, John, had walked out never to be heard from again. Laura had found out she was pregnant two weeks later.

The court had granted her a divorce by default after an expensive lawyer, every reasonable attempt to find him, and a waiting period. Full custody of Holden was awarded to her, terminating any parental rights should John ever reappear—not that she thought that would happen. At first, she had searched and waited, but now presumed him dead. Laura hadn't found her life to be much different without him. It hadn't been a happy marriage and was heading toward divorce when he had walked out of their small rental house for the last time.

Laura walked to the kitchen and started a pot of coffee before walking the nine steps it took to get back to the living room and sit in her recliner, the one splurge item she had bought herself as a new mom. It had come in handy on those seemingly endless nights when Holden would only sleep against her.

She rested her eyes and listened to the sound of the Mr. Coffee heating the water. The knots in her shoulders relaxed from the tension they had been clinging to. She didn't have to work tonight, which meant she could catch up on sleep after her night shift. The remainder of the evening hadn't been memorable, with only a couple of calls that required a vitals check but no transport, but that wasn't what had occupied her mind.

It was Carter. The man who had broken her heart back in high school. In hindsight, he was probably the reason John had seemed like such a great idea at the time, and look how that had turned out.

But it wasn't bad memories that were weighing on her. Why hadn't it worked?

Laura had been able to heal everyone she touched except for Holden and her mom. Given they were both family, she had written them off as exceptions. After all, there wasn't a handbook to this kind of thing, and she had never told another soul, especially since Holden had come along. A single mom with a low credit score who started talking about X-Men powers was not going to have many fans in Child Protective Services.

Besides, she wasn't hurting anyone. It was the opposite. She quietly helped everyone she could, while scouring the internet late at night to find anyone else like her who didn't live in a fantasy novel.

While Laura didn't know where or how or why, she had based her life's work around it, wanting to become a doctor or nurse since she was a young girl. Money, timing, and an unexpected baby had all been bumps in the road, but some day she would make it.

The coffee pot beeped, but Laura's eyelids didn't flinch. Just a little rest was all she needed before—

"Mama!"

Laura drew in a breath and tried to open eyes that somehow had become magnetic and were now glued to each other.

"MAMA! I pooped!"

That got her up.

She headed for the hallway lined with pictures of Holden, pulling her uniform top off and slipping out of her pants before reaching for an old cotton robe in the bathroom. God, her clothes still smelled like smoke from the crash. Carter's crash. She needed a shower and a long sleep before she gave him any more thought.

"Coming, baby!" she said, cinching the tie tight around her middle.

"Mama! I'm taking off my Pull-Up!"

"Here I am! Good morning—" The smell almost knocked her flat.

"It's a big poop," Holden said, his brown eyes growing wide to clue her in to the magnitude of what awaited her.

Five minutes later, after she had cleaned and dressed Holden for the day, Laura carted out the carnage that was the diaper in a grocery bag she threw on the outdoor step to take to the dumpster later. Armed with enough room spray to blind a moose, Laura ushered Holden out toward the living room, much to his cranky dismay, and let loose.

"Alright, let's get you some cereal."

"'Eerios! 'Eerios!" His cheeks jiggled as he ran over to the table and scrambled up into his chair.

Laura laughed at Holden's interpretation of the name just like always, imagining him going into marketing to rebrand the General Mills cereal for Halloween. She poured out the honey-nut circles into Holden's favorite Mickey Mouse bowl before getting the matching spoon, one of his Christmas presents.

She sat with a cup of coffee and watched the toddler dig into his breakfast with delight, milk dribbling down his chin.

"How was last night with Ms. Jessica? Did you have fun?"

Holden looked up, chubby cheeks filled to the brim like an adorable chipmunk. He bobbed his head. "We watched Mickey Mouse and she made mac and cheese!"

"Was that yummy?" Laura asked, taking a sip of her coffee.

Holden shrugged, his new favorite move. "A little bit. I wanted ice cream." He shrugged again bringing his shoulders clear up to his ears.

Laura chuckled and was going to ask another question when the phone rang.

"Hang on, sweetie." She jogged over to the door and dug in her purse to find her cell, tossing out pouches of apple-sauce, fruit snacks, and a couple of used tissues. She really needed to clean this out. Finally, her hands touched the glass.

"Hi, this is Rachel. I'm calling from Goldvein Apartments, LLC. Is this Laura Burton?

Holden let out a shriek in the background and started banging his spoon on the table to what could be considered the alternative rock ABCs.

"Holden! Inside voice! Sorry, This is Laura Burton. Let me just go into another room." She slipped into her bedroom and shut the door behind her, which only managed to muffle the LMNOP. "How can I help you?"

"I'm calling because we have not received your rent payment—"

Laura strained her neck back and up toward the builder-grade, so-called white, painted ceiling as she mouthed a very bad word.

"I'm so sorry. Time just got away from me. I'll drop off a check this afternoon."

"Mama?"

"Hang on, buddy, Mama's on the phone," Laura called through the hollow core door. "Hi, are you still there?" she said into the phone.

"Yes, ma'am. I also wanted to let you know—"

"MAMA!" On the other side of the door, a chubby fist rapped on the wood before shaking the doorknob with persistent determination.

"Just a second, buddy! Listen, I'm sorry this isn't a great time. Can I call you back?"

"Ms. Burton, it's urgent that I speak with you today."

"MAMAMAMAMAMA!"

A loud phwap shook the door, followed by another—the sound of an empty Mickey Mouse bowl colliding with the wall, no doubt spraying bits of milk everywhere.

"I understand. I'll call you back." Laura didn't wait for a goodbye before she ended the call.

She tossed the phone on her unmade bed, thought better of it, and plugged it into the charger, before raking a hand across her hair and pulling it down her face. Not great for skincare, but hey, who cared at this point? How could she forget the rent again?

"Okay, baby!" she said, opening the door. "What's wrong?"

"Quick! Come see!" His chubby little feet covered with Goofy socks sprinted back toward the dining table before he clambered back up to his seat. "See!" He gasped and puffed out his cheeks, pointing at an apparently offensive speck of milk almost invisible to the naked eye. "I spilled!"

Laura drew in a long breath. "It's okay... Mistakes happen. The important thing is,"—she reached over to the counter and grabbed a dish towel—"that we clean up."

Ten minutes later, breakfast was all cleaned up, and the melodic and maddening sounds of Mickey Mouse cartoons filled the apartment. Holden had proceeded to dump his basket of toys all over the floor. Combined, the toys and the show bought Laura twenty-two minutes of peace where he could entertain himself.

Laura grabbed her phone of its charger and eased into the recliner, holding a now-cool-to-the-touch cup of coffee. She could get up and microwave it, but she was so exhausted, she was just going to call it iced coffee to make herself feel fancy.

"Miska Mouska Mickey Mouse!" Holden called out right on cue to the TV, while holding a car in one hand and his stuffed rabbit in the other.

In lieu of a coaster, Laura set the mug down on the worn Disney World planning book and felt her eyelids droop. A little rest wouldn't hurt anything.

The phone buzzed again in her lap.

Laura didn't move. They could leave a message. She'd drop off the rent check after she took a shower, to hopefully wear out Holden for a nap. A long walk should be enough to get him to go down. She wouldn't take the stroller.

"GRAMMA!"

Holden grabbed the phone with her mom's picture on the screen and slapped his little hand across it like he had seen Laura do many times.

"No, no, no. Bring it here."

Holden grinned like he was going to make a run for it, but Laura faked him out and grabbed the phone, hitting the green button to answer. Her mom's face popped into view with a smile.

"Hey—"

"Hi, Gramma! Look, Donald's so silly!"

"Is that Donald Duck? I know him! He is silly. Did you put some money in the bank that I gave you?"

Holden's eyes got big and serious. "Yeah, five monies!" He held up his chubby little hand, splayed out to show all five fingers.

"Hey, Mom."

"Hey, yourself. Just wanted to call and check in."

"We're okay here. How are things going over there?" Laura sat up in the chair and considered Holden for a moment, who was still transfixed on whatever puzzle was on the screen. "Therapy still going well?"

"Slow, but I don't want to talk about that."

"You sound good." One of the many things Laura had to be grateful for was that her mom hadn't lost much of her speech with the stroke. She had been moved to a rehabilitation facility in Missoula about a six-hour drive away.

"Thanks, been trying to keep busy. I spoke with your aunt earlier."

Laura listened to her mom fill her in on all of the goings-on in the family and the rehab facility, which she had chosen because it was one of the best in the state. She and Holden missed seeing her but made the drive as often as they could and called with video almost every other day. Thank God for technology. It was so much easier than a twelve-hour round-trip drive with a three-year-old. Hopefully, her mom would be out soon, and they could all be back in the same town again.

It wasn't that her mom didn't know how to live on her own. She was still sharp as ever and had been doing as well as could be expected after Laura's dad died of cancer a few years ago, but the stroke had taken the left side of her body, and walking, dressing, and even making a cup of coffee was all a slow battle to relearn. The goal was that her mom would get a small apartment and become independent again, but there was a long road ahead of her.

Laura listened and chatted until Holden's show ended, promising to call tomorrow.

"It's overrrr!" Holden announced as she disconnected the call.

"How about we clean up and go on an adventure outside?" Laura said, leaning forward.

"YAY!"

Thirty minutes later, they were walking hand-in-hand outside around the apartment complex in the sun. Montana was known for fierce winters, but the summers were gorgeous. Blue skies that went on for miles were a welcome reward after the heaps of snow.

They took the long route, avoiding the community playground on their way to the leasing office. Laura figured business before play. Once Holden was on the slide, there was no coming off without a tantrum.

"Good morning," she said as they walked into the cheery office where Rachel sat behind a counter. They were about the same age, but Rachel put way more thought into her clothes. Today she wore a maxi dress and jean jacket. Her hair was always the same, pulled back into a tight bun.

"Good morning! Hey, Holden. What do you have there? A flower?"

Holden clutched a dandelion in his fist and hid behind Laura's legs, peeking out and giggling.

"I see you!" Rachel pulled out a basket filled with lollipops and glanced at Laura, who nodded. After a short-lived game of peek-a-boo, Holden had an orange sucker balancing out the flower.

"I'm just here to drop off my rent check. Sorry about that. Time just got away from me," she said, passing it over.

"Thank you," Rachel said as she reached over. "I'm glad you came because I have some paperwork for you."

"Rent going up? Isn't it time to renew my lease?" Laura

asked, keeping an eye on Holden, who was walking in a circle by the door.

"Well, actually..." Rachel pulled her lips tight like someone does when they're about to give bad news. She pulled an envelope from a stack and passed it to Laura. "We're renovating the basement properties, so we need them empty for three months. Failed inspection and we have to do it now. Old pipes, and some of the units had traces of lead paint."

Laura's stomach dropped a little, but she tried to stay calm. "Okay, do you have another property available?"

Rachel pulled her lips tight again, and Laura's body felt like it got hot all over. "That's why I was calling earlier. I just leased the last one."

Laura's heart started to pound, while she processed this. "So what does this mean exactly?"

Rachel looked like she might be sick and looked down at her desk before looking back up. "I'm really sorry, but you're first on the list to get your place back in three months. They need the apartment clear no later than thirty days from now, so I'm sorry, but you'll need to move out."

CHAPTER 3

"Alright, where is it?" Jordan said as they pulled into the park with the siren going. Laura was back on call after a full twenty-four hours of worried attempts at packing and falling asleep, neither of which she'd made any progress on.

"There's the party," she said, pointing toward a pavilion decorated with pink balloons for a child's birthday party. A crowd of people crouched around what looked like a child lying on the ground, while some adults ushered a few tear-stained kids toward the playground.

Jordan pulled up as close as he could. Laura jumped down and jogged over with her bag.

A woman rushed over, eyes wide with panic. "Thank God you're here. She's never had any allergies before, but we gave her some trail mix maybe fifteen minutes ago. She said she felt tight and that she couldn't breathe."

"Okay, what's her name?"

"Katie. She's my niece."

"And you're sure there aren't any known allergies?"

The woman hugged herself and started rocking. "Not that we know of. Her mom's right over there."

Laura thanked her and found Jordan had already reached the mom, who was crying and shaking her head. She went right to the little girl on the ground and knelt before her.

"Hi, Katie. My name is Laura and I'm here to help you."

Katie looked to be about seven and was wearing a unicorn T-shirt and jean shorts. Her black hair stuck to her tear-stained cheeks and had bits of mulch stuck in it. A quick check of her vitals revealed an elevated heart rate, low blood pressure, and wheezing.

"Does your throat feel tight?"

Katie nodded.

"Can you tell me what happened right before you felt this way?"

Her voice was hoarse, high-pitched, and Laura couldn't understand what she was trying to say. Katie's eyes started to panic as her breathing picked up.

"Stay calm. Just look at me," Laura said, seeing Jordan already pulling out a syringe and a vial of epinephrine to the side. "My friend Jordan is here to help too. He needs to poke your leg."

Katie shook her head and grabbed Laura's hand, tugging it toward the back of her calf, which was red and swollen.

"Did you get stung?" Laura asked.

Katie nodded as two more big tears fell from her eyes down her cheeks.

"Have you ever been stung before?" Katie shook her head back and forth.

"Okay, I'm going to need to check that, but first Jordan has to give you a shot. I'm going to count to ten. Hold my hand."

Katie's mom knelt down now too and took hold of her other hand. Jordan administered the shot while they counted to ten together. Laura had to hand it to the girl—she was a trooper and didn't flinch after the first shock of the needle.

"We're going to need to take her to the hospital. You can drive her or we can transport her," Jordan said to the mom, who nodded and swiped away her tears.

"Okay, let me grab my purse from my car and tell the other parents."

Jordan and Laura helped Katie onto the stretcher and moved her into the back of the ambulance. Jordan talked with the mom and the dad once more, giving Laura a few minutes alone.

Katie watched Laura with big eyes, tracking her every move. It was so much easier to heal patients who were unconscious.

"I'm going to wash my hands and take a look at your leg now."

"Will it hurt?" Katie croaked out.

"No, I'm just looking. If it hurts, just tell me and I'll stop, but I'm really just looking." She waited until Katie nodded.

Laura pulled off her gloves and cleaned her hands. "I'm going to touch your leg and tilt it toward me to get a better look at it."

Katie nodded and watched. Laura drew in a breath. She was nervous, this being her first attempt to heal since Carter. She had so many questions, but mainly—would it work again? There was only one way to find out.

She touched her hands to Katie's calf, pulling it slightly to reveal the red welt. Laura took another breath to quiet her mind and closed her eyes, visualizing the swelling going down. The familiar warmth and tingling started in her chest again before she opened her eyes and saw the red blotch retreating slowly. Laura could hear Jordan and the mom coming closer, so with another breath, she steadied her mind and visualized Katie's airway opening back up.

Katie took in a deeper breath than before and blinked a few times.

Laura let go as the mom stepped up, then turned to pull on a fresh pair of gloves.

"Can I sit by her? I've never been in an ambulance before."

Laura spent the rest of the ride keeping an eye on Katie and her mom. Katie was improving with the medicine and the healing, but her mom hadn't improved much, still choking back sobs and apologizing to Katie about her birthday party.

"Happy Birthday, Katie," Laura said. "I didn't know that was your party."

Katie gave her a shy smile and murmured a thanks when her mom prompted her.

The tell-tale sign of the speed bumps announced their arrival at the hospital. Katie's mom thanked them both several times before she followed her daughter inside with the nurses.

"I'm going to grab a quick bite. Want to come? It's roasted chicken today," Jordan said, walking backwards toward the door to the cafeteria.

Laura waved him on. "You go ahead. I'll grab something from vending."

"Alright. See you in twenty," he said, taking a left down the hallway into the belly of the hospital.

Laura shut the doors to the ambulance and walked inside, veering right instead of left. The little girl named Katie was going to be fine, but any calls with kids made her nervous and really brought all the mom-guilt right to the forefront of her mind.

She slid her phone out of her pocket and checked the preschool's app for updates on Holden, who apparently had not eaten his vegetables again today and had a bathroom accident. There was a picture of him coloring something that resembled a Jackson Pollock, and another shot of the playground with a blur of him mid-run.

Laura popped the phone back in her pocket and headed to the vending machine just as her stomach squirmed audibly. She was starving, and the roast chicken at the hospital wasn't bad at all, but she needed money for whatever deposit she was going to have to make. The last time she looked for an apartment, she had picked something she liked that was almost the cheapest on the list, which meant no matter where she went, it would be more money that she really didn't have.

It wasn't that she was totally broke. She had cash— enough to keep her car in working order, save a little, and feed Holden's Mickey Mouse addiction. But no one said paramedics made great money, and the lawyer's fees had wiped out most of her savings from before she had Holden. She wasn't in the hole, but she wasn't very far ahead either, and every time she had a little cushion, something always came around to take a bite out of it.

Laura bought a peanut butter candy bar, figuring it at least had some protein that might get her through until she could go home and eat something real. As she nibbled away, she found a bench to sit on, waiting for Jordan to finish off his lunch.

At least she had one thing going for her. She had been able to heal Katie at least a little—enough to know her powers were there. When she hadn't been able to heal Carter, a small part of her had worried she was losing it. If she wasn't able to heal, her job would take on a much different meaning. Not that she hadn't been trained for it, but having her power as insurance helped her sleep a lot better at night. It was one of the few things she hadn't lost in her life. Her ability to heal was a constant, and without it, she wouldn't know who she was or what she would do.

The thought niggled at the back of her mind. Except for Holden and her parents, she had been able to heal everyone else. She had tried to heal her dad. He was the only one who had ever found out. When she had first learned of the ability with a friend who fell off her bike, he had been the first one she had told in the garage when handing him her helmet. Laura still remembered the concerned, fearful look on his face, as he held her hand in his own and told her in a low voice to never tell anyone about what she might be able to do.

Might. Even then she knew he was too afraid to admit to the possibility. She wanted to show him, but he shook his head and warned her to be careful and never let anyone see. For a confused and curious child, seeing her brave, gregarious father shaken haunted her.

He never spoke about it again, but he offered a quiet smile filled with pride but laced with worry every time she spoke of going into the medical field. When she was older, she tried to assure him no one would find out, but he held up a hand and shook his head before asking her just to be careful.

She was. Since then, there had been countless people, and the process was always so effortless that it was easy to lose track of how many people she had helped. No one suspected a thing.

Laura glanced up and down the corridors and started walking, tossing her wrapper in the trash can as she passed.

She knew the hospital's layout after having spent a fair amount of time there, so she soon found the unit she was looking for—post critical care.

Two oversized doors blocked her entrance with a keypad on one side. Laura bit her lip and started to leave. It was a stupid idea to see if she could try and heal him now to show herself she could do it, so she could put this whole thing behind her.

One door swung open and a nurse walked out, and it was someone she recognized.

"Hey, I think I know you," Laura said before she could stop herself.

"Hi…yes, I think we've crossed paths before. I sometimes work down in the ER. How can I help you?"

"I'm looking for a patient we transported here a couple of nights ago. Burns and a broken tibia."

"Oh yes, he woke up and is doing well. Would you like to visit? I heard through the grapevine one of the paramedics knew him before."

He was up?

"Word gets around fast," Laura said.

"I'll take you back. He's been asking about what happened to him. Doesn't remember a thing."

"Oh, no, that's not necessary," Laura said. "I just wanted to make sure he was okay and stuff."

"You sure? I don't mind." The nurse pulled her badge with the white keycard hooked on it. "Might help him get some questions answered."

Laura glanced at the clock on the wall. Jordan wouldn't be back for another ten minutes, and with any luck, Carter would be asleep, so she could test herself and get out of there before he woke up. After what he had been through, he would almost certainly be knocked out by medicine.

"Well, okay, but I only have a few minutes."

The nurse smiled and touched her keycard to the pad, escorting Laura inside.

The unit looked like most others with the nurses' station in the center and doors all around to various rooms.

"He's right over here in this room."

What in the hell was she doing here? Laura visiting a

patient who was her ex-boyfriend was *so* not a good idea. "Look, he's probably sleeping. Maybe I'll just come back another time."

The nurse opened the door, and there was Carter. He looked like he was asleep, reclined, but not quite flat on his back, his leg in a cast and parts of his face and hands covered in bandages.

Laura stopped and stared, a cocktail of emotions flooding her chest. Regret? No, that wasn't it. Revenge wasn't right either. Remorse for not being able to heal him was the loudest and the only reason she took a step forward.

His head turned to her, and those dark green eyes zeroed right in on her, stopping her midstride.

Laura opened her mouth and closed it, not knowing what to say.

Carter shifted and blinked as if trying to sit up and say something to her, not that he had much success. The nurse pumped the hand sanitizer on the wall and rushed over, rubbing her hands with the foam.

"This is one of the paramedics who brought you here. She stopped in to see how you're doing."

He kept blinking and squinting at her with his brows furrowed.

"Um...hi. Look, I've got to get back to work. It's nice to see that you're awake, and I hope you get some rest and have a smooth recovery," Laura said, stepping backwards. "Thanks for your time and for letting me on the unit," she added to the nurse. "I've gotta run." She darted out of the room and out of the unit to save herself the embarrassment of any further conversation.

As she raced back to the ambulance, she figured she had been right. Laura Burton really was the last person Carter Price wanted to see.

CHAPTER 4

"That was nice of her to come and check on you," said the nurse, who began checking his vitals for what felt like the fifteenth time that day.

Carter tried to sit up, but his head was pounding, his leg was throbbing, and the only feeling he recognized was pain, but he knew who he'd seen.

Laura had just been standing in the doorway of his hospital room, looking like she had seen a ghost from the past. She was probably right to look that way, considering how things had been left between them.

There was certainly no love lost there. At least, not on her part anyway.

Laura had been great. Funny, beautiful, smart, a little shy to go on adventures in a pickup truck deep into the country. For a while, things had been amazing between them—or so Carter had thought. He had been chasing her since sixth grade when they first met in history class. Their teacher, Mrs. Mildrew, had paired them together to work on a project on Abraham Lincoln. Laura had done most of the work because Carter had been too busy sitting staring at her dark hair up in a ponytail and her huge brown eyes framed with perfect black lashes, trying to figure out how to untangle his tongue.

They had received an A on the project, which was purely because of Laura, and Carter had set out on a quest to learn everything he could about her. While he was at it, he tried anything to get her to notice him, which unfortunately meant he got more attention from every teacher than anyone else in his class. His mom hadn't noticed, as she was too busy being a waitress after his dad walked out. Carter craved attention from Laura and a glimpse of her soft, pink smile, all kindness and warmth. Any chance he had to act a fool, he relished in before glancing over to catch her giggle, which resulted in a lot of detention...which resulted in a lot of hanging out with kids who thought the rules were suggestions...which resulted in a slow slide into breaking other rules.

Carter had pulled it together for a little while, however, with Laura's help. Thank God for Mrs. Nelson, who had partnered them up for a chemistry lab right before the homecoming dance. By this point, Carter'd had over four years of practicing confidence, and when he asked Laura out over the Bunsen burner, the pink tinge in her cheeks and delighted smile were the sweetest rewards he could've counted on. They had dated for what would turn out to be an incredible school year and the kind of summer kids remembered for the rest of their lives. Until it ended.

It had been in August and they had been to a bonfire on his friend Bradley's family's property. No one lived there, they just owned the land, which is why it was the perfect hangout for a bunch of teens. Carter had met Bradley and his girlfriend in detention, forming a fast bond over too many poor choices to count. They had never liked Laura, worried she'd call the cops, but Carter had promised them she would play it cool and wouldn't snitch. Turns out they'd been right, but not for the reasons they'd feared.

Carter closed his eyes against the memory, but the vision was seared into his mind. He had just gotten his license and bought an old truck earlier that summer before his junior year. Carter didn't remember most of the bonfire other than Bradley laughing until he cried over something stupid Carter had said. Laura had been cool, and everything was going well until the accident. It was the trip home at the end of the night that changed everything. Bradley's Bronco in front of them, speeding, taking a curve too fast, smashing into a tree. Bradley and his girlfriend were thrown from the vehicle. Carter took off toward them. And that's when Laura called 911. When the cops came, they found all the drugs Bradley had been selling stashed inside the back seat. He had been high and drunk while driving, and his girlfriend was dead.

They read Bradley his rights while the paramedics checked him over, and the whole time Bradley was screaming every name in the book at Laura, who stared with glassy eyes in shock at the drugs on the hood of the cop car. That's when Bradley outed Carter too.

Lying in the hospital now, tears stung his eyes as he remembered the look of betrayal Laura had given him when the cops found the additional drugs in the very seat she had been sitting on. Her expression as the police car pulled away with him in the back seat was forever burned into his memory. He and Laura hadn't communicated again—until today.

"Oh, I'm sorry. That hurt you," the nurse said, seeing his tears and offering him a tissue, which he accepted. "Let me go and grab your pain medicine. It's about that time anyway. I'll be right back," she said as she pumped the sanitizer and left the room.

Carter sighed and looked around the room. It reminded him of juvie.

Bradley had been tried as an adult and had gone to jail for a long time for killing a passenger while driving under the influence. Carter got a misdemeanor for possession and spent a little time in juvie before heading to the alternative school across town where he probably belonged. The whole situation just about killed his mom. She couldn't look him in the eye for a long time. That's when he met Coach.

Carter shifted in the hospital bed and let out a sigh of relief when he saw the crumpled paper that had been in his pocket on the night of this most recent crash. He reached out, straining his muscles and skin to the point of agony, and picked up the program from Coach's funeral.

The former marine turned math teacher had coached the alternative school's intramural football team and had taken Carter under his wing, taking him to get burgers and fries once a week so they could talk on the hood of his old beat-up truck. They kept the routine up, even when Carter had earned his way back into his old high school where he spent his last year on the honor roll and football team. Laura had still been there, but he was too ashamed to talk to her. Instead, he focused on school, with Coach's help.

It was because of Coach that he got into Stanford, graduated with an MBA, and had started his own tech company. Carter owed all of his success to Coach and had invited him on a trip to Wall Street to see him ring the bell on the floor of the Stock Exchange. After, Coach insisted on taking Carter out to get burgers and fries. The next day, Carter returned the favor by treating the closest person he had to a father to a real pastrami sandwich.

He had stayed sober until after the burial.

God, it was some kind of irony that Laura had pulled him out of whatever fiery crash had happened, bringing them right back to where they started. Her doing the right thing, him a drunk screwup.

His phone buzzed next to him on the nightstand. One of the nurses had even been kind enough to plug it in for him. Checking the number, Carter shifted as much as he could with his leg in a cast to grab it.

"Hey, Mom," he said, trying to disguise his labored breathing.

"Oh, I'm so glad to hear your voice. I've been calling the nurses twice a day, trying to get through to you. Do you need me to come up there?"

"What? No, I'm fine. Just ran off the road, got banged around a bit."

He could almost hear his mom chewing her nails. "I don't mind coming up there. I already talked about it with Fred."

Carter's mom had married Fred and moved to Florida a few years ago. Most of her time was spent trying to learn how to crochet and sending him pictures of the flowers on her patio. She was truly happy for the first time in years, probably because she had money ahead of her and didn't have to worry about Carter. Until now.

"No, seriously. I'm okay."

"The doctors told me you have a broken leg and a lot of burns. Are you sure? I don't mind. Really."

"Mom, it's fine. I'll send you a picture to prove it."

"Okay. If you're sure." His mom sounded anything but sure.

"I'll call you every day. I'd rather you come visit when I get home. You can help me with my garden."

"Say when and where and I'll be on the first flight."

"Okay, sounds good."

"Carter?"

"Yeah, Mom?"

"I love you."

"I love you too."

"You scared me."

"I'm sorry. I'll be okay and I'll call tomorrow."

"Only if you feel up to it. I don't want to bother the doctors."

"I'll make sure to call when I can," he said before promising her two more times and ending the call. He held his phone in his hand and let his head fall back. He hated worrying his mom, and though he'd been past that for fifteen years since the arrest, all it took was one crash in Goldvein to bring back the not-so-good days. Then again, his mom always worried.

Carter's phone rang again. Mom almost always called back after hanging up. He rested his eyes and answered.

"OH THANK GOD YOU'RE OKAY." The screeching on the other end had him jerking the phone away from his ear. The distance didn't lower the volume.

It was Ruby, his VP. "I have been trying to get ahold of you for two days, and you know how I get when you ignore my texts. Where the hell have you been?"

"It's nothing, really. Car went off the road—"

"WHAT?! You were in a wreck and you didn't even bother to tell me? How am I supposed to find these things out? Why did you even go back there for so long? Could've flown in and out for the funeral. Done. You said you hated that place and never wanted to go back—"

"It's fine, I'm okay, but yeah, I guess things have been a little crazy around here. I just have a few scrapes and bruises," he said, frowning at the bandages covering most of his arms where he could feel the tightness of the skin starting to sting again. Thank God the nurse was coming back with the medicine. He didn't think now was a great time to bring up his broken leg.

"Okay, great. So when are you coming back? We have the board meeting to prepare for. We cannot mess this up."

"I'll make it back. I just need a few days to sort some things out."

"I can fly out there, you know." Her voice softened, like it always did when she changed gears.

Ruby was always so willing and eager. She had been dropping hints since day one about the two of them working late together and maybe grabbing dinner. She always wore the tightest dresses with staggering, red-soled heels. At first, Carter had been interested, and they grabbed dinner a few times, spent a few late nights together, but after a long weekend away with her, he had seen her true colors start to peek through and had tried to let her down and distance himself. She was smoking hot, funny, and smart, but there was just something that rubbed him the wrong way, especially given she was his employee.

"Look, there's no need for that. Just give me a few days to get things straightened up and I'll be back in California in no time," Carter said, tamping down her repeated offers.

A dull ache was beginning to form at the base of his head. Did he have a concussion? He hadn't thought to ask the nurse. Ruby's overwhelming concern wasn't helping. He cut her off midword.

"Well, thanks again for calling." He glanced at the still-closed door. "The nurse is coming in now—"

"YOU'RE STILL IN THE HOSPITAL?"

Carter jerked the phone away from his ear again. "I'll give you a call in a few days." He hit the red button to end the call and let his head fall against the almost paper-thin pillow.

Everything ached, and Carter knew his body needed rest, so he let out a slow breath and tried to relax. Carter had two thoughts as he drifted off to a restless sleep. He needed to thank Laura—and at least this trip couldn't get any worse.

CHAPTER 5

The rest of Laura's shift was spent routinely as no more calls came through. She was both disappointed and grateful. She needed some time to rest, even if she couldn't sleep, but no calls meant she couldn't heal anyone to verify she still could, and she didn't have any distractions to keep her from her real problems.

After enough pestering from Megan, Laura started to call around to a few other apartments, most of which were way out of her price range. Still, she noted down numbers and the appointment times for when she could go and see them in person.

At the end of the day, she drove the two miles to Sunflower School where Holden was enrolled in preschool and afterschool care. This was part of the reason her budget was so thin—she had put him in one of the best schools she could afford. Her money had paid dividends too.

Through the windows of the building she could see art made out of handprints that turned into everything from jellyfish to suns and even birds. Laura parked and jogged up to the front, tapping her unique number on the keypad outside the door. The door swung open, revealing a welcome desk with a huge bank of TVs overhead, showing all the rooms from infant to after-school care, as well as the playgrounds.

After she had signed him out on the tablet and paid for the week, she scurried to the back classroom. Through the glass window, she could see Holden and a dozen other kids involved in what they called "free play," code for chaos.

Sound exploded out of the room when she cracked the door, waving to the teacher standing to the side, talking to a child while holding another.

"MAMA!" Holden yelled, running toward her with his chubby arms outstretched and what looked to be the remains of some sort of red sauce down his shirt. One of his kind teachers had made an attempt to clean him, but still it looked like the image of Mickey Mouse had been attacked.

"Hey boo boo! Did you have a good day?" Laura said, swinging him up onto her hip and planting a kiss on his cheek.

"We played outside today! Look! Mulch!" Sure enough, Holden was holding up a shard of wood, staring at it with a look of benevolent awe.

"That's great. Do you want to leave it on the playground?"

He snatched it back and lowered his brows in a menacing glare. "Mine!"

"Right. Let's grab your bag."

With a sling of a backpack and a thank you to the teacher, they were back in the parking lot. Laura wrestled Holden into his car seat, ultimately winning through bribery, the promise of Goldfish when they got home.

Laura checked the clock, and even though she hadn't been late to get Holden, it was still almost dinner time. Her urge to hit the drive-thru was strong, but she gripped the wheel extra tight as she drove by, thinking of all the pricey apartments she had called that day.

Fifteen minutes later, Laura pulled into her parking slot at the apartment complex.

"Look, Mama! Ooooh trucks! It's so big!"

Holden was right. The lot was filled with trucks. Construction had already started. Laura parked and stepped out of the car and into the open air, which filled with the sounds of saws and hammers breaking up tile. She grabbed Holden and walked hand in hand on the sidewalk that led to the basement apartment, facing the back.

With every step, the noise got louder. Laura bit her lip and checked her phone for the time, hoping work would stop soon. Rounding the corner only amplified the sound.

"Potty! Why is there a potty in the grass? That's so silly!" Holden giggled while pointing to the broken toilet lying on the grass by the open door of the apartment they shared a wall with. The sounds of tile shattering rang out from within, right before a sheet of what had been a wall was thrown out next to the sidewalk.

"Someone's making a mess. They're not following the rules."

"I think they're fixing it, buddy," Laura said, walking to their own door and pulling out her key, afraid of how much she would hear through the walls.

When she opened the door, Holden ran right to the little table and chairs in the dining room where he liked to color and picked up the remote.

"Mickey Mouse? Goldfish?"

The screaming sound of a saw that would have woken the dead shook the wall next to Laura. It was fine now, assuming they left soon, but on days when she needed to sleep after a night shift and Holden needed to nap, this wasn't going to work anymore. They needed to move ASAP.

Laura let her purse, an old brown leather one she'd acquired after having Holden, slide off her arm and down onto the floor where she kicked off her boots.

"A promise is a promise."

She turned on the TV, cranked up the volume, and headed to the kitchen to pour little orange fish into Holden's Mickey Mouse bowl. She placed the offering on the table in front of him, reminded him to say thank you through his transfixed stare, and headed back to the kitchen to start dinner.

The sound of the saw started up again, punctuated by a few loud bangs for good measure. She could already feel the dull ache at the base of her skull and glanced at the clock on the stove. Any minute now, they would stop, and she could get some peace.

Laura preheated the oven and was laying out some frozen chicken on a baking sheet when the phone rang. She answered and, thinking better of putting her mother on speaker, wedged the phone between her cheek and her neck.

"Hey, Mom."

"Hey, sweetie, just...God, where are you?"

Laura sighed. "Home."

"What in God's name is that awful racket?"

"You mean other than a pain in my ass? They're remodeling all the basement apartments, apparently starting with the one next door."

"Oh, that'll be nice! A fresh coat of paint just brightens a room right up. So when are they doing yours?"

"As soon as I move out."

"What are they moving you into? Another unit?"

Laura glanced over at Holden, still fixated on Goofy, while she opened a can of peas and put it in a saucepan. She didn't like the idea of upsetting her mom who was a worrier anyway, but there didn't seem to be any way around it.

Sooner or later she'd find out, and she'd be even more upset her daughter hadn't told her in the first place.

Laura drew in a breath while stirring the peas.

"No, actually. They don't have any left."

"What? A big place like that?"

"I was the last to get back to them, but I've already called a few places and scheduled some tours."

There was a pause on the other end of the line.

"Mom?"

"Laura, the last time you looked for an apartment, you told me how much they all were."

"Yeah, I know, but it'll be okay. Besides, what choice do I have? Construction started today, and Holden and I won't be able to sleep on the days we're home. It'll work out. It's going to have to."

Her mom made a noise of agreement but didn't sound convinced. Laura changed the subject. "So, tell me what's new?"

"Well, I got a call from my old friend, Harriet, and she had gone to Phil's funeral. Do you remember me talking about him? Worked at the alternative school?"

"Uh-huh," Laura said, putting her mom on speaker and digging around in the cabinet to pull out plates and cups.

"Well, Phil was her neighbor and was always so nice. He'd come down and chop trees for her and shovel snow in the winter. I was so sad to hear that he had died. He went quick, though. Went to bed and didn't wake up."

"That's the way to go."

"Right. Well, anyway, Harriet told me that the service was beautiful, and so many nice people from the community spoke about the impact he'd made. You know, he was a marine, so they had the flag and the trumpet. She went on about how lovely the whole thing was."

"Sounds like it."

"Harriet also told me that Carter Price was there—"

Laura dropped a sippy cup that clattered across the cheap linoleum floor. Her mom didn't even take a breath with all the racket.

"…that's what he said in the eulogy. You know I guess he met him at that school they sent him to—"

"After the accident, you mean," Laura said, knowing exactly what had sent him there and who had called 911. She really didn't want to get into it, but she knew there was no stopping her mom once she was on a path of sharing good gossip.

"Yes, but he's really turned himself around. He's a billionaire now, with a B. Can you imagine if you had stayed with him?"

Laura knew that wasn't possible after she had been the one to call the cops that night. She shuddered when she remembered the angry glare he and his friends had given her all those years ago.

"Yeah, well, I don't think he'd like me anymore."

"I always liked him. Such a nice young man, and the two of you looked so good together, all dressed up going to homecoming. Such a shame his dad had walked out, but you know his mom did such a nice job with him on her own."

"Mom, raising a drug dealer isn't exactly a nice job."

"He just fell in with the wrong crowd after his dad took off. It isn't like it happened again. We can't hold people to one mistake they made in high school."

Laura wanted to point out to her mother that it was clear Carter Price hadn't changed his stripes when she'd found him reeking of alcohol after a recent crash.

"Maybe if he's in town, the two of you could get together…"

Laura let out a bitter laugh. "Mom, I'm one hundred percent positive he doesn't want to see me any more than he

KATHRYN K. MURPHY

has to. Besides, he's not my type anymore, and I'm too busy to see anyone. Instead of talking about old boyfriends, why don't you fill me in on your therapy."

Laura finished the call with her mom after hearing about the latest equipment her mom was using. According to her, the doctors found her strength to be improving a little bit each week, which was the first good news Laura had heard in a while.

The night passed in the usual way. She and Holden ate dinner, he with copious amounts of ketchup. Then he colored while she did the dishes, followed by bath, bedtime stories, and a good night kiss.

Laura walked out of his bedroom and eased the door shut behind her, shuffling over to the recliner in the living room. She flopped down in her robe that she had changed into when she got home and picked up the remote to channel surf, hoping to find something happy that didn't involve ex-boyfriends, money, construction, or apartments.

Honestly, that was what she liked about being single. Everything was simple, and she controlled how much drama was in her life. As much as any one person could control their life. In simplicity there was peace.

She wanted to watch a cooking show, but they always made her hungry, so she clicked the remote a few more times until she landed on a travel show. The soft, even voice of the host washed over her while the sunny landscapes made her long for a vacation. Laura didn't care where as long as it was far from here.

She tried to keep up with the history portion on some cathedral, but her mind wandered back to what her mom had said about Carter Price. Billionaire *with a B*. Who would've thought that Carter, the class clown, who had a car seat full of drugs that had sent him to an alternative school, would make something of himself? Laura had done everything right in school, and any reasonable person probably wouldn't have bet she'd be the one trying to find the cheapest apartment in town.

Her mom's memories took her back to that homecoming. Laura closed her eyes and remembered the laughs and the sweetness of their first kiss on the way back home. She had liked Carter for so long at that point and never thought he'd see her as anything other than a project partner. Everything involving him had felt like a dream until that last night, which had managed to tarnish every other memory Laura had of Carter Price.

CHAPTER 6

The next morning, a knock on the door to his hospital room had Carter turning off his phone and looking up, expecting a nurse, only it wasn't a nurse who walked in. A cop, with short black hair and almost violet eyes walked into the room with her hands on her belt. She was followed by a larger male cop with glasses.

"Hello, sir. I'm Sergeant Ashleigh Myers, and my colleague here is Officer Bryce Johnson. We reported to your crash. I'm glad to see you're awake."

Carter shifted slightly so he could sit up as much as he could to face them.

"Thank you," Carter managed, already dreading what was coming next. He shouldn't have been drinking, and he shouldn't have left the bottle in the car. Maybe it had been destroyed in the crash. God, what would Coach have said? Carter hated the old bastard for dying only because he had loved the man so damn much. His absence had left Carter right back where he was as a troubled teen.

"I'm sorry to report we haven't been able to recover the

vehicle. It was a total loss. I'll write up a report for your insurance."

Carter nodded once, not wanting to talk. He unfortunately had experience with this.

Those violet eyes didn't leave his face once. "Given the nature of the crash and the bottle we found in the car, we had enough evidence and probable cause to get some bloodwork done. Do you have any questions for me about that?"

Carter started to shake his head no and then stopped. "Actually, I do have one, but it's not about the tests." He could already hear what his lawyers would be saying if they knew he had chosen to speak, but he'd had a lot of time to think, both in this bed and on the way to Coach's funeral. He had remade himself and achieved everything he had ever dreamed of and more, but there was one thing that still bothered him. One person from his past who had found him again and saw him not as what he'd become, but as what he'd once been. Maybe it was something he should discuss in therapy, but he always hated the idea of someone not liking him, so the face Laura had made when she had walked into his hospital room had been weighing on him, and he had to do something about it.

"Okay."

"I want to contact one of the paramedics who saved me," he said, watching the cop raise her eyebrows in surprise.

"May I ask why?" she said after a beat and narrowed her eyes.

"To thank her for everything she did for me. Her name's Laura Purcell, or now it's something else, yeah…after she got married, I think."

Sergeant Myers studied him a bit more. "I'll mention it to her. She'll contact you if she has the time."

"Okay," Carter nodded. "Can you please tell her I'd like to talk face-to-face? If she doesn't want to come back here, maybe I could get her phone number or she could call me. I have cards in my wallet."

The cop tilted her head to one side. "Sure, I can pass along a card."

"Great, thanks." Carter propped himself up on his hands and scooted toward the bedside table, opening up the drawer where he had asked the nurse to put his wallet after she had shown him where his clothes had gone. He rummaged inside the leather that still smelled like smoke and pulled out a bright white card with his personal number on it. It was a little bent at the top, but didn't look too shabby considering it had been in a car that had rolled God knew how many times down a hill before slamming into a tree and bursting into flames.

"Thank you again."

"You're welcome," Sergeant Myers said, sliding the business card into the pocket of her dark blue uniform. "Do you have any other questions?"

Carter shook his head. "No."

"Alright," she said, pulling out a notepad and pen, clicking it open. "We have a couple of questions for you."

Carter nodded, the sinking feeling in the pit of his stomach returning.

"We already have information from your license, registration, and insurance from your wallet, but we need to follow up on the crash. Where were you coming from?"

"A friend's funeral," he said, trying to ignore the lump in his throat that appeared when he thought of Coach in the ground.

"Alright, walk me through what happened right before the crash."

Carter thought for a moment and chose his words carefully. "I was driving. It was dark. I saw a deer, swerved, and lost control." No need to mention the alcohol, loud music, and tears streaming down his face.

Sergeant Myers made some notes in her pad. Her colleague's phone pinged. The large cop pulled it out and started swiping and typing away on the smartphone, tapping her shoulder once for her to read what the screen said. She looked up from her notepad, gave a quick nod, and went back to writing.

"Alright, and can you tell me, did you hit the guardrail on any part of the road other than where the car went over the embankment?"

Carter arranged his face to look like he was remembering that night, knowing full well he had been buzzed and had a hard time putting all the pieces in place. "No, I don't believe so," he said, hoping he hadn't failed some gotcha test they were trying to pull.

Sergeant Myers finished jotting down what he'd said and God knew what else. "Will you go grab the nurse?" she asked her colleague, who nodded once and stepped out.

"Do you know when you're going to be released from the hospital?" Sergeant Myers asked, looking up at him, her violet eyes giving nothing away.

"Actually, the doctor said later this afternoon. May I ask what all these questions are for?"

The door opened, and the other cop came back. "She'll be here in a minute."

"Good to go?" Sergeant Myers asked.

He gave her a thumbs-up, and she closed her little notepad, tucking it away.

"Alright sir, we reported to the scene of your crash and found you unconscious and your car on fire. You were removed from the fire and treated by the paramedics for what looked to be burns and a broken leg before you were transferred to the hospital. Once the fire was out, we found a damaged liquor bottle in the passenger seat, with the top seal broken. There was also a pungent smell of alcohol. This evidence combined with the crash gave us enough probable cause to order a blood draw to determine your blood alcohol content, which was .10, and over the legal limit. Because you are scheduled to be released today, we have a warrant and are placing you under arrest for driving under the influence."

Carter sat in stunned silence while Sergeant Myers pulled out her handcuffs from behind her back, reciting his Miranda rights. Just when he had thought this trip couldn't get worse, he felt the cold metal of the cuff against his wrist, trapping him in the last place he wanted to be.

CHAPTER 7

C arter climbed out of the rideshare he'd hired and propped himself up on his crutches on the curb of the one of the biggest houses in the nicest part of town. Spending the previous night in a hotel had been fine, but he was going to need something more long-term, thanks to the judge's bail conditions. He couldn't leave the state, drive, or consume any alcohol until his trial. Carter didn't mind the last condition as he'd already planned to avoid it again in tribute to Coach, but the first two conditions were outrageous, in the words of his lawyer who, despite his best efforts, was powerless to change the judge's mind.

He would've come back for his court date in two or three months and had even talked about his business back in California, but the judge wasn't having it. The road and guardrail he had been on when he crashed needed to be repaired, and even though Carter had offered to pay for everything himself, thinking the small town could use the money, the judge wouldn't budge.

At first it didn't make any sense until Carter recognized the older judge with gray hair as the one who had handled his possession trial fifteen years earlier. In his eyes, Carter Price was probably the teenager who had gotten off easy, made too much money, only to come back home and get up to his old tricks again.

Carter let out a sigh and looked up and down the street. At least he had found a fully furnished house to rent on one of those vacation property sites, although in Carter's opinion, anyone who elected to vacation in Goldvein, MT needed to take a long hard look at their life.

At least that meant the price was right and everything was already in place, right down to the sheets on the bed and the spoons in the drawers. As it was, Carter's overnight bag had been burned in the fire. Last night, after the arraignment, Carter had gotten a lift over to the shopping center to pick up some clothes and toiletries before heading back to the hotel. Even that small task had proved exhausting. Not only had his leg started to throb, but he had to get into one of those beeping carts reserved for old people and kept dropping his crutches in the aisles. The pharmacy had taken forever to fill the prescription for his pain medicine, but at least he used his time to buy everything from a phone charger to socks and shoes as well as a few groceries.

Getting them to the hotel was only slightly easier because he had hit the ATM and paid the rideshare driver cash to bring all the bags of groceries and clothes into the room and put them on the counter. He had paid again today to have them all moved into the house he had found online last night.

Even with this help, though, the events of the past week had wiped him out. He swung himself up the driveway with his crutches and to the front, where the driver had already opened the door using the code the owner had texted Carter.

Carter used his crutches to get from the kitchen to the living room, which had a huge TV and a leather living room set he actually liked, and he sat down to rest, grabbing the remote. He flipped through the news and business channels, while checking email on his phone.

Ruby had been busy handling everything on her end while copying him on emails. Apparently, she had also made it very clear he'd been in some sort of life-threatening accident, and Carter had over twenty-five best wishes emails.

"Better let them know I'm alive," he said to no one in particular as he drafted an email calling a virtual staff meeting where he could video conference with the whole team. He scheduled the meeting and sent out the calendar invite in his email. With that dealt with, he checked the time. He hadn't bought a full load of groceries, and the sandwich he'd grabbed at the hotel was long gone.

With his leg propped up, Carter searched for his favorite old Italian place from when he was a kid. If he was going to be stuck in Goldvein, he may as well enjoy it as much as he could. Seeing they still delivered, he dialed the number and muted the TV.

"Pascal's, this is Rob, can I help ya?" a rough voice answered on the other end.

The voice sounded familiar. "I want to place an order for delivery."

"Great. What's your phone number and address?"

Carter rattled them off, having to read the address off his phone screen. While the man on the other end of the line took them down, he placed the voice and asked, "Is this Rob Cassandro?"

"Yes, sir."

"Hey, man, how are you? It's Carter Price."

"Hey dude, I haven't seen you since you went to college. How are ya, man? Visiting your mom?"

"No, she moved to Florida. I came back for a visit,"— Carter did not want to say or even think of the word *funeral* more than he had to—"and I got in an accident."

49

"Oh, shit. Are you hurt?"

"Broken leg, so I'll be around a bit."

"Damn. Well, maybe we can catch a beer or something. I saw your old man a few weeks ago."

Carter's gut turned to stone. "Oh, yeah?" he said, his voice flat.

"Yeah, he's doing better. Started to turn himself around and all that."

Too little, too late, Carter thought. He had zero interest in seeing the man who had never been around. There wasn't much in this town, including his dad, that still held his interest—except for one person.

"Hey, speaking of the past, do you ever run into Laura Purcell? I want to get in touch with her."

"Yeah, I know Laura. Last name's Burton now. Every now and then she comes in to pick up dinner. She's a paramedic. Her husband went missing a few years ago. Just took off one day and poof."

That got Carter's attention. "Where is he?"

"No one knows. Laura's made a go of it, though. Actually, hang on a second," he said, putting Carter on hold. "—yeah, okay, thanks. Carter, you still there?"

"Yep."

"Sorry about that, one of my waitresses just heard me talking about Laura. Told me her apartment is being renovated."

"Really?" Carter said.

"Yeah, hang on again...What? No, it's not about that."

"What's that?" Carter asked.

"No, apparently, Laura put on social media last night that she needs a place to stay. Do you want me to tell the waitress to pass on a message?"

Carter thought for a moment. "Yeah, actually. I just want to thank her for saving me. She's the one who pulled me out of the crash."

"Small world."

"Indeed it is."

"Yeah, I'll let her know. Ah hell, I should've gotten your order while we talked so they could put it together."

"No, that's fine," Carter said, thinking through what he had learned. "Let me get a baked ziti and an order of garlic knots. Can you throw in a soda or two?"

"You got it."

"Alright, thank you."

"Cash or card?"

"Either way is fine."

"Cash helps us more."

"Deal."

"Alright, should be twenty minutes. Also, I'm kind of slow right now. Do you want me to send over that waitress, so you can chat about Laura?"

Thirty minutes later, Carter was back on his couch with the same amazing baked ziti he remembered as a kid—and he had Laura's number.

He shoveled in more food while watching the news but not really seeing it. Instead, he rehearsed what he wanted to say and how he could say it.

The truth was, he had no idea what to say. He wanted to apologize for everything that had gone down fifteen years ago but didn't know how to even start. She hadn't done anything wrong, and a small part of him had always missed what he'd lost that day.

He stopped that thought by shoving another garlic knot in his mouth and punching the number into his phone, his thumb hovering over the green call button.

It would be better to just thank her for getting him to the hospital, wish her well, and hope that was enough. He tossed the phone to the side, trying to focus on the news while he finished his dinner and got his thoughts in order.

After dinner, he put his phone in his pocket and gathered up the trash, tossing it right back in the bag the girl had delivered it in. He hooked it over his arm and used his crutches to move him toward the trash can under the sink. Dinner was done, but without a rideshare he was kind of stuck, and while he had made a go of it thus far, taking a rideshare for every trip and ordering for every meal were going to get old soon.

He used his crutches to go up the stairs to the bedroom one step at a time, with two bags of clothes in each hand. Reaching the top of the stairs felt like a marathon, and only then, after he caught his breath, did he look around and realize the laundry room was on the main floor. He headed over to what looked like the master bedroom, passing four other rooms, all of which were ready for guests.

Opening the double doors to the master revealed a king-sized bed with a gray comforter facing a TV mounted on the wall. Next to the dresser and desk, which matched the dark wood bed, two doors stood, one on either wall. Carter went to the right one first and found what he would've called a closet, but really was probably a dressing room, complete with an island and drawers. He tossed the shopping bags on the floor and headed back over toward the other side of the massive room. This time, when he pushed through the door, he found a master bath fitted with double sinks, a soaking tub, and a glass shower with all the bells and whistles. The ad had said it was renovated, but Carter had to admit, this exceeded his expectations.

His arms sore, he hobbled back over to the bed and eased down, taking care to leave the crutches where he could grab them easily. He pulled over one of the many pillows and propped up his leg before easing back into the bed for a rest.

He needed a shower, and apparently, to order a new laptop. His bills at his old place were all on autopay, and he could have his mail forwarded...

He was stalling and he knew it.

Carter pulled out his phone, saw Laura's number was still there, typed on the screen, and hit the green call button.

"Hello?"

God, her voice hadn't changed at all.

"Hi, is this Laura?" he asked, falling back on his years of business calls.

"This is. How can I help you?"

He cleared his throat and reminded himself it was just a phone call, nothing special. "This is Carter Price. I wanted to thank you for um...taking care of me after the wreck."

"Oh...you're welcome. Part of the job. How did you get this number?"

"Friend of a friend. I hope you don't mind. Um, actually, I was wondering if we could speak in person."

There was a pause on the other end of the line.

"About what?"

"After fifteen years, I guess we have a lot to catch up on, but—"

"Carter, listen, this is a bad time right—"

"I heard you need a place to rent." The words came out of his mouth before he realized what he was saying.

"Yeah, like I said, I'm in the middle of—"

"Well, I'm going to be staying in town for a while now and I'm renting a house for the next few months. It has a bunch of bedrooms, and I need some help with my leg and all, and I was wondering if you'd like to move in and maybe we could help each other out."

Silence.

"Laura? Are you still there?"

"I'm sorry, Carter. I appreciate the offer, but—"

"I'll pay you for your trouble, and you can live here rent free. I owe you after…well, after everything."

"I'm sorry, Carter. Things have changed. Thank you again for thinking of me, and I hope you have a quick recovery."

"Okay. In that case, about what happened in high school—"

"I'm sorry. I've got to go. Bye."

Carter stared at his phone in his hand after she ended the call until his eyes felt heavy.

As he lay there, trying to sleep, Carter did what he always did at night. He tallied up how much good he needed to do to outweigh his past.

CHAPTER 8

The next day Laura let the last and heaviest box fall out of her hands onto the carpet. "Thanks again for all this," she said, wiping her brow.

"Oh, of course! I'm so excited you and Holden get to stay with me. I'm sorry I don't have room for your furniture." Megan had practically jumped at the chance to offer up her apartment after the construction had gone well into the night only to start up again at seven the next morning. Laura had called to complain, only to have no one answer. Figures everyone had gone home for the day. Must be nice, she thought, and refocused on what Megan had said. Oh right, all of her furniture.

Laura forced a smile she hoped was nonchalant and waved it off. "We can leave it at the apartment until I get a new place. I'm just so glad we have somewhere to sleep that doesn't have a jackhammer next door."

Megan's one-bedroom apartment was not big, but it was quiet, at least assuming the cats didn't start meowing. She had two—a teddy bear of an orange tabby named Lincoln and a small brown shorthair named Popsicle who was a year old and followed Lincoln everywhere. Both were rescues, along with two parakeets and a turtle. It went without saying that if Megan had the room, she'd have a whole farm. She had always wanted a dog, but her shifts at the station were too long to be fair to one, given she lived alone.

"It'll be like a party!" Megan said. "I need to run to the store anyway, so I'll pick up some veggie sticks for Holden and a few more options for fruit. He likes mac and cheese, right?"

"Adores it."

"Okay, I'll pick up some of that too. Here's my spare key, so you can get back in after you grab Holden, in case I'm not back."

Laura accepted the key and looked at it in her palm. "I really can't thank you enough."

"That's what friends are for. We girls have to stick together. Alright, I'm off to the store. Bye, boys," she said to the cats.

Laura and Megan had been friends ever since Laura had started running calls. It helped that Megan was the only other girl her age. All of the guys adored Megan and for good reason. She was tall and thin with gorgeous hair, but that was nothing compared to Megan's marshmallow personality. She was the bubbliest, friendliest, kindest person Laura had ever known. She never ate meat and adopted any animal in need of a home regardless of how many she already had.

When they'd first met, Laura hadn't known what to make of the real-life, blue-eyed doll. She didn't exactly scream firefighter, and for a brief moment, Laura thought she might just be there to get a boyfriend. That thought vanished the first time she responded to a house fire with Megan, who had no fear when it came to running into the flames.

It had been a family home, and everyone was out, thanks to Megan and the other guys on the call. But when the little girl started crying about her pets, Megan darted back inside to find the family's dog and cat, managing to carry both of them out as the house started to show signs of collapsing.

The image of her in her equipment, carrying those animals out of the flames, had banished any doubt Laura had in her mind that Megan was the real deal.

That night had left an impression on the guys too. They all adored her, but she would never date any of them, not even for coffee, so after a few years, they gave up and started treating her like a sister.

Laura got to work, unpacking the dozen boxes they had managed to squeeze into both of their sedans. Most of it was clothes, toiletries, and toys. The rest of her things would need to be moved with a truck once she had a place of her own.

She started laying out Holden's favorite toys and stuffed animals in the little living room. Megan had offered Laura her own bedroom, but that was a bridge too far, and Laura already felt terrible for intruding as it was.

Once she had everything arranged as neat as it could be, she pulled out the sofa bed and fixed it with some sheets she had brought with her, taking special care to lay out Holden's favorite stuffed animals. Laura hoped he wouldn't mind the change too much. Hopefully he'd go right to sleep beside her.

The phone buzzed in her back pocket.

"Hey, Ash," Laura said, answering with one hand while trying to break down boxes with the other.

"Hey. Heard you moved in with Megan."

"Yeah, the apartment next door is all torn up with construction, and the noise proved my original thought that there never was any insulation between the walls to begin with."

"That bad, huh?"

"Oh, yeah."

"Well, I'm glad she had the room. I'd offer mine, but you know mine's smaller than hers."

"Thank you anyway. I really appreciate you guys having my back. I need to figure out what to do for Holden's birthday. I had wanted it to be special, but you know how that goes."

"Don't mention it. And we'll figure something out. By the way, I have a message for you."

"Oh, yeah?" Laura frowned to herself while trying to pound at the stubborn cardboard with her other fist to get it to fold. One last punch did it, and her victim collapsed in on itself, the last of its kind.

"You working out over there?" Ash asked with a laugh.

"Not even close. Trying to get a box to collapse," Laura said, standing up and puffing out a breath, making her bangs fly away from her eyes. "So who's this message from?"

"Carter Price."

Laura froze. Why was it that all of a sudden, everywhere she turned, he was around?

"When did you see him?"

"A couple of days ago when I took him into custody. I asked if he had any questions and he asked about you. I had debated whether or not to tell you, but since he's staying in town for a while, I figured I'd better."

"Why doesn't he just fly home?" Laura asked.

"I heard through the grapevine this morning that at the arraignment, the judge gave some conditions, one of which is he's not allowed to leave the state. I don't know where he is, but he won't be leaving Montana for at least another couple of months, after his next court date."

"Wow. Maybe I should've been a judge."

"Yeah, I see you more as a doctor."

Laura shrugged and smiled before realizing Ash wasn't in the room with her. "Thanks," she added.

Laura drew in a breath, trying to tell herself he couldn't still be mad at her after all these years, and that his opinion didn't matter.

"Well, what did he say?"

"He just asked if I knew how to contact you, said he wanted to thank you for everything you did for him."

"He already tracked me down. Did you give him my number?"

Ash scoffed. "Of course not. I'm not surprised he found it though. He seemed pretty persistent."

It wasn't easy to make an impression on Ash since she was pretty tough, but Carter must have hit a nerve or something. Either way, Laura had too much to deal with already without bringing up the past.

Laura wrapped up the call with Ash and grabbed her car keys to get Holden. She locked up Megan's apartment and headed out to the parking lot to find her car with the visitor tag hanging from the rearview mirror. The sight of it was a punch in the gut. She pulled the thing down as she cranked over the engine and headed toward the school.

She hadn't done anything wrong and even had a small savings account to show for her efforts, but with one letter from her apartment management, she was going to be homeless in a few weeks.

Ten minutes later she'd signed Holden out, grabbed him and his bag, and was jogging back to the car.

"So how was your day?" she asked, climbing back in and grabbing her seatbelt.

"Good. I played on the slide."

"Oh, that's fun."

"Yeah, we got messy."

"I can see that," Laura said with a glance in the rearview

mirror. "Hey, buddy, what do you say if we stayed at Ms. Megan's house tonight?"

Holden's big brown eyes looked over at her in the rearview mirror. "Ms. Megan? She has curly hair like a princess."

"Yes, she does. Do you want to go sleep at her house? It'll be like an adventure."

Holden did his signature shrug and smiled. "Sounds good to me!"

Laura let out a bark of a laugh. "Buddy, I love you."

"I love you too. Can we listen to music?"

"Sure thing."

After two rounds of the same Mickey Mouse song, Laura pulled back into the parking lot next to Megan's car.

It wasn't until now that Laura realized how deep Megan's kind-hearted nature went. She insisted on cooking them all dinner, which concerned Laura at first when the smoke alarm went off, not to mention the limited array of healthy snacks in the pantry, but she made a pretty tasty quiche with egg substitute and carrots. Thankfully, Holden ate most of his portion and even said thank you on his own, which was a win for the day in Laura's opinion. When Holden stood up after he finished eating, he even started to laugh at the cats after they almost knocked him flat rushing to get their own dinner.

After dinner, they went to take a bath only to realize Megan's bathroom was not only filled with essential oils on every flat surface, but the tub stopper was broken, meaning Holden was going to have to take a shower. Laura drew in a breath and tried to calmly prepare Holden for the spray. He nodded and held her hand, but once the water was on, he turned into a thirty-five-pound screaming banshee, allergic to all water, dancing around as if it was acid.

Hearing the chaos, Megan rushed in with a Tupperware

lid, which fit perfectly inside the drain. It worked, and slowly, warm water rushed in to fill the tub. When it was full, Holden looked suspicious and tested it before shaking his head. It *was* perfect, but Laura didn't have the energy to fight over the meaning of room temperature water with a tired toddler.

"Okay, fine. Let's just take a break and go get ducky."

"Ducky!" Holden said, running back to his packed bag with the towel still wrapped around him. Once they had retrieved the small rubber duck, Holden led the way back to the bathroom to show off the new digs to his favorite bath toy.

A loud splash came from the bathroom before they even rounded the corner. Holden shrieked and jumped back as a large orange cat went flying by, flinging water everywhere.

"What's wrong?" Megan asked, coming running again, before she shrieked too. "Lincoln! No, no, no!" She grabbed a towel and started mopping up the wet trail that led back to the guilty party.

"He wanted a bath! That's so silly!" Holden said, laughing, but then the smile left his face. "Uh-oh. What's in here?"

If Laura had been smiling, it would've left as soon as she saw what was left of the water. Orange cat hairs and little bits of what looked to be cat litter and kibble were in the otherwise perfectly warm, full bathtub.

She hid her sigh and reached for the Tupperware lid to drain the tub. "Well, that's okay. We can run another one. She cranked the water for the third time, but instead of warm water, the tap was tepid at best, and the water turned ice cold.

Damn.

"Megan? I think we might've used all of the hot water."

Megan came back in the room holding the wet towels. "Oh no. That's okay though. It should reset in about an hour."

Her smile faded a little when she eyed Holden still partially naked in his towel. As if on cue, he let out a big yawn.

Megan pulled a face. "I could heat up some water on the stove, though, if that would help."

"If that's not a huge pain, that might help get him down faster."

Fifteen minutes later, Holden was finally in a few inches of room temperature water. The seal from the Tupperware lid wasn't great, so it was the fastest bath in history, which meant Holden didn't get to play. Since he was already tired, that meant more crying and pouting, as Laura hauled the sopping wet, reluctant little boy out of the tub and wrapped him in one of Megan's remaining towels.

"Holden, look at me."

"No." He pouted while clinging to his ducky.

"Look at me."

"NO!"

Laura drew in a steadying breath. "I'm sorry you didn't get to play in the water. Maybe tomorrow."

Big brown eyes looked at her while his last tear slid down his damp, red cheek. His lower lip puffed out in front of his face as he did his best sad face, which, unfortunately for her, he had learned and mastered at school.

"Come on," she said, toweling him off, "let's get you dressed and into bed."

An hour later, Holden had finally fallen asleep next to her after three stories, a sip of water, and a trip to the bathroom where the two cats joined them.

Once Holden had exhausted all of his many attempts to avoid sleeping on the pullout couch next to her, he started tossing and turning. He flopped around and had accidentally kicked her so many times that Laura wasn't sure her kidneys could take anymore.

Finally, he settled, and she turned slowly to watch him

sleep. Dark lashes against perfect skin without a wrinkle or worry in the world. He looked so at peace.

Laura released a silent sigh and rose, planning to finally grab a shower of her own. By now the hot water heater should've caught up. She considered skipping, but her back was killing her, and she just wanted to wash off the day.

Standing over him, Laura looked down at him, asleep on the big pullout bed in someone else's living room. It was quiet, but he deserved so much more.

Laura crept into the shower, making sure she closed the door before turning on the spray. She pulled down her ponytail and ran her hands through her hair before stepping under the water. While she stood there, letting the hot water run over her back, she let so many things course through her mind, but Carter Price looking at her in the hospital kept coming back to the surface.

After all this time, why did he still want to talk to her? What could he possibly have to say after fifteen years?

Fifteen years. Surely any bad blood they still had between them couldn't be worth losing some disposable income. What was worse, after all? Holden sleeping on someone else's pullout sofa in someone else's apartment or her getting some money out of a very rich man she just so happened to date in high school? Megan was great, but Laura hated to put her out, and it was clear this wasn't going to be a suitable long-term arrangement.

Laura let her head rest on the side of the shower as she thought through her decision. She still didn't know why she couldn't heal him, but she could deal with that later. Holden mattered more. Laura needed money and a place to stay, so first thing tomorrow morning, Laura was going to call Carter back.

CHAPTER 9

C arter stared out the window and pulled out his phone to dial Laura again. She had called him that morning, saying she'd changed her mind and would be over today. The call had been short, but what had astounded Carter the most was when she had said the last part.

"I'm not sure if you know or not, but just so you aren't surprised, I have a three-year-old son named Holden, so I'll need two rooms and can pay my way for both."

The sentence had shocked him, but recovering quickly, he had managed an okay before Laura laid down terms. There were to be no alcohol or drugs on the premises as long as she and Holden were there. He didn't actually have issues with either of those things, anyway, but the deal made complete sense. After he agreed, Laura had ended the call, saying she would see him at three, which had been thirty minutes ago.

As he had already been to physical therapy that morning —with the help of another rideshare—Carter didn't have anything else to do except wait.

He was nervous. His hands were slick as he kept adjusting his grip on the handles of his crutches, maneuvering to and from the window in an awkward lurching shuffle. He'd thought about getting to speak to her again for years, but never could face it. Once at college, he'd focused on school, then his MBA, then finally, the business, but through it all, thoughts of her occasionally crept up to haunt him in the middle of the night. He felt he'd gotten a chance to make everything right in his life—except for her. Laura was the last memory he stayed awake to at night. It didn't matter whom he was dating or where he was. A smell, a song, or a memory with Coach or his mom would bring back an image of her and the time they'd shared together, as well as the regret he had over the way it had ended.

They'd been so in sync in high school, and he had spent most of his secondary education studying Laura, but still, people changed. Carter realized he wanted her to be the same person he had known, who would laugh at his jokes and finish his sentences.

Carter also hoped her son liked him. He didn't have any experience with little kids. That Holden was three meant nothing to him. Was he potty-trained? Could he talk? He had no idea.

He hobbled over to the window again to see an unremarkable Toyota Camry pull up, Laura behind the wheel. A yellow VW Beetle followed, driven by a fiery redhead. Both cars were packed to the roof with boxes.

Laura stepped out first, her chestnut hair pulled up into a high pony. She wasn't in uniform today. Just jeans, a black T-shirt, and sneakers. Carter smiled to himself. It was just the kind of thing she'd worn growing up. Not too girly or sporty. Laura's friend, in a pink T-shirt and with red hair bouncing out of a pink headband, was already setting down boxes next to her car. Laura ducked into the back seat and, after a longer time than he'd expect, pulled out a little boy who looked just like her. He waved to her friend and then squinted up at the big house in front of him. Laura set him down and held his hand. The little boy bounced up and down and wrinkled his face while flopping his arms, until she produced a stuffed Mickey Mouse that had seen better days. The pair of them walked up the walkway and then the steps while the redhead stayed behind to unload.

Carter hobbled over to the door and swung it open. Laura gave him a tight smile and a quick nod.

He opened his mouth to speak, but before he could, she looked down and jiggled the hand of the little boy.

Carter tried to crouch down, but the best he could do was lean. "Hey, buddy."

The little boy clutched Mickey tighter, made a face, and retreated behind his mom and looked at the ground.

"Sorry," she said. "He's tired. Didn't get much sleep last night. Could do with a nap. Can we come in?"

He stumbled backwards as they stepped into the two-story foyer. "Oh, yeah, um, do you want a tour?"

"Did you hurt yourself?"

"What?" Carter asked, looking down.

Holden pointed at Carter's leg in the cast and his crutches. "Do you have a boo boo?"

"Um, yeah I do."

"Does it hurt?" Holden asked, holding Mickey and furrowing his little brow like he really understood pain.

"A little bit, but I have medicine."

Holden considered this. "I take Tylenol. My mommy makes people feel better."

Laura shifted from one leg to the other and put her car keys in her purse, which was still on her shoulder.

"I know. She's very good at it."

Holden shrugged. "Yeah, I know."

"I like your doll."

"This is Mickey Mouse. He has a lot of friends."

"That's good."

"Do you have snacks?"

"Holden, I have Goldfish in the car."

"I don't like Goldfish anymore. They're not my favorites."

Carter looked from Laura to Holden to try and figure out what to do. Laura sighed and looked bone-tired. She had said Holden hadn't slept much, and it didn't take a baby expert to figure out that when a kid didn't sleep, neither did the parents.

"I have snacks in the kitchen. Want to see?" Carter asked.

Holden nodded and watched as Carter maneuvered his way down the hall to the huge kitchen. Even Laura's eyes got big as he turned around to face them.

"Wow, I've never seen an island that big."

"Yeah, I know. I just needed something furnished. Your key is right here," he said, picking up the piece of brass and passing it over. "Hey, that reminds me. Do you have furniture too?"

"Yeah, it's still at my place. I need to get a storage unit," she said, raking her hands through her hair, as if adding yet another thing to the list.

"Well, you don't need to do that. I think there's an empty basement if you'd like to store stuff down there."

"Thanks, but I think I'm good. Already called a place."

"Oh, okay." Carter tried to ignore the sting of disappointment with her words and put on a smile for Holden, who was orbiting the island like a little alien with light-up shoes that echoed in the open floor plan.

"Can he have chips?" Carter asked.

Before she could answer, Holden yelled, "Chips?" and ran toward Carter, knocking into him. The move caught him by surprise, and he dropped one crutch with a clatter, started to fall backwards, but caught himself just in time on the handle of a double oven. Searing pain made him see stars as the move stretched the tender burned skin under the bandages on his arms and chest.

"Oh, Jesus, I'm so sorry," Laura said, rushing forward to grab Holden's arm, pulling him backwards. While crouched down, she picked up Carter's crutch and passed it over. "Holden, I told you in the car. He has a lot of boo boos. You have to be gentler."

Holden looked like he might cry as he looked up at Carter and murmured, "Sorry" over a fat, quivering lip.

Carter took a moment to catch his breath and right himself on his crutches. "It's okay. I'm good. I'm good," he said to try and convince himself it was true. "Alright, buddy, let's find you a bowl and get some chips."

"CHIPS! Do you have a Mickey Mouse bowl?"

"That's packed up, honey. Actually, can you watch him for a second? I need to help Megan." Carter nodded, and Laura gave Holden a quick peck on the top of the head. "Be right back, buddy."

"Mama?" Holden looked unsure. "I come with you?" He raised his arms up and hopped up and down.

"No, no, no. I'll be right back."

Holden started to whimper, jumping faster and faster. Carter didn't know much about kids, but he was a quick study and could see a tantrum coming.

"Hey, who needs a bowl? Let's pop open some chips," he said, grabbing a bag and tearing the top open.

Holden glanced over at him, unsure but intrigued. "I have a TV too," Carter offered. That did it.

As if transfixed, a little alien being led toward the mother ship, Holden took the bag and followed Carter toward the living room. He shoved chips into his face, leaving a trail of crumbs in his wake as they walked.

"Let's see what we can find."

"Mickey..." Crunch, crunch, "Mouse."

Carter looked at him and started to laugh.

Holden must have thought he was waiting, because after a moment, he swallowed and added, "Please."

A few minutes later, Holden was on the couch, hugging a half empty chip bag, staring into the screen as the "pals" as he called them danced around and sang while solving little puzzles. Thank God it was a smart TV, and Carter had been able to find the beloved mouse within minutes.

A loud thump had him getting up from the chair, and with a quick glance at Holden, who hadn't moved a muscle, Carter grabbed his crutches and moved over to the door.

Laura and the redhead—Megan, he'd heard Laura call her —were stacking boxes inside.

"You sure you'll be okay?" Megan asked, looking wary.

Laura propped her hands on her hips and wiped her brow with the back of her hand. She looked completely drained. "Yeah," she said, nodding. "We'll be fine. Thanks again for everything."

The pair embraced, the redhead's pink shirt a total contrast to Laura's black, but it was clear they were friends. Carter couldn't hear what they whispered to each other.

The redhead saw him when she stepped back from the hug.

"Hi, you must be Carter." She stepped forward with a hand outstretched. "You look a lot better than the last time I saw you. I'm Megan."

He gladly accepted it and realization dawned. "Are you a paramedic too?"

She laughed. "No, that's just Laura, but we're out of the same station."

"She's the best firefighter we've got."

"Oh you!" Megan said with a wave of her hand that made her red hair bounce.

"Did you come to my call?"

69

"Pulled you out of the car myself. It's a good thing you wore your seatbelt." She whistled. "I'm glad I was able to get to you as soon as we could. Those electric cars are terrible. Yours kept burning for days."

Carter had no idea what to say, but the best he could manage was, "I didn't know that."

"Yeah, each battery fuel cell catches after the one behind it. Anyway, I'm really glad to see you up."

"Thank you so much. I don't even know what to say."

Megan waved another hand and then her ice-blue eyes caught his and got serious. "Be nice to my Laura and my Holden."

"I will," Carter said with a nod.

"You better," she said with another bright smile. "Alright, well, I'll see you tomorrow at work."

"Thanks again," Laura said, before waving her off and shutting the door behind her.

"She doesn't seem like the firefighter type," Carter said when they were alone.

"Yeah, I know, but she's great." Laura propped her hands on her hips and looked at the boxes before meeting his eyes. She was beautiful, just like she had always been to him. The years hadn't diminished her one bit, taking her from a young girl to an accomplished woman. If anything, she looked sexier now than he remembered.

"Holden's watching TV?"

Carter nodded.

"I need to unpack, but we need to talk about the terms of this arrangement first," Laura said.

"Sure, yeah, I understand. Let's go into the dining room."

He led the way on his crutches toward the back, through the expansive kitchen, into a side dining room with a dark wooden table set for eight. He pulled out an upholstered chair for her, which took longer than it should

70

because of the crutches, and sat down next to her at the end of the table, so he could face her and stretch out his legs.

"How long will you be here?" Laura asked, jumping right in. She was a lot more confident than he remembered, but then, neither of them was in high school anymore, and he could see the mama bear in her now.

"At least two months, maybe three."

"Until your court date," she said, nodding once.

"Word travels fast."

"I know people," she said. "How much is two rooms going to cost me?"

"What were you paying at your old place?" Laura said the number, and Carter could've fallen over from shock at how low the number was. She couldn't afford a shed for that price in California.

"How about half, since we're sharing the house."

"Utilities?"

"All-in already."

"That's too low."

"Not considering you'll be helping me," he said, watching her fold her arms and narrow her eyes. She glanced down at his leg, and her eyes skimmed over his burns on his arms.

"What kind of help do you have in mind?"

"It's hard to get around with the crutches. I can't drive, and getting groceries and clothes almost killed me."

Laura nodded and waited for him to continue.

"I need help around here too. I don't need a maid, but cleaning and laundry are hard enough, and I could use some help with that."

"Seems fair. What else?"

Carter thought for a second and had to look away to clear his thoughts. He was no stranger to business negotiations, but he hadn't wanted his first conversation with Laura to go like this. Still, it was clear she wasn't going to relax until things were settled.

"Did they go over how to change your bandages?" Laura asked.

Carter had to think. The whole discharge had been rushed and under the watchful eye of Sergeant Myers.

"Yes, but I can't remember."

"Have you changed them since you left the hospital?"

"Only once. It took me forever."

Laura nodded again. "Should we write all this down so both of us are on the same page?"

"If that would make you more comfortable, we can do whatever you want."

Laura seemed to relax at that, nodding once and letting her arms drop to her sides before she ran a hand through her hair.

"Okay, we'll draft something up." She glanced over her shoulder toward the hall where the echo of Mickey Mouse continued. "While I have a minute, let me go unpack."

CHAPTER 10

L aura had tried to play it cool, but when she was alone upstairs and laying out Holden's clothes in the dresser in what would be his room, she didn't know what to think. The house was massive. She'd counted at least five bedrooms, and all of them must have been furnished by a decorator. Whoever rented this out had excellent taste and a whole lot of cash.

Carter had said he didn't care which rooms she took, and Laura had found one designed for kids, with a bunk bed and trundle that was low enough to the ground for a toddler. The whole room was outfitted in a woodland theme, with decals of moose on the walls and furniture designed to look like it was in a log cabin. The buffalo-plaid drapes were blackout too, which was perfect for Holden, since he was quick to wake up with the slightest light or sound.

Laura finished placing his clothes in the dresser and arranged his toys on the bed, taking care to display the piggy bank her mom had made in pottery class for him on the dresser, so he would feel as at home as possible. She placed his favorite books on the nightstand and stood, surveying her work.

If they had to leave their apartment, this wasn't a bad place to come to. Even if it was only for two months. And with her ex-boyfriend. At least it would feel like a vacation until she could move back into her old place. The leasing office had said the renovations would take ninety days, and with the reduced rent, Laura figured she could probably afford to stay here for the third month even after Carter had left, and everything would work out perfectly, or at least, as perfectly as things could with her life.

Laura broke down the boxes and jogged down the stairs to see Holden passed out on the couch. Carter was in the recliner, resting too. On the TV, the news was muted while stock prices scrolled on the bottom of the screen.

Relieved to have extra time to unpack herself, Laura crept upstairs and found her room. She hadn't been picky, but when searching for a suitable room for Holden, Laura had looked in all of the rooms, finding Carter had taken the master, which made sense, though he should make his bed and pick up his clothes. Laura didn't know if that was part of her new job description and figured it may be since Carter had a hard time maneuvering around with his crutches.

The other rooms each had their own theme and vibe. Laura had taken one down by Holden's room which faced south and was filled with sun. After a basement apartment, the golden glow of the afternoon had drawn her into the yellow room with white bedding. It felt like a more feminine room, and even though she would've been fine with anything, it felt nice to step into the dreamy bedroom, which even included a plush, tan couch by the window along with a TV on the wall.

Laura got to work unpacking her clothes, taking care to put pictures of Holden and her mom and dad on the nightstand. Because her outfits only ranged from jeans to her uniforms, she was done in a few minutes and sat down on the bed to test it out and look around, letting the silence envelop her.

She still felt like a failure. Ever since John had taken off, she had sworn she'd be independent and wouldn't need to rely on anyone. Looking around at this beautiful room, which Carter was practically giving her, made her antsy. To add insult to injury, her car had been acting up on the way here, and her bank account couldn't take much more.

Laura glanced down at her hands and closed her eyes to calm her mind, trying to visualize herself healing. The warmth tingled in her palms, and the knots in her shoulders melted away. When she opened her eyes again, she was more awake. It felt so natural to her, and yet, when she had tried to heal Carter, it hadn't happened. Just like Holden and her mom, no amount of visualizing brought that familiar, comforting glow. It just didn't make any sense. At least now that she was in the same house, she might get another chance. That had been the only reason she had asked about his bandages.

Looking forward to getting another crack at it, Laura grabbed her purse and keys and jogged downstairs. The sun was starting to fade, and she knew they needed groceries. There was a grocery store at the entrance to the neighborhood not even a five-minute drive away. Laura peeked in on Holden and Carter from the stairs, and they were still both passed out.

She tiptoed to the kitchen and opened the fridge to find not much of anything. A few takeout leftovers and a couple of sodas, but no milk or anything for Holden.

Laura debated leaving, knowing full well that Holden would wake up petrified without her. She shook her head and decided it'd be best to wait until he woke up. From

75

where she stood in the kitchen, Laura could see Carter sleeping.

He was still just as handsome as he had been in school, but older and without that same cocky grin. But getting a DUI, crashing a fancy car, and being tied to crutches for a couple of months would knock anyone down a peg or two. She had always believed him to be a good person, but that had been her downfall. He might be good-looking, charming, and rich, but he was the same person who had a passenger seat full of drugs in high school. Her mom might've thought he'd changed, but the crash had proven otherwise, so no, she would certainly not be leaving Holden alone with him.

The thought of the drugs made her mad all over. Once the betrayal and shock had worn off, she had been convinced he was a dealer. She hadn't been a paramedic long before she'd seen her share of overdoses from people who had no defense against the chemicals people sold to them.

A knock at the door sprang her from her thoughts. Neither Holden nor Carter moved, so Laura walked toward the front entry. Maybe it was the landlord, coming to drop something off. Laura checked the peephole. A man in a jean jacket stood outside. Laura felt like she had seen him before but couldn't place him.

She eased the door open and poked her head around the side.

"Hi, can I help you?" she asked, with a good ninety percent of her body still behind the door.

"Sorry to bother you, ma'am. I thought someone else might be here. Have a nice day."

"Oh, um, this is a rental, but maybe I can pass along the name. Who were you looking for?"

The man stopped and turned around. His hair was gray and his face lined, but his green eyes were still vibrant. "Carter Price."

Carter hadn't mentioned a man, so Laura went with her gut. "He's here, but he's asleep at the moment. Did you want me to take a message, or is it urgent?"

"I'll just come back another time."

"Oh, okay. He'll be here tomorrow. Can I tell him who stopped by?"

The man looked down for a second before meeting her eyes again. "Tell him his dad came looking for him."

The wind left her lungs. When they had grown up together, Carter never mentioned his dad and had idolized his mom, who'd a been a waitress at the local diner forever. It was only after they had been dating for six months that Carter confessed, with tears in his eyes, that his dad had taken off when he was a baby.

"Was he expecting you, Mr. Price?" Laura asked, not caring about the venom in her voice.

The older man laughed. She could see the resemblance immediately when he smiled. Carter looked just like him. "Call me Frank, and after all this time, no, I doubt it. I heard he was living here through a friend at the police station. I just wanted to talk to him. I've tried to call him before, but he never picked up, and well, with him being back in town, I thought this might be a chance for us to get to know each other."

A protective instinct came out of nowhere. Laura didn't care much for Carter anymore, but as a mother to a son whose dad had vanished, all of her emotions ran to the surface. "You're about thirty-one years too late. He needed you when he was younger. He wasn't hard to find then. Captain of the football team, and even stood up on stage when he won a scholarship to Stanford at graduation. It would've been nice if you'd made an appearance before now."

The man looked down at the ground, hanging his head in shame, nodding slowly. "You're right."

"So now you hear he's in town and made it rich, and you come knocking on his door? That seems a little convenient to me. If you had actually wanted to be a father, you should've been there for him sooner." Laura's face was hot, and her eyes were beginning to water with angry tears that she wasn't sure were only for Holden anymore.

"I had to fix myself for a long time."

Laura blinked fast and shot back from the hip. "That's a lot of time wasted."

"I was ashamed, but that's in the past. I don't know if he'll see me, but I'll come back tomorrow. When I heard about the accident, I just felt like I should come. Didn't know you were with him. Thought he was alone."

"So you could ambush him?"

His head snapped up and pain etched into the lines of his face from the nerve she had struck. "No, because I am his father. I was a worthless father, but I still love my son."

The dam broke. Laura ducked behind the door to swipe a hand over her face. "I'll let him know you came by."

Before she could shut the door, Frank Price put his hand against it. "It's not my business, but who are you?"

"A mother to a fatherless son," she said and slammed the door shut.

CHAPTER 11

Carter watched as Laura carried in the groceries after letting Holden back into the house after their trip. He and Holden had slept until almost five, at which point Laura had asked him about a grocery list. Carter gave it to her and offered her money for his share of things, which she declined.

Part of him wanted to go with them if for no other reason than to have an outing, but while they'd been gone, he had taken the chance to head upstairs and wash up with a rag, which, with his injured leg and arms, took a long time. He looked forward to the day when he could hop in and out of the shower like he was accustomed to.

Holden waved and carried in a half-eaten banana, while Laura heaved at least five bags on either arm. Carter's gut reaction was to help her carry things, but with his crutches he didn't even know how to start, so he just nudged the door shut behind her with his crutch.

"How was the shopping trip?" he asked, following them both into the kitchen.

"Good," Holden answered with a mouth full of banana. "Mama bought snacks."

"Oh, yeah?" he asked, sitting across from Holden at the kitchen table.

"Yep. I got more chips to replace the ones he ate, and everything else you had asked for, except the ice cream. They had cookies and cream, but no cookie dough." Laura swung open the fridge and added a gallon of milk, some eggs, a loaf of bread, and cold cuts, before filling the fruit drawer with oranges and baby carrots.

"That's okay," Carter said. "Feels like it was easier to find back in the day."

Laura didn't respond, but kept unpacking while Holden sat across from him, watching with those big eyes and big chipmunk cheeks, which puffed out when he chewed.

"Did you want to order in some dinner?" Carter asked.

Laura turned and looked at him. "I picked up a frozen pizza and some nuggets, so we can heat those up."

"It's almost six. We could get Chinese here in twenty minutes. Do you still like that?"

Laura gathered up all of the plastic bags and stuffed them into the pantry below the chips, cookies, cereal, and microwave popcorn. "I do, actually, but we don't have to—"

"My treat," Carter said, pleased he could do something. He wasn't used to sitting around, watching someone else work. "I'll order now. General Tso's Chicken or Beef and Vegetables?" he asked, remembering what she had always liked.

"I'm impressed you remember, or maybe I'm just so dull that I like the same things."

"No, they're great. And I do remember. What does Holden like?"

The little boy perked up at his name. "Who, me?"

Carter smiled, not sure how this worked with a three-year-old. "Yeah, do you like Chinese food? It has rice and vegetables."

"He likes pork fried rice."

"No veggies," Holden said, wrinkling his nose with a funny shrug that made him look like a little grown man.

"Yes, veggies," Laura said, looking under the sink and assessing the stash of cleaning supplies and paper towels.

Carter looked back at Holden, who shook his head and whispered loudly, "No, thank you."

He sucked in his lips to cover a laugh and pulled out his phone to place the order.

Twenty minutes later, he had paid and carried in a bag with the goods, while Laura laid out the plates she had found in the cabinets. He had been in the house for two days, and this was the first time he had eaten on a plate or at the kitchen table for that matter. Most of his time had been spent on the couch in the living room, scraping the edge of the Styrofoam containers with a plastic fork.

Laura wrangled together drinks while Carter put the bag of food on the table. Holden had been getting cranky and managed to demolish another banana while watching some kids' show involving puppies on TV. Even so, once she spooned out some pork fried rice, he wiggled in excitement.

"Oh boy," he said, looking at Carter. "Look at all this food."

"I know. I'm hungry," Carter said and picked up his fork.

"Heeeeey," Holden said with a furrowed brow that actually looked pretty menacing. "You didn't wait for us."

"Holden, he doesn't need to do that," Laura said, mumbling a "Sorry," in Carter's direction.

"No, no, it's fine. I just forgot."

Holden glared at him. "DON'T touch your food until we all do."

"Yes, sir."

Laura looked up toward the ceiling and gave him a pained and patient smile, thanking him for playing along.

"Holden, really. Enough is enough."

"I didn't say, 'You may eat,' like my teachers at school. Those are the rules," he said to Carter with another one of his little funny shrugs.

Laura let out a long sigh. "Holden, please just eat your food."

He shrugged again, and they all dove in, eating with children's cartoons in the background. When Holden's plate was clean, Carter motioned to Laura, who hadn't looked at him once.

"Can he have a doughnut?" he mouthed to her, sliding over a Styrofoam container of the sugar-covered dough.

Laura cracked the barest whisper of a smile before it vanished when she cleared her throat. "You didn't need to do that. I'm also happy to chip in for our meals."

Carter wanted to tell her not to worry about it but didn't think making a fuss would stop her. He had already decided he didn't want her money, but she was so concerned with being independent and not taking one thing for charity, he hadn't figured out how exactly he would do that.

"I'm happy to," was all he could manage to say.

Carter cracked open the doughnut container and won a lifelong friend in Holden with the sweet gesture. Apparently, chips were the way to buy his trust, but sweets were the way to friendship.

Laura declined a doughnut at first, which disappointed Carter a little. He and Holden ate all but one, and when he offered it to her again, she considered for a moment and accepted. The whole exchange felt like he was making progress on breaking down the walls built by old wounds and time.

After dinner, Laura cleaned up while Carter tried to help

by wiping down the table. She bagged up the trash and tossed it into the garbage can in the otherwise empty garage, then moved her car inside. With dinner out of the way, she told Holden to say goodnight and hauled him up for a bath. Carter maneuvered over to his comfy chair and grabbed his phone to check his email.

Most of his employees had already accepted the meeting invitation and sent along a few well wishes. He checked some more accounts and logged onto social media, but after a few minutes, nothing felt that relevant. He could hear Holden upstairs, singing loudly and off-key while sloshing around in the tub. He sat there and listened to the pair of them talking, their voices muffled. Laura said something in a silly voice, and Holden giggled. They went back and forth a few more times before she pulled the plug and released the water. Somehow, what they were doing seemed far more important, and he wished he could be a part of it.

Carter turned on the TV, but after channel surfing, he was restless and felt...lonely. Back home, he'd always have on the news, stocks, a game, and his phone would be blowing up with plans and things he used to think were important. After last week's events—a funeral, car crash, and arrest—Carter's email didn't seem as important. Things that had been stressing him out had worked out on their own, or a decision had been made in his absence.

He could hear Holden come out of the bathroom. "Where's Mr. Carter? Is he still downstairs?"

"Holden, he's a grown-up—"

"What's up, Holden?" he called back.

"Why aren't you upstairs? Do you sleep downstairs?"

"Holden—"

Carter smiled and left his phone charging before grabbing his crutches and rounding the corner to look up the stairs.

Holden stood there in a hooded towel, trying to squish his face through the rails of the landing to see him.

"I'm coming."

"Okay!" Satisfied, Holden turned on his heel and ran back to his bedroom down the hall.

Carter took his time getting up the stairs, the effort and Chinese food conspiring to make the trip even more exhausting than usual. When he finally reached the landing, he ignored his own room and went down the hall to find Holden and Laura curled up in one of the rooms, while she read a story.

"Hi!" Holden said. "You can sit by me." He patted the side of the bed next to him twice.

"Holden, Mr. Carter can't because of his leg."

Holden looked back down at his leg. "Oh."

"Sorry, buddy, maybe next time."

"Do you want to see my book?" he asked, grabbing it and holding it up. "It's *Twinkle, Twinkle!* That's a star."

"Good job! That is a star." Carter took his hand off the crutch.

"You didn't need to come up here. Sorry about that," Laura said, looking like bedtime couldn't come soon enough. Carter dropped his hand.

"Oh, sorry. I didn't mean to interrupt."

"No, it isn't that. I just feel bad about Mr. Bossy Pants."

"Hey! I'm not bossy."

"I've never taken orders from a three-year-old before. He'll do great in business. Got upper management written all over him."

Laura let out a hollow laugh and stroked Holden's hair. "Yeah, maybe. Let me tuck him in, and I'll come out in a minute so we can talk."

"Okay, sounds good. Night, buddy!"

"Good night!"

Carter didn't know where to go after leaving the room but settled on his bedroom, since it seemed far enough from Holden's room that they could talk without making noise. It wouldn't be his first choice, but he didn't think he could take another round trip on the stairs.

To make it less awkward for them both, he sat down on the couch in the sitting area of the massive bedroom and turned on the TV, making sure to mute it for Holden.

A few minutes later, he heard the soft close of a door and peeked down the hall to see Laura standing there. Carter waved her over, and she walked into his bedroom, glancing around at the enormous space around them before stopping in front of the sitting area.

Carter waved his hand awkwardly. "Would you like to sit down? I'd say we could go into the living room, but I'm trying to avoid the stairs again so soon."

"This is fine," Laura said, easing into the chair that matched the sofa. "Did you have a chance to draw up the paperwork?"

"I emailed it off to my lawyer to check it over."

Laura gave a prim nod. "Would you like some help changing your bandages?"

Carter opened his mouth to decline, but then reconsidered. "Yeah, actually."

Laura stood after he directed her to the bag he had left the hospital with. "This won't last too much longer, but I can pick more up for you at the store."

"I'll make sure to give you some cash," he said, and Laura nodded, laying out the supplies on the side table in the room, pulling out a pair of gloves first and snapping them on.

The sun had gone down, and the lights from the bedside table across the massive bedroom were casting a warm glow. Laura clicked on the floor lamp next to them so she could see better. The light caught her brown hair and smooth skin.

She was just as beautiful as she had been, and just as focused, if not more so. Holden clearly took a lot of her time, but Laura seemed to manage it all in such a low stress way. Carter marveled at her. He had so many questions about the last fifteen years he wanted to ask, but he didn't know where to start.

Laura peeled back the bandages, and Carter looked away while she worked. Her touch was so light, he almost didn't feel any pain other than the raw skin touching air. When she was done with one arm, she came around to start on the other. Carter shifted his head so he wouldn't have to see any more.

"What about your chest?" she asked.

"Not as bad," Carter said, knowing he knew nothing about burns. "At least that's what the nurses said."

"Still bandaged?"

Carter nodded.

"Alright, your arms are done. Let me take a look at your chest." She slipped a button through the hole on his shirt and opened it up just enough to reveal the large white gauze. She peeled it back just like she had on his arms, but with nowhere else to turn, he saw the yellow ooze cling to the material. He didn't look down, not wanting to think about his skin. He had been told his arms were second-degree, and his chest was first, but as he was naturally squeamish, he hadn't wanted to spend more time than he needed to on the subject. He had managed to change his gauze only once since leaving the hospital, and the experience had left him light-headed.

"You okay?" she asked, seemingly distracted by the ointment she was applying to the fresh gauze. To calm himself from thinking about his skin, he focused on the intensity in her eyes.

"Yeah, I'm good. Thank you." He meant it. Never in his

wildest dreams did he ever think he'd be this close to her again.

She didn't respond but stood up and surveyed her work while pulling off her gloves. "Is it alright if I touch you without gloves? To look at your leg, that is."

The question seemed odd to Carter, as did the look in her eye. They had touched each other plenty years ago, but now they were almost strangers. Carter chalked it up to her being a medical professional and nodded. "Yeah, of course."

"My hands are clean," she said, falling back on her medical training.

He watched as she leaned down to his right leg in the cast. He wasn't sure what she was looking at or if there was anything she could do, since the bone wasn't out of position. He watched as Laura placed her hand right above his cast, the heat of her touch warming his heart. She shifted her face away from him, so he couldn't see her eyes, and paused with her hand on his knee.

Carter opened his mouth to ask what was wrong when she pulled away, her lips drawn tight as if she wasn't satisfied with something.

"What's wrong?"

She shook her head. "Nothing. I just...remembered something."

Carter would've bet everything she was lying, but before he could press, she spoke again.

"I wanted to tell you that while you were asleep this afternoon, you had a visitor," she said, gathering up the packaging from the bandages.

"Oh, yeah? Someone from school?"

Laura carried the trash over to the can. When she came back, she wiped her hands on her pants. "Your dad." At last, those brown eyes he'd been desperate to see met his.

"My dad?"

She nodded.

"What the hell did he want?" Carter said, not fully believing what she was saying. "Are you sure it was him?"

"I thought about that too, but he looks just like you, or I guess, you look like him. Said he wanted to check on you. Get to know you."

Carter snorted. "What did you tell him?"

"That you weren't available." Laura stared right back at him.

"Well, good. I have enough trouble as it is."

"He did say he'd be back tomorrow."

"Well, I hope he enjoys looking at the yard because that's all he's going to see. He's about thirty years too late for a game of catch."

Laura let out a smile. "I may have said something like that too."

Carter looked back over at her, raising his eyebrows in surprise. "Really?"

Laura shrugged. "It brought back a lot of emotions."

Carter blinked, not sure what she meant. "Like what?"

"Holden's dad disappeared before I found out I was pregnant."

"I'm sorry."

She nodded. "Thank you. It wasn't a long or happy marriage, and if I'm honest with myself, it wasn't a great relationship before that. What little relationship was there was just us using each other as a distraction. We had talked about getting divorced. Fought a lot. With all of the stress, I didn't realize until after he was gone that I was three months pregnant."

"I'm sorry he left you like that." Carter's heart broke for her over what had happened.

"I don't miss him, which is probably telling, because my

life without him wasn't much different. But I'm sad for Holden."

"What about your in-laws? Are you close with them?"

Laura shook her head again. "No, John didn't have any close family. Foster kid who had aged out of the system. A friend set us up a few years ago. So, it's just Holden and me. Mom adores him, but she's in Missoula right now and has been for a while."

Carter didn't have the words to describe what he wanted to say to her about Holden, her husband, all of it. He had been through the wringer, but through it all, he'd had people to stand by him. His poor mother had been right there with him, and though his dad hadn't been around, his grandparents had worked extra hard to make up for the effort.

"Well, I didn't mean to go on about it. I have to work tomorrow, so Holden and I will be out of here by seven. I'll let you rest. Thank you again for letting us rent here."

Carter wanted to stand and struggled to grab his crutch, propping himself up on only one. "Of course. I'm glad to see you, Laura. I really am."

She gave him a small, tight smile before shutting the door, leaving Carter alone with his memories.

CHAPTER 12

L aura spent the next day in a complete blur. After one of the best night's sleep she'd had in a long time, she'd woken up late in the sumptuous room bathed in the early morning sunlight. Normally she was up well before dawn, so the light in the room was a little disorienting and left her feeling behind schedule. At least she had showered last night after leaving Carter in his room.

In addition to the room being the prettiest and the closest to Holden, it also had the added benefit of having its own bathroom, complete with the most gorgeous shower she'd ever seen. The long, hot spray had been the perfect fix to the day after she had moved all of her essential things twice in twenty-four hours. Her muscles were sore, and she had been exhausted from not sleeping so great the past two nights, first because of the construction and second because the pullout couch she'd shared with Holden at Megan's had a bar that hit right on the center of her back.

While moving in with Carter had seemed like a step backward, this room and shower were a great consolation prize. He hadn't been angry or as arrogant as she'd expected, and he was so good with Holden that Laura could feel herself beginning to relax around him. She didn't believe for a second he had changed, but the memories of what had made him so kind in the past started to bubble to the surface. While that was at least a positive, one thing that was still upsetting her was her inability to heal him.

Last night had been a risk for sure. The paramedic in her didn't mind changing bandages for someone who had been a patient, but asking to touch his leg had been a purely selfish move to see if she could heal him. Still, as much as she'd tried to calm her mind, the warm glow she was so used to never came, and though she had wanted to try for longer, the awkward five seconds it took for her to decide nothing was happening was about as long as she could stand. She wasn't going to get another crack at it until tonight when she offered to change his bandages again.

What had happened after the bandages, though, had shocked her. Laura hadn't expected Carter to be interested in his dad, so no surprise there, but she hadn't expected him to consider her feelings about Holden. His eyes held a note of sincerity as he listened to her talk about John. While she didn't need pity from anyone, Carter's heartfelt words rang true and meant something to her. It felt good to be understood and have someone notice everything she was going through so they could appreciate her.

The trip down memory lane had kept her company in the shower, ending almost as soon as her head had hit the pillow. She fell asleep in an instant.

This morning had become more chaotic than she'd intended. Rushed for time, she had gathered her clothes and raked a brush through her hair before slapping some water on her face and darting over to Holden's room.

Thankfully, Holden had slept in as well. He must have slept hard too. Not one to be rushed, Holden fussed while she tried to wrestle him out of pajamas and into clothes and then combed his hair, which was standing on end from being smashed against the pillow in a weird way.

Carter had already been up and, bless him, had made a pot of coffee. Laura grabbed a cup, threw a handful of cereal in a bag for Holden, and practically fireman carried him out to the car while he wriggled to get out of her grasp.

Laura was late to work and almost ran into Megan when she burst through the door.

"Hey, Laura! How's the new living situation working out?"

Laura could've collapsed on the spot but took a breath and grabbed another cup of coffee from the station. "Good, actually. Holden loves the room he's in."

"That's awesome!"

"Yeah, it's got a cute little woodland theme. We're getting two rooms for the price of one, and I think I may ask to take over the rent for the third month to cover us until the apartment is finished."

"Hey, that's a great idea!" Megan said, getting a cup of some fragrant tea and curling up on the couch they had pulled into the kitchen.

"Yeah, thanks again for letting us stay the night."

Megan waved her hands, shooing away the offer of thanks. "No biggie. Was Mr. Green Eyes DUI okay with Holden?"

"Yeah, actually, he was. I was kind of surprised because, you know, kids can be a lot. He proved that this morning for sure."

"Who? Holden? He's an angel."

"Uh-huh," Laura said, making a face and putting back the creamer she had taken out to fix her cup. "Well, yeah, I think it's going to work out."

"It's not weird living with your ex-boyfriend?"

"Not as weird as I thought it would be. He's like anyone else. I mean, it was so long ago, we hardly know each other anymore. It's just like sharing a space with and assisting anyone else."

"I can see that," Megan said, nodding to herself. "I wonder what it would be like to do that?"

"Do what?"

"Rent a big place with another person."

"Your place is cute," Laura said, sitting down for a minute of peace. The first sip of coffee was always a blessing.

"Yeah, I know, but I'd like to meet someone."

"You've already met Mr. Green Eyes as you called him."

"Yeah, he's not my type. I don't want some business guy."

"I'm not the one to ask about men. You know I have horrible taste."

Megan opened her mouth to say something but got cut off by a call coming in. They both sprang into action, Laura leaving her still steaming coffee on the table.

From that first call, the rest of the day was a blur. They were out almost all day, running all over town for various calls before having to respond to an accident on the highway a little farther away. Before she knew what had happened, the day had ended, and she was back in the station when she realized the time.

"Is that clock right? There's no way it's five forty-five," she said to Megan, who was storing her equipment in the locker. An icy feeling dripped down her spine.

"Yeah, don't you have to get Holden?" Megan asked with a confused look that Laura didn't have time to process. She snatched her purse and her keys and took off running for the car. She hopped inside and cranked the engine over, spraying gravel in her wake.

Goldvein wasn't a large town, but anytime she was in a hurry, traffic snarled, locking up the one main road and

KATHRYN K. MURPHY

blocking her way. It didn't help that thanks to the town council, the traffic lights had been changed to a full minute each way.

Laura drummed her fingers on the steering wheel, adding up the minutes while drowning in mom guilt. Her phone buzzed in her bag. The screen showed the school's number. She rummaged around and answered it with one hand.

"Hi! I'm on my way now—"

"Oh, hello, Ms. Burton. How are you?" answered the always cheerful secretary.

"Good. Sorry I'm late. I'm so sorry. How much do I owe for the late penalty?" she asked. Normally, if she was late, it was an additional twenty dollars for every ten minutes.

"Well, there's no late penalty if you can get here in the next four minutes. We tried to call you about an hour ago. Holden is having a rough day and is a little upset."

"Poor buddy. We've had a few off days and been out of our routine," said Laura, still sitting in standstill traffic. Apparently, the summer meant it was time to pave the road, dooming her to an extra-long wait.

"Ah, yes. I see."

Laura could hear Holden in the background. She couldn't make out his words but could tell it was his little whimpering voice, asking, "Is my mom coming?"

"She's on her way now," the secretary said to them both in a kind, calming sort of way. "Would you like to talk to him?"

"Of course. Yes, thank you."

"Come here, sweetie. Yep, hold it like that, okay. Go ahead, she's there."

"Hi, Holden! I'm coming, buddy."

"Where are you?"

Laura could tell he'd been crying and was about to again, when he sniffed at the end of his question.

"I'm driving to you, and I'm coming as soon as I can."

"All of my friends are gone, and Mickey got a stain on him." He whimpered and sniffed again.

"I'm sorry, baby. I know that's tough. We can wash Mickey when we get home."

"Okay, are you here yet?"

Laura looked at the road ahead of her, watching the line of cars crawl forward.

"Not yet, but I promise I'm coming."

"I want to go home," he said in a small voice with a choked sob.

"It's okay. I know. I know. I'm coming as soon as I can."

"Ms. Burton? Hi, it's Lynne again. I'm going to set up a little cot for him next to my desk for him to lie down."

"Okay, thank you. I'm so sorry. I'm coming as soon as I can."

"Sounds good. We'll keep an eye on him."

Laura thanked her and ended the call. As she reached to put the phone down, the traffic crept forward.

"Thank God."

Her car lurched forward with a bang that threw her into the seatbelt. She glanced up into the rearview mirror and saw the driver of a truck look at her and pull a face before smacking the wheel and opening his door.

Panic bubbled up as he and a few other people around her got out and headed toward her car. This was so *not* the time for an accident.

Laura jogged back to see two large dents in her bumper but no other damage. "It's fine. No worries. We don't have to call anyone," she said in a rush to the driver who had rear-ended her.

"Sorry, ma'am. I need to call. It's my company's truck and that's the rule. I'll dial the police now. Are you hurt?"

While she waited for the police, Laura paced and tried to

think of a way to get Holden home. She had gone round and round when her phone buzzed.

"Hello?" she said more aggressively than she wanted.

"Hi, just checking on you guys. I thought you said you'd be home by now." Carter's voice sounded clear and held a note of genuine concern.

Laura explained the situation while pacing and straining her ears for the sound of a police cruiser cutting through the traffic.

"Where's the school? I can go and grab him while you sort things out there."

"No, it's fine. I'll get there when I can." Putting her son in the car with someone who had gotten a DUI a few days ago was a new low for her that she was not willing to explore.

"Seriously, I don't mind. I can get a car seat with the rideshare app."

As much as she didn't want to sign over permission, the idea of Holden upset and having to wait longer than he needed to fueled her flaming mom guilt. At this rate, Laura wouldn't make it there for at least another forty minutes, and that was the best-case scenario. She closed her eyes and prayed for strength, luck, and a new situation before she drew in a breath to speak.

"Okay, I'll text you the address and pay you back."

"No prob. Consider it done."

"Thanks, I'll call them and let them know you're coming."

She ended the call and dialed the school.

"Hi, Ms. Lynne? It's Holden's mom." She rattled through the next chapter in a series of unfortunate events.

There was a lengthy pause. "Oh no, I hope you're okay."

"I am, thank you. I know there will be a penalty."

"Yes, ma'am. Is there maybe someone else you can call? We need to get going now, and I'm not sure how long it will take for you to deal with the police and get here."

She could've died from mom guilt alone when she answered, "Yes, I give permission for Carter Price to take Holden home. Uh, he'll be coming in a rideshare."

Lynne thanked her and got off the phone almost immediately, no doubt to pack up the last child there, put him in a strange car seat in a strange car, and send him home with a man who unbeknownst to them had been arrested a few days earlier.

All of it weighed on Laura and brought her down to her lowest point in a while. She tried to cheer herself up on the way home but had little success, letting the tears slide down her face while berating herself for taking care of other people more than Holden. The best she could do was get home as fast as possible and give him the biggest squeeze she could when she got there. After that, she'd apologize to Carter—who clearly had gotten more than he'd bargained for—pay for the rideshare, and offer to move out if it wasn't working. She hadn't actually signed any of the paperwork yet, but she'd be glad to pay him for the time she had stayed. The idea of moving all of those boxes again made her already aching head start to throb.

To add insult to injury, the ride home took more like sixty minutes. Laura threw the car in park, ran up the steps, and threw the door open, ready to console a screaming child, but the house was void of tears or tantrums.

"Holden?" she called out. Her anxiety had started to take a nasty hold of her with terrible images of what might've happened on their ride home, when she heard the familiar sounds of the Mickey Mouse song from the living room.

"Hey, we're in here," Carter called out.

Laura walked in to find them both sitting on the couch eating McDonald's, Holden hugging a Happy Meal on his lap, picking up another chicken nugget when he saw her.

"Mama!" He jumped up and ran for her, arms outstretched, a fry in one fist and a nugget in the other.

"Hey, baby!" She gave him a big squeeze and didn't let go, trying to soothe her anxiety with his touch.

"Did you have a good day?"

"Yes! I was worried I would have to sleep at school, but Carter came and got me and we got nuggets! And I got a cookie!"

"Oh, that's nice," she said, relieved that Holden appeared to be happy as ever. As if to prove it to her, Holden lost interest and went back to eating fries and watching the rest of his show.

"I hope that's okay. Wanted to smooth things over with him and cheer him up. I got you a couple of cheeseburgers too. Figured you might be hungry," Carter said, standing up with his crutches and passing over a bag of food.

Laura accepted the bag and wanted to cry on the spot.

"I'm sorry. I'll pay you for the food."

"Don't be sorry. It happens."

"I should've been there," Laura said. "I'm just so sorry."

"Really, it's okay. How's the car?"

"It's fine. I'm not."

"Look, I think you're being a little hard on yourself. We just walked in and started this episode. If you want to drop off your things, I can watch him, or if you'd rather I give you guys some space, that's fine too."

His green eyes looked at her, and though she tried to see something malicious or mocking in them, there was nothing.

"Did you have a busy day?" he asked when she'd said nothing.

She nodded, probably looking every bit as run-down as she felt. "Let me change out of this and then I'll come back down to eat."

CHAPTER 13

The truth was that Carter had nearly fallen out of his chair from shock when she had agreed to let him go get Holden. He ordered the rideshare with his app while they were still on the phone together. He didn't judge Laura at all, though it looked like she had done plenty of that for herself.

If anything, he liked Holden, and having a little guy around the house seemed far more important than any of the emails he had answered on his phone. Once everyone had found out he had been in a car accident, they must have had some meeting and decided to take it easy on him because he truly had nothing to do. He had been sitting around thinking too much about the past, so the trip to get Holden had been the first excitement since Laura and Holden had left in a whirlwind this morning.

To be honest, he was in awe of Laura. After what she'd told him last night about her ex-husband, he appreciated everything more now. He would've never believed the sweet girl he had fallen in love with in middle school history had nerves of steel to face the kinds of challenges she was up against, but then it was clear he had underestimated her and what she was capable of.

Carter hated to see her beat herself up. He got the impression his presence wasn't helping the situation, so when she came back down in a cotton robe over her pajamas, he had made room on the massive couch so she could snuggle with Holden and eat her cheeseburgers while they finished the rest of the show. After dinner was done, she picked up all the trash and ushered Holden upstairs for his bath time ritual.

Carter said goodnight to Holden and stayed downstairs to check in on the markets, even though he had been watching them all day. Laura came back downstairs about an hour later, looking totally worn out. She sat down on the couch and looked at him.

"I am sorry," she said.

"I told you, I really didn't mind. It was kind of fun going to McDonald's with him. He insisted we buy the driver an apple pie. I don't think she really needed it, but we got her an apple pie anyway."

Laura smiled, but in the kind of way that broke his heart. She looked to be on the verge of tears.

"Did your dad come by again?"

Carter rolled his eyes and puffed out a breath. "Nope, and I was here all but the hour or so I went to get Holden. I wouldn't hold my breath. It isn't like he's a reliable person. The past certainly proved that."

Laura nodded. "I'm sorry if I scared him away."

Carter waved a hand.

The pair of them watched the muted TV. On the national news, the president was being quoted about a tragedy that had happened in a nursing home somewhere in Virginia.

"Why a paramedic?" he asked.

Laura shrugged. "I like helping people."

"Why not a doctor or nurse?"

"That's the plan eventually."

"Oh yeah?" Carter said, shifting so he could see her better than the TV.

"Yep."

He was disappointed when she didn't elaborate. Part of him wanted to dig and get an answer, but it didn't take a genius to figure a single mom might struggle with that amount of schooling. People under the best circumstances found it difficult. Instead he took another route.

"Is it because of the accident?"

She turned away from the TV again. "Which one?"

"You know the one. After the bonfire."

Laura drew in a slow breath and curled up into the couch, tucking her legs under herself. "What do you mean?"

"Bradley's girlfriend. She didn't make it."

"I know," Laura said, her brown eyes now serious and flat. The medical professional in her came forward. It wasn't a look of someone who was uncaring, rather the look of someone who had seen far more than their share of death.

"I just didn't know if that might have something to do with it."

Laura stared at him.

"I also wanted to apologize to you."

She frowned, her dark eyebrows coming together.

"I want you to know I'm sorry I lied to you. I'm sorry I didn't get out of that shit sooner. I'd say I'm sorry the whole thing happened, but if it hadn't gone down that way, I'd never have been sent to the alternative school where I met—"

He couldn't bring himself to think of Coach. Every time he did, it felt like an ice pick had pierced his heart.

"Who?" she asked.

"Someone who turned me around," he finished. "I'm a

better person because of him, but I am sorry the way it worked out between us. I've always regretted that."

Laura blinked twice and studied him.

"That was a long time ago. We all make mistakes," she said, looking down at her hands.

"I am also sorry I've waited this long to apologize to you. I know you avoided me like the plague our senior year, but I should've said something sooner."

Laura swallowed and nodded.

Carter didn't feel any better. He wanted to but didn't. After all this time, he wanted her forgiveness more than anything. He wanted her to see that he was a changed man.

"I'm not like that anymore," he said.

She turned back to him and looked down. "You don't have to prove anything to me, Carter."

It was the first time she had said his name like that, her voice filled with exhausted pain.

"No, I mean it. It's important you know. I'm not like that."

"Carter, you really don't have to explain, but either way, you're the one who's sitting here, by order of a judge."

"I know that, and I know how that looks. But you need to understand. I haven't touched drugs or alcohol since the crash. I didn't even want the pain meds at the hospital."

"Okay." She didn't believe him. He could see it in her face.

"I'm serious. I know I reeked of alcohol when you...when I...crashed because I was having a really shitty night, okay?"

"We all have bad nights."

God, the disappointment in her voice was salt in the wounds. "I know that. And I know I was wrong. And don't think I miss any of the irony of the fact that the first time you see me in all these years, I'm drunk and almost wrapped around a tree or whatever."

She was watching him now, with a look of concern that made him want to rip something apart.

"I know how it looks. I get it. My mentor died, and I was coming from his funeral. He was like a father to me, and I have him to thank for the way I turned out. Well, him and my sainted mother, who was at the end of her rope and didn't know what to do. I met him at the school and he took me under his wing. We've stayed close, and with him gone, I just…I got lost."

"I'm sorry for your loss," Laura said. She looked like she meant it, and the light was too dim to tell, but he thought he saw the glimmer of tears in her eyes.

He then felt tears of his own and pulled a hand over his face to wipe them away.

Carter sucked in a breath. "So yeah, you're not the one who needs to apologize."

"I do, though."

"What happened today with Holden—" he started.

"Shouldn't have happened and won't again," Laura said. "And I am sorry. I want to pay you for the rideshare and for dinner tonight and last night."

Carter sighed. He wanted to pick up where they had left off all of those years ago. He wanted so badly to make amends and didn't understand why she refused to break down the professional wall between them.

"Look," Carter started. "I know that's important to you, but it's also important to me that you don't."

"Why?" Laura said with a frown. "I'm not a charity case. Just because I'm a single mother who happened to be in need of two rooms does not mean I don't have money in the bank."

"I'm not saying that at all," Carter said, cutting her off. "If I'm being completely honest, I want to make it up to you because when you called the police all those years ago, you helped me turn my life around. I shouldn't have been involved from the beginning, but be that as it may, you helped get me out of it."

"I wasn't calling for you," Laura said, her voice quiet.

"I know that, but I guess the point I'm trying to make is that I wanted to get out of it when we started dating, but I didn't know how. Had we not been in the truck together that night, I don't know what would've happened to me, so I owe a lot of the last fifteen years to you."

"I didn't do anything that wouldn't have happened anyway, Carter. You don't owe me." She stood, ending the conversation with her body language. "I need to get some sleep. Can I change your bandages before I do?"

Carter nodded and followed her up the stairs to the bedroom where he kept the medical supplies. Just like before, he sat in the sitting area and turned on the TV. She pulled out the bandages and laid them out on the table. Laura went to the bathroom and washed her hands. When she walked out, she was carrying a basket of laundry he had been collecting.

"I think I have enough already for a load, so I'll take these down."

"Laura, can I ask you something?"

"What?" she said, opening the fresh gauze so it was ready to go.

He wanted to know so much about her and tried to sort through his thoughts to figure out which question he wanted to ask first.

"Is this about John?" she said, when he didn't talk. "Or about something else in the past?"

Carter opened his mouth and shut it, not sure what she meant. "Okay, well, I was going to ask about him, but if you don't want to talk about him, we don't have to."

Laura shrugged and adjusted the light so she could see

better. "I don't know what I could tell you. I don't know anything. He's presumed dead. In order to divorce him, I had to spend a lot of money trying to find him. Never did. Neither did the police." Carter nodded and shifted when she looked at him. "Did that answer your question?"

"One of them."

"Okay, I'm going to start on your arms now."

"Okay."

While she got to work, he watched the careful attention she gave to his arms. Just like before, he turned away when she started to remove the gauze, the idea alone making his stomach flip in his gut.

He drew in a shaky breath.

"You're doing good. It is healing."

"Okay, that's good. Did you love him?" he blurted out, putting his finger on the feeling that had been bothering him in the back of his mind since learning about her. He was jealous, and angry on her behalf.

"Thought I did."

"Date a lot of guys before him?"

"Nope."

He could tell he wasn't going to get anywhere with the line of questioning, and her answers had done enough to soothe the curiosity that had been plaguing him. It had already been a deep enough night, so he changed tactics.

"What do you want to do in the future?"

"Is this about the doctor or nurse thing again?"

"It could be. Just making conversation."

"Well, I'd eventually like to go back to school once I have enough saved. I'd also love to take Holden to Disney World or Disneyland."

"Oh, yeah, he'd freak out."

Laura let out a laugh. "Yeah, I know. Alright, other arm."

He shifted around to give her better access and repositioned his head away from her and the bandage that wrapped around the better part of his forearm.

"What about you?" she asked.

"What do I want to do?"

Carter didn't know the answer. Before, the answer had always revolved around money and material possessions. Once he had made his mom and Coach proud, the goals had always been the next merger or newest model of car.

"I'd like to not go to jail."

"You probably won't, so what else?"

"Um, I guess I'll head back to California."

Laura made an mhmm sound with her mouth shut, and he heard the sound of the ointment tube hitting the glass top of the coffee table in front of him. "Any other big plans?"

"I guess I haven't thought about it," Carter admitted to himself. "Wanted to climb a few mountains, but that's out of the plan for a while. Maybe I'll get a dog. It'll be good to have someone else in the house."

"I was wondering if you were single," Laura said.

Carter's head turned right back around to study the top of hers—shiny, red flap of flesh be damned. He was disappointed when she didn't look up. "I am."

"That's surprising but explains a lot," Laura said, standing back from her work and admiring the fresh gauze. "Alright, now for your chest."

"Yeah, I haven't had a girlfriend in a while. Been too busy. What do you mean that explains a lot?"

Laura shrugged and started unbuttoning his shirt. "I was surprised you asked me of all people to help you. Figured you'd have a bunch of people flying out here to help take care of you, or at least a girlfriend."

Carter thought of Ruby, who had been ready to jump on a plane the first she'd heard of anything going wrong. The idea of her changing his bandages made him cringe. "I guess I'm lucky you were available," he said, giving her a smile.

"Because I'm a paramedic?"

"No, because you're you."

Laura stopped peeling away the edge of the tape and looked up at him with the same sarcastic look of disbelief she'd had in high school whenever he'd said she was pretty, but there was a glimmer. Her lips turned upwards just the barest amount.

"Your skin does look better. You probably won't need the bandages soon." Meaning, of course, she wouldn't need to change them. Carter's momentary high from her smile dimmed a little.

"That's good."

"It is."

The warmth of her hands touched his skin, and he realized she had taken the gloves off. Just like last night over his knee, she pressed her palm into his chest, and he felt the contact down to his soul, making a thrum of excitement dance across his spine. Laura closed her eyes for a few seconds, then pulled back, looking distant and disappointed as if he had failed some test, just as she had before.

"What's wrong?"

"Nothing," she said, standing to collect the trash.

"No, I'm serious. Something's up and you're not telling me."

Laura pulled her lips tight and shook her head. "Nothing you would understand."

"Try me."

Laura took the wrapping for the supplies and dumped it into the trash can, then picked up the whole can and set it over by the laundry basket to take downstairs and empty.

"It's nothing. I'm fine. Your skin really does look good. Alright, well, I'm going to go start this—"

"Laura…"

"Yeah?" she asked, turning around to face him with the basket on her hip. Her pale blue cotton robe was cinched at the waist, hiding almost everything but her forearms and a V at her neck. Still, from what he could see, she looked just like she did in high school. Her shape was the same, and her skin was still a delicate pale, flecked with two or three little brown freckles here and there. He could see the column of her neck and the delicate line of her jaw as her brown hair was swept up in a ponytail, almost identical to the one she wore back then. She looked exhausted, strong, determined, and absolutely stunning all at once.

"I recognized you when we were in the ambulance."

Something flickered in her eyes, but she slid her calm mask of professionalism back into place before he could study it.

"You were unconscious."

"I must have woken up for a second, because I saw you watching over me, and you know what I was thinking?"

She shook her head no.

"That you were beautiful and that if I was going to die, I was so glad I got to see you at least one more time."

CHAPTER 14

L aura hadn't known what to think of what Carter had said last night, but unlike the night before, she had lain awake revisiting every memory she had of him. Through the shower and when her head hit the pillow, she stared at the wall, picking each memory up in her mind and examining it like an antiques dealer unpacking a long-lost trunk.

It wasn't unheard of for people to want forgiveness from everyone they had hurt or let down in the past after a near-death experience. At first, Laura had thought this whole situation had been a ploy to do just that, so that Carter could heal up and head right back to California, never to think of her again.

Frankly, when she had first seen him, if he would've wanted that, she would've given him a thumbs-up and sent him packing back to his own life and out of hers, regardless of whether or not she could heal him. When she had tried that approach downstairs, however, Carter was unmoved, still wanting to talk to her about his past, her past, and where they were now.

She didn't have time to think about the past with Holden

around. Part of her envied Carter and part of her pitied him. Laura hadn't given a lot of thought to Carter after he had spent his whole senior year avoiding her through his newfound popularity. The next time she had seen him was the accident. He had been her first love, and his betrayal and then avoidance had left her with no closure and that ultimately had made her stronger. Laura didn't need him anymore. She wasn't the same eighteen-year-old girl who wanted an explanation. She was a grown woman with real problems and actual goals.

Hike a mountain? *That* was his big goal? It struck her as the kind of thing people said when they didn't have real perspective. Those were rich people goals, and rich people problems. Carter clearly had forgotten what it was like to have to budget your time and your money.

It should've been easy to write him off as just another person who had been in an accident, out to balance the past, but something was stopping her from answering his questions and moving on. And so, she lay awake most of the night, revisiting the past and trying to decide for herself what kind of person Carter Price really was.

She must have fallen asleep though, because the next thing she knew, the alarm was ringing on her phone, and unlike yesterday, Laura didn't need to work, meaning she could take her time in the morning and be the mom she wanted to be.

Already dressed in jeans and her favorite blue top, Laura had just finished making the coffee and finding a skillet when Carter came downstairs, growing more accomplished with his crutches.

"Good morning," he said, swinging himself toward the mugs she had laid out. "Work today?"

"Nope, so let me know if you need anything in particular. I plan on running a few errands and calling the movers,"

Laura said over her shoulder, grabbing the eggs. "Scrambled or over easy?"

"Scrambled if you're offering."

"Cheese or no?"

"Either way is fine."

"Cheese it is," Laura said, already cracking the eggs into a mixing bowl she had found. It was weird not using her own cooking equipment, but when in Rome. It wasn't like her stuff was top-notch or anything, but she was used to it.

She could hear Carter pour himself a cup of coffee and move over to the table to sit.

"Did you sleep okay?" he asked.

"Meh. Had some trouble falling asleep but got there eventually," Laura said, pouring the eggs into the hot pan she had coated with oil and melted butter. She took out some bacon and put some slices of bread in the toaster but didn't start them. "How about you?"

"It's hard to sleep."

She glanced over at him. "Is it your leg or the burns?"

"Both, I guess. I'm not used to them."

Laura stirred the eggs and microwaved some bacon. "Makes sense. Have you talked to the doctor about it? You could see if they could give you something to help you sleep."

"Nah, I'll be okay. I don't like taking meds like that because I don't want to get addicted."

"I understand." Laura shrugged in agreement and finished putting breakfast together. She could now hear Holden playing upstairs in his room. He had been fast asleep when she had checked on him before. "Let me go grab Holden—sounds like he's getting into stuff." She quickly grabbed the cheese and sprinkled it over the eggs in the pan before taking them off the heat and turning on the toast. She placed a cover on the eggs and bacon and went upstairs. Carter had moved on to work on his phone.

Pushing through the door, she found Holden stacking his pillows on the ground to put Mickey to sleep, but after a quick hug and kiss, she carried him and three of his stuffed animals down to breakfast.

"Hey, Holden!" Carter said, turning off his phone and putting it to the side, far out of the splash zone.

Laura let Holden slide down her into a chair at the table. He put his finger in his mouth acting shy. "Hi."

"Do you like eggs?"

"Mhmm.

"And bacon?"

"MHMMMM."

"How about toast?"

"Ummm…"

Laura laughed while she plated up the food, listening to Holden tell Carter all about his feelings on toast, which included opinions on jelly, crust, and what the other kids at school ate.

"Alright, breakfast," Laura said, coming to the table with both of their plates. "What do you say, Holden?" she said on autopilot.

"THANK YOU!"

"You're welcome. Here you go," she said, putting down Carter's plate in front of him. "I didn't put any jelly, but I'll bring the jar."

Carter took the plate and locked eyes with her. "Thank you, Laura."

She gave him a tight smile and walked back across the kitchen to grab her own plate. When she sat down to eat, there was a cup of coffee waiting.

"Oh…thanks."

Carter gave a little shrug with a smile. "Least I could do."

Holden led them through the prayer, which meant he stopped and started three times because Carter wasn't doing exactly what the teacher did at school. Finally, they all were able to eat.

In between bites, Holden asked Carter about Mickey Mouse and if he had a school too. Once they had finished, Laura cleared the plates and ended the interrogation by picking Holden up to get him ready for school.

Since she wasn't working, they didn't need to rush, but rather than keep him home, Laura still liked him to go because she paid either way, and she used the time to get errands done. They grabbed his school bag and walked down the stairs hand in hand, while Holden counted each one.

"Alright, we're ready to go," Laura said, grabbing her purse and keys.

"Do you want to come?" Holden asked Carter when she opened the front door.

Carter sat in the living room with the TV on mute, looking at his computer, but something about him told Laura he really did want to come. "You need to ask your mom."

Holden looked up at her and gave his signature shrug, as if that settled the matter.

"Honey, Mr. Carter's working. He doesn't have the time—"

"Actually, I am free this morning—that is, unless you don't think there's any room in the car. I mean I would understand completely."

Laura looked at him. She hadn't considered having a shadow with her as she had a quiet weekday morning filled with errands, but Carter looked like he desperately wanted to get out of the house.

"Yeah, we have room. Are you ready to go now?" she asked. He was dressed in a button-down shirt over dark blue jeans. His leg with the cast wouldn't need a shoe, but he still needed something on the other foot.

"I bought some shoes the other day. They're right behind you."

A few minutes of furiously clearing out the front seat of her car later, they were all in the car, heading toward the school. Laura felt a little strange driving with someone else besides Holden in the car. Because Goldvein wasn't a large town, she was able to get to Holden's school in only fifteen minutes, even with the morning construction.

"I'll be right back," she said to Carter then brought Holden inside just in time for the craft they were doing. With a quick kiss and hug, she was out again in a flash.

"That was quick," Carter said when she got back in the car.

Laura pulled her seatbelt over her chest. "Yeah, it's so much easier when they're about to start an activity because otherwise he gets shy and doesn't want to jump in."

"Ah, yes, I can see that. Alright, so where are we off to next?"

"Well, I need to grab a few things from the apartment before I call the movers, and then after that, I need to go and pick up some more groceries. What about you?"

"I'm flexible."

"Don't you have physical therapy?" she asked, pulling out of the parking lot and onto the road.

"Yeah, but they're coming to the house for now. I think they come tomorrow actually."

"Okay, sounds good."

"I'm just happy to be along for the ride." Laura could feel him looking at her, and while she knew a near-death experience made people do strange things—like want to run out and profess love to the first person that showed them kindness, or to right a wrong—a small part of her didn't mind the attention or the company. She had gotten used to being alone since her mom had moved to Missoula and had managed to find peace in the few quiet moments she had on days off, when Holden was at school. Still, having Carter in the car hadn't dampened the mood.

They drove to the grocery store, where he declined any of the scooters or wheelchairs and followed her around, up and down the aisles on his crutches.

"Do you like salad?" Laura asked him, throwing a head of iceberg into her cart.

He shrugged. "Yeah, I'm fine with salad. I don't get too fancy with them."

"How do you mean fancy?"

He followed her over to the fruit. "You know like greens and fruits on them with cheese I can't pronounce."

"I bet you get a lot of that in California."

He let out a laugh. "Yeah, I do. There's a lot of great food, but also a lot of those overpriced places where you get a leaf on a steak the size of a chicken nugget with a swipe of sauce."

"You don't sound like you enjoy it," Laura said, grabbing a few strawberries, then changing her mind for a watermelon.

"I mean I have to. I have clients and stuff there, and it's nice. The food is good, and I've never left hungry because they throw in a lot of little courses, but, well, you know I didn't grow up like that."

Laura nodded, and they walked over to the meat section, where she grabbed a chicken that was on sale and some hamburger.

"What do you like to eat out there?"

"Oh, that's easy. Tacos."

"Oh yeah?"

Carter nodded and smiled while he maneuvered on his crutches next to her. "I mean, I haven't met a taco I didn't like, but I didn't realize there were so many until I went to school there."

"What was that like?" she asked, now turning down the aisles to grab a few more pantry items.

"Stanford? It was awesome. Different than anywhere I'd ever been before. You know, at first, I felt out of my league, but I was able to hold my own in the classes, and my confidence started to really go up. Made a lot of friends, did well."

"That's good. I always wondered what it would've been like to live in a dorm, eat in the dining hall, and all that."

"You never went away?"

"Nope. Just to community college. I didn't get enough aid to make the move worthwhile, and I didn't feel that taking out a bunch of loans was a good idea at the time. Wanted to work for a few years first. Medical school is a tall order."

"But I thought you had been planning to go when we were in high school."

Laura threw some more chips in the cart and stopped to turn around and face him. "It probably sounds like an excuse, but my dad died and the wind went out of my sails a bit. I'm getting back to it though. Slowly. Had enough for a whole year saved when John disappeared. Things got complicated after that."

"I'm sorry."

Laura shrugged and moved toward the baking section. "I'm doing okay."

"I'd say, given the circumstances, you're doing better than okay."

Laura smiled at him and went back to studying the cakes and candles. "Holden's happy and we get by. That's all that matters. I'm on track to have enough saved for him to go to school, and really, that's more important to me."

Carter nodded and looked like he wanted to say something, but instead, he followed behind her, agreeing to everything she asked him about in the store. When it came time to check out, he paid for it all, even though she had her card out. The only way she allowed it was when he was quick to point out that he was going to be eating all of it too, and she'd already done all the cooking.

"I'm heading back home to drop this off and make some lunch before I go back out again. Do you want to take a rest or…?"

"Actually, I was wondering if we could go out to lunch? My treat."

CHAPTER 15

Carter hadn't been much help with carrying the groceries inside or unloading them, but he at least thought he made good company. After everything was put away, they were back in the car, and Laura hit the bank to get some cash. She made a point to go inside, which Carter found strange considering there was a drive-through ATM and window, but he figured she wanted some privacy, so he was content to wait in the car. While he did, his phone rang.

"Hey, Mom."

"Hey, how are you feeling?"

"A lot better actually."

"Oh, good. I was so worried. I can still come up there if you need me to."

Carter smiled to himself. "Mom, it's fine. I'm okay, really."

"Well, that's a relief. When are you heading home?"

He didn't want to tell her about the arrest and worry her, but he didn't want to lie to her either. "I'm actually going to stick around for a little bit, just until the leg heals up some more. Take some time off."

"Oh? That's surprising."

"Yeah, you know, meet some old friends, maybe catch up, that sort of thing," Carter said, studying his casted leg. "Mom?" he asked when she didn't say anything.

"I'm here, just a little surprised. Unless you were visiting Coach, you never liked to go back there."

Coach's name was like a punch in the gut, bringing back a whole wave of grief Carter hadn't revisited in at least a day, now that he thought about it. Laura and Holden had been a welcome distraction.

"I'm sorry he's gone, honey. I know how special he was to you."

"Yeah, he was one for the books."

"Well, listen, if you change your mind about me coming, just let me know. I'm a little worried you aren't heading back home. If you'd rather I come there, I'm happy to do that. Frank and I were thinking of coming for the fall anyway."

"Yeah, you got it, Mom," Carter said, seeing Laura come out of the double doors. "Alright, I'll call you later. Love you."

"Love you too."

"Everything okay?" Carter asked when he had ended the call right as Laura opened the door.

"Yeah, why wouldn't it be?"

"You just looked like you were thinking about something when you walked out."

"I guess the markets aren't doing too well; the funds I'm in for my retirement and for Holden haven't been performing like I wanted." She frowned again and cranked over the engine.

"I'd be glad to take a look at them or give you a few names of people who could, if you'd like."

Laura pulled out of the parking lot on to the road, and he could see she was mulling it over.

"Just think about it and let me know. I understand if you already have someone in mind."

"I have a guy who also does my taxes, and he's been good to me before, but maybe."

Carter recognized progress when he saw it. "Just say the word."

"Sorry for keeping you."

Carter waved a hand. "I'm just along for the ride and the company. Mom called while you were in there. She's been checking in every other day or so."

"How is your mother? Didn't she move down south or something?"

Carter watched as they turned back on the main road. "Yep, got married to a nice guy named Frank who retired from his small appliance repair shop, and they moved to Florida. She's really happy."

Laura gave him a smile, before putting her focus back on the road. "That's nice. Where do you want to go eat?"

"You pick."

"No, I'm not picking."

Carter shifted to face her. "Well, we're just going to ride around in circles until you say something."

"I would've been fine with a sandwich at home."

"Nah, let's get something and then we can head over to the apartment."

Laura sighed and slowed for a red light and construction. She tapped one finger on the wheel. "What are you in the mood for?"

"I can go for anything."

"Not helpful," she chided.

"Well, we got cheeseburgers last night, and Chinese the night before that."

"So those two are out."

"Before that, I had Italian."

Laura cranked up the A/C. "That's a cold weather food for me."

"Yeah, I ate a bunch of pasta and fell right asleep after climbing the stairs."

"You are still recovering. You need to give yourself credit."

Carter didn't want to get into that. He didn't want Laura thinking about herself as a caregiver any more than she needed to. He wanted to be something more. Friends again, for starters. "Well, at any rate—"

"You know what sounds good?"

"Hmm?"

"A milkshake," she said, easing off the brake to crawl through the construction zone where part of the road was completely removed to install pipes.

"That does sound good. Joe's it is."

Laura turned into the old 1950s style diner that everyone in town loved and that had long been the hangout for teens, families, and retirees. It was a legend and leaned toward traditional diner decor, which meant when they parked and went inside, they had their pick from all of the red vinyl booths. They chose the one closest to the door, and he positioned himself against the wall and raised his leg onto the booth seat. As unattractive as it was, he needed the elevation as the throbbing had come back with the activity and car ride —not that he'd tell Laura that.

For some reason, he was compelled to see her apartment and know everything he could about her, from what she liked to what she didn't. He wanted to know what every second of her senior year had been like, what she was like in her twenties, and how she felt when she brought Holden home.

The biggest emotion had been a sense of regret, but now that he felt he had her forgiveness, even if it was just surface level, he realized they still got along, fit together. Being with her felt natural and exciting and comfortable all at the same time. Sitting on the couch watching Mickey Mouse with a Happy Meal felt better than most of the meals he'd had in California. It was like he had been living in a fantasy and now—coming home, back to Laura—he felt real. Whole again.

"Alright, can I start you off with some drinks?" said the waitress with short gray hair who reminded Carter of his mom when she had been a server.

"A chocolate milkshake and water for me, please."

"Can I get a root beer float?"

The waitress started writing before she answered. "You sure can."

"Thank you, and a water as well."

"Alrighty, will this check be together or separate?"

Laura shook her head at him when he met Laura's eyes and grinned. "Together."

"Great! I'll be right back with your order."

Laura held his gaze across the table covered in paper placemats. "Carter, what are you doing?"

He flipped the utensils wrapped in the paper napkin in his hand a few times. "I believe it's called eating."

Laura shook her head and leaned forward with her elbows on the table next to the mini jukebox that could order music into the whole restaurant. He had loved flipping the panels inside, featuring all the song choices, when he had come here as a child.

"What?" he asked.

"I don't understand you."

"What's not to understand? I'm hungry."

"No, it's not that."

"Well," he prompted, "what is it?"

"I figured I was the last person you wanted to see in this town. Now, you're following me around while I do errands and buying me lunch."

He stopped messing with the utensils. He peeled away the paper ring that held the napkin together.

"Do you not like being around me?" he asked, his voice low.

"I wouldn't say that."

"What would you say?"

She folded her arms again and considered him. Her brown eyes drew together while she puffed out a breath and blew her bangs away from her forehead. She had worn her hair down today, and the dark chestnut brown was shorter than he remembered, hitting just below her collarbone, but even more beautiful than before. The blue of her shirt made her skin glow, setting off her perfect pink lips.

"I guess I'm just surprised."

The waitress came back, landing the thick glasses filled with frothy cold drinks in front of them. Next came the water glasses that were so full, when she set them down, the water sloshed a little and made a puddle. "I'll be right back to get your orders."

"I told you I was sorry," Carter said when she left. "And that I was so glad I got to see you. I've always regretted not seeing you sooner, owning up to everything. Getting a second chance."

Laura's eyebrows drew together. "Second chance?"

"We were good together. I had liked you since middle school, and I always felt like that year we were together was one of the best."

"You had a great senior year. Football, scholarship, took the captain of the cheerleading squad to prom," Laura said, giving him a pointed look and taking a sip of her milkshake.

"I should've asked you, but I was too ashamed." He stirred the float, watching as a dribble of ice cream ran down the side of the fogged-up glass. "All I could see was your face when I was put in the back of the cop car."

"Well, I'm sure Cindy the cheerleader, who had a line of disappointed prospective dates, was a real comfort to you."

Carter leaned back and groaned. "She was nice."

"And pretty."

"Yeah, but she wasn't very smart. She just wanted to date me to make the quarterback jealous."

"Uh-huh. That's what it looked like while you two were on the dance floor, glued together."

"You were there?" Carter asked, then seemed to remember. "That's right. You wore a blue dress."

"I did. I'm surprised you saw anything besides Cindy's D cups."

The waitress came back and cut off Carter's shocked reply. Laura smiled sweetly at the waitress and looked smug as she placed an order for the special, which was roast chicken. He ordered the steak and handed over the menus.

"That dress looked good on you."

Laura blinked at him. "You're good, but you're not that good. I'll bet you couldn't remember one thing about the dress you *allegedly* saw me in at prom."

"It sparkled."

"Lucky guess. All prom dresses are sparkly."

Carter tilted his head to the side and smiled. She truly had no idea how much he had missed her. The opportunities he had missed haunted him. "Alright, you don't believe me?"

"Nope. Not one bit."

"Your hair was up and you had a blue clip in it that looked like a butterfly. It was off to one side, like it had just landed."

Laura cocked a smile. "Not fair. Everyone wore butterfly clips back then."

"Told ya."

"Well, I didn't think you noticed me. You didn't look over at me all night."

"How would you know? You were always talking with your friends. Came in a big group."

"Yeah, because no one asked us out."

"You danced with a couple of guys."

"Yeah, Todd asked me to dance."

"He always had a crush on you," Carter said, leaning back into the booth.

"Not enough to ask me out, but yeah, he asked me to dance, which was cool. I guess."

The waitress came back with the food and set it down between them. Carter had eaten there enough times before to know that it was going to be great, but still he dug in with relish to the familiar tastes, which hadn't changed no matter how long he'd been gone.

Carter watched Laura chew and wipe her mouth.

"What?"

He smiled. "Just looking at you. You look the same as in high school."

"Wow, okay. First you try to impress me with a butterfly clip and now this? What do you want, Carter?"

He held up his hands in defense. "Nothing. It's true."

"I don't know why you keep bringing up the past between us," Laura said, shaking her head. "In a few months, you'll be out of here and back to California. You don't need to flatter me while you're here."

Carter waited a beat, mulling over his thoughts. "I'm not flattering you. I wish I'd asked you to the prom."

"Carter—"

"I always put you on a pedestal. You were so good and made the right decisions. I felt like I had blown my chances with you and that you wouldn't want anything to do with me after that."

Laura shook her head. "I haven't made all the right decisions. You're doing better than me—aside from the whole DUI arrest thing. If you take that away, you're doing much better than I am."

"If you're talking about money, I can't take credit. Most of that is luck and being in the right place at the right time. Hiring the right people. Being a good negotiator. Most startups fail anyway. What I meant was in school, I felt like I had blown it with you. You came from a good family and followed the rules."

Laura tilted her head to the side and took a drink of her water. "True. Dad probably wouldn't have let me go to prom with you even if you'd asked. But my mom still likes you. Said so the other day."

"Oh yeah?"

"Yeah, she heard you were back in town and mentioned how you were always a nice guy."

Carter raised his eyebrows in surprise. "Wow. I didn't expect that. How is she doing?"

Laura shrugged and took a bite of her food. "She's okay."

"You said she's in Missoula. When did she move there?"

"About six months ago. It's not permanent, I hope. She had a stroke, and the best place for her is there."

Carter froze with his fork midair and slowly felt his hand lower it back to the plate. "I'm so sorry to hear that."

Laura stiffened up and focused on pushing her food around the plate, her lips locked in a tight smile. "Yeah, she's doing better, but it's slow. She can still talk, but she's having to relearn a lot of motor skills."

"I don't know what to say."

She shrugged again. "Not much to say. It is what it is. But we talk on the phone and video chat. I'll probably call her tonight." Laura gave him a smile. "Do you want me to ask her if I could've gone to the prom with you?"

Carter cracked up, and Laura laughed along with him.

"You know, maybe we should just focus on right now," Carter said, holding her gaze until she returned his smile.

CHAPTER 16

C arter felt the success of that smile all the way through lunch and to her apartment, where she had finished gathering up a few more things and packing some of the more delicate items for the movers. Once inside, he'd felt the glow dim only a little with the sense of how much her apartment brought him back to his own childhood, with his mom doing the best she could to stretch a dollar until the next pay period.

When they had turned into the neighborhood, he recognized it as one where a friend had lived while they were in elementary school. They pulled up to a small townhome with a statue of a little fat frog holding a welcome sign. All of it had looked cheery and positive until Laura started walking down a sidewalk to the back. That was when he realized she lived in one of the smaller, darker, basement apartments.

She let them in with the key from her pocket and quickly set to work, suggesting he sit on the one couch in the living room next to a small side table. The only other furniture was a recliner, a coffee table that bore the marks of crayon, and a medium sized TV.

While Laura worked, Carter maneuvered his crutches around the few stacks of boxes. The apartment was small and dated, but clean and surprisingly well-planned. Despite it being in the basement, the layout gave it an airy and open feeling.

There was nothing to suggest any sort of male presence over the age of three, which brought up mixed emotions. He wanted to feel encouraged that Laura was available, recognizing his old feelings lighting back up when he was around her. But the lack of a father figure for Holden broke his heart and angered him on behalf of Laura, who had done nothing to deserve her circumstances.

The sight of the two chairs at the dining table was a window into his past. He had been so desperate for someone to come back into the house one day. He, like other children, had often daydreamed about what his dad was really like, and how one day he would come back, embrace Carter and his mom, and all of their problems would vanish overnight. In his childhood memories, Carter had dreamed of playing catch, fishing, changing a tire, running home in the rain laughing, and most of all, buying an ice cream cone, which his mom never could afford.

Carter blinked fast and turned away from the little chair. Everyone wanted a happy ending, but that's not how life was. There never was a day that his dad came back. Carter had grown up learning things the hard way, until Coach had found him and done his best to polish what Carter had become into something close to a success story.

Now, years later and without Coach, he felt that loss of a parent all over again. There was no coming back from the dead. Coach was gone. The only person who could save that little boy in Carter's memory was himself.

To think that his dad had shown up allegedly wanting to reconcile—to make up for all of the wasted years and build a relationship with him now—was ridiculous in its irony. He didn't need a father figure anymore.

Carter glanced up at the cheap refrigerator. There were a few pictures drawn by Holden in crayon. One looked like a firetruck or police car, but it was the other that held his attention. In crayon, there were two stick figures holding hands inside the shaky outline of a heart. One had long brown hair and a smile. The little one had short brown hair and an even bigger smile.

"I think that's everything," Laura said, coming back inside. "Oh, I forgot about these. We left so quickly to get to Megan's."

Carter did a quick swipe over his eyes when Laura wasn't looking as she went to pull off the papers. He coughed and said, "They're really good."

"I think so too. He did them a few months ago without any help," she said with a genuine smile.

"You're doing a good job with Holden."

Laura's lips formed the thin-lipped smile laced with worry he was more accustomed to seeing. "Thank you for saying so. He's so smart." She carefully put the papers into her purse, careful not to crush them in the worn brown bag. "I see friends, well, acquaintances really, online and some of their kids are sick. And then of course, you know in my line of work, I see a lot of hurt kids, and the parents are dealing with so much. It's unimaginable, but somehow those parents pull through because what choice do they have? They love their kid and will do anything for them, but still, it's not easy to see children who are medically fragile. It makes me grateful. I really have it easy by comparison."

"Laura, you need to give yourself some credit."

"I can't. Like you said at lunch, I'm just lucky."

"Holden's lucky to have you."

A shadow crossed her face, and her lip quivered before she clenched her eyes shut and choked out a sob.

"Hey, hey, what's wrong? Come here," Carter said, dropping his crutches and pulling her in close. He held her against his chest, resting his chin over her head. He rocked them back and forth while feeling the silent sobs shake out of her body.

"It's okay," he said, smoothing his hand down the back of her head. "Just let it out."

Carter's leg started to ache while they were standing there, but he wasn't about to let go of her when she needed this.

She pulled back eventually, sniffling and taking deep breaths. Her pale skin was red and blotchy while tears like crystals hung onto her dark lashes before falling down her cheek.

"Talk to me," he said, looking at her.

"I'm scared for him to be alone."

"What do you mean by that?" he asked, smoothing her hair away from her face while she stared at his chest, still crying, each tear falling when she blinked.

"He only has me. What happens when I'm gone? Who will love him? I'm not going to live forever. I can't have any more children. When I had Holden, something went wrong. I hemorrhaged. Couldn't stop bleeding. The doctor put me under but couldn't fix it. Mom was there, the doctor asked her, and she agreed. When I woke up, they had taken everything. Found precancerous cells in all of it."

"Hey, you can't dwell on what you don't have—"

More tears came, and Laura tried to pull them back. Carter reached over to a box with some paper towels in it and pulled one out for her.

"His dad is gone. My dad is gone, and now my mom…"

Carter didn't know what to say, but he held her again

while she cried. The reality of her situation hit him then, as did her strength. More sniffles came while he smoothed her hair, thinking through everything she had just said.

"I just don't want him to be alone."

"He won't be. He's a great kid. Smart, lovable. He will have friends and family who surround him all the time."

"But what if that's not enough?" Laura looked up into his eyes, her warm brown eyes swollen with worry.

"It will be, because he has a great mom who loves him and that's enough. Believe me. I know."

Laura swallowed and nodded.

"And before you bring it up, that doesn't mean he'll get involved in the wrong stuff like me. He's too smart for that."

Laura took a step back and let out a laugh and blew her nose on the paper towel. "You read my mind." She blew it again and took a deep breath.

Carter's hands missed her, but she seemed steadier and she spoke again. "Sorry about that. Thanks. Here, let me get your crutches."

He accepted them and propped himself, giving his aching leg a break. "Thank you. You're doing enough, Laura."

"Thanks for saying that and,"—she waved one hand around—"you know, putting me back together. Let's get you home. The movers will be back for the rest of this tomorrow."

"You like to take care of everyone," Carter said when they were back in the car.

Laura smiled and threw her arm around the back of her seat to reverse. "Yeah, I guess it comes with the job."

"You've always been like that though," Carter said, looking at the rest of the neighborhood. "Ever since school."

"How do you mean?"

"Well, I remembered you were always the first to run up and help anyone who got hurt at school."

Laura shifted in her seat.

"I remember there was this little girl in elementary school who was running during PE, and someone pushed her down. She skinned her knee pretty bad, tore up her tights. Do you remember that?"

"I think so."

"Fifth grade, before we even really knew each other. You ran up to her and put your hands on her knee before any of the teachers got there."

Laura hit the brake to stop at a light but didn't turn to look at him. She sat still, as if someone had frozen her.

"Do you want to head back and pick Holden up early?" Carter asked when she didn't say anything else.

She nodded and turned on the radio until they were back at the school with Holden in the car.

Twenty minutes later, they walked back into the rental house, Holden bouncing off the walls with energy, telling her about all of the crafts he had done at school.

Laura's smile radiated love mixed with worry and hope all in a cocktail of emotions that Carter was now starting to understand.

He left them alone together and made his way upstairs with his laptop, one slow step at a time. Finally reaching his bedroom, he opened his computer and began to scroll through the day. He was getting more emails now, which was a double-edged sword. In the business world, being left alone too long was never a good thing, but then, getting those emails meant he needed to respond to them.

Ruby had cc'd him on several in a row, all about a possible merger he had been working on before Coach had passed. That had been the big-ticket item on his to-do list. Something about the deal rubbed him the wrong way, but with the company going public, he couldn't steer the ship himself.

Despite the fact that it was more or less his child, the board and shareholders had to be considered.

Much like Laura was already worried about Holden growing up, Carter's business now had reached adulthood with a mind of its own, no longer in his control. He made a few notes and replied to emails, negotiating more time. Ruby had sent him a personal email, offering to come out again, but the sheer idea of that was enough to make him vomit. If she or the board found out about his DUI, he likely wouldn't have any sway with them in the merger.

"What's wrong?"

Laura was standing in the doorway, looking at him. "You're frowning. Everything okay?"

"Just work stuff."

"I'm sorry I kept you out so long."

Carter shook his head and set his laptop to the side. "Nothing that can't wait."

"Dinner's ready. Do you want me to bring it up here so you don't have to walk back down?"

"Do you want to have some alone time with Holden? It's okay if you do."

Laura smiled. "That's very kind of you to offer. He was actually just asking about you. No pressure. I can tell him you're resting."

"No, I'll come down. I could use the company."

He made his way down slowly, feeling the exhaustion starting to kick in. He was going to sleep well tonight with all of this activity.

Laura had baked chicken and made macaroni and cheese with some peas so something green would be on Holden's plate, even if it was swimming in cheese. Carter ate, savoring every bite of normalcy while listening to Holden talk about his day in response to Laura's questions.

After dinner, he helped clean up by washing a few dishes

at the sink, figuring out how to prop himself up with the crutches while having his hands free. Laura popped some popcorn and followed Holden into the living room where they had queued up a kid-friendly movie. It was one of the newer movies Carter had heard of but had not seen.

He considered going upstairs, but right as he turned to do so, Holden called out to him.

"Carter, you can sit by me."

When Carter came around into the living room, Holden had made a spot and patted the couch next to him. The movie started and Laura got up to dim the lights and grab a throw from a basket on the floor.

It was the best invitation Carter had gotten in a long time. He sat down next to Holden, who promptly said, "Here, you can share my blanket."

"Thank you."

"You're welcome," Holden said with his funny little shrug.

He glanced at Laura, who rolled her eyes and shook her head with a silent giggle.

The movie kept Carter's interest, but also gave him a chance to think about Laura again. He kept stealing glances at her and Holden curled up together on the couch. The sight of them snuggled up together relaxed him, like a balm had been smoothed over his stressors and worries.

When the movie finished, Holden was asleep. Laura gathered him up, which sounded easier than it looked. Holden's legs dangled limply from Laura's arms, bumping against her sides as she carried him up the stairs. Carter came up behind her on the crutches, the stuffed animals in his hands. Holden woke up halfway and sat there in a daze while Laura peeled him out of his shirt and pulled on pajamas in the dim light before laying him down and tucking him in with a kiss. Carter placed Mickey right next to him, and as if he could smell his favorite toy, Holden reached out and pulled the worn mouse into his chest. With a sigh, he fell back asleep before they left the room. Without a sound, Laura shut the door.

"Like I said, you're doing an incredible job." Carter's voice was low.

Laura didn't say anything but walked to his bedroom and went to get out the bandages. Carter sat down in the now-familiar spot and turned on the light, but not the TV. Unlike before, he didn't feel the need to have something between them to fill what had been an awkward void. Instead, he undid his own buttons, his fingers now getting back some of the dexterity that had been lost with the crash. He had been able to manage the crutches and his phone fine; getting dressed with the buttons had taken him the most time, though he was getting quicker.

Laura didn't say anything this time, just sat across from him, pulling out the fresh gauze they had picked up while they were out. As always, her touch was light and she worked methodically, taking time to apply the ointment to the gauze before touching it to his damaged skin. The pain had lessened, but whether that was the over-the-counter pain meds or the healing process, he couldn't say.

He watched her while she worked, touched that she was able to care for him when she had already given so much to those around her.

"Laura?" he asked, his voice sounding strange to his ears in the quiet.

"Yeah?" She looked up and turned her attention to his already exposed chest.

Words failed him. He wanted to say so much but didn't know where to start or what he could say to describe his feelings.

She stopped and looked up at him with her big brown

eyes that had been red rimmed with tears a few hours earlier.

His eyes dropped to her lips, and she didn't move or pull back. If anything, he felt the slightest shift as she watched him dip his head low toward her, so slowly he wasn't sure if he was moving or she was. They drew together by a magnetic force he couldn't see.

Their lips met light and tender. Like strangers for the first time. He felt her body relax, letting out a small sigh of contentment. He didn't want the moment to end but pulled back before it could go on. Laura's eyes fluttered open, and a pink tinge of blush hit her cheeks while her eyes met his again. Her brows dipped slightly as if she was as confused about what had just happened as he was.

Carter offered a warm smile. "Thank you."

CHAPTER 17

L aura walked into the station the next day after
dropping Holden off at school, still trying to figure out
what was happening between Carter and her. Jordan was
outside, washing off the ambulance. He gave her a wave as
she walked, and she returned the wave.

Yesterday had been a whirlwind of emotions, but last
night had been a surprise. She hadn't wanted to admit to
herself that she had feelings for Carter anymore, but the
previous night had proven otherwise. His leaving her with
the lie—that he was using and dealing drugs—in high school
had left its mark. Many nights after Carter had been taken
away, she had gone to sleep with a pillow damp from her
tears. Then when he had come back to school and pretended
she hadn't existed, the tears had come faster, before she
eventually toughened up and moved on.

She wasn't a teenager anymore, and to think that the
emotions had once again bubbled to the surface felt like a
betrayal of her independence. The kiss had left her breathless
and excited. She felt warm and wanted for the first time in a

long time. After being left behind by the death of her father and a husband who vanished, the comfort of Carter's presence offered her more than she wanted to admit she needed. He had been so gentle with her when she had broken down at the apartment. He'd melted her jealous heart over lunch, when she realized she was apparently still upset about him going to prom without her. Everything he had done had been exactly what she'd wanted him to be when she was younger.

He was still handsome and kind. Funny and thoughtful. And he noticed and remembered everything about her, which made her feel like a teen all over again. The giddiness and excitement she didn't want to admit to herself were in complete contrast to the mom-ness of the last three—almost four—years. Not that she didn't love being a mom, but being desired and seen by a very good-looking, charming billionaire was not a topic that came up in of a lot of mom forums online.

The kiss had given her the chance to get close to Carter without gloves, and at first, as selfish as it was, she had tried to heal him then, with her hands on his chest while their lips were pressed together. But just as before, nothing happened, until she felt the shift within herself moving from professional healer to something deeper. Just like with Holden and her mom, Laura had started to accept that she wasn't able to heal Carter—she just didn't understand why.

Still turning over her thoughts, Laura walked in to drop her lunch off in the fridge in the break room and found Megan sitting there again, eating.

"Hey, Laura, how's it going?"

"Good. How are you?"

"Good. I'm watching my neighbor's dogs and took them out for a run today in this beautiful weather. I saw a kitten under a bush and tried to get the little guy but couldn't."

"Maybe you'll see him again on the walk tonight."

"Yeah, I hope so. What plan did you figure out for Holden's party?"

Laura opened a cabinet and pulled down a mug to get some of the leftover coffee. "Yeah, I'm having something at the rental house. It's big enough, and I have some of the kids from his class coming over. Crap. I need to send an update on where the party will be since I wasn't sure when I sent the invitations."

"I can't believe he's going to be four! Such a little man. The house is still good then?"

"Yep." Laura didn't want to elaborate because as it was, Megan had an uncanny ability to get information out of her.

"Uh huh. What about Mr. Green Eyes?"

"He's okay. Burns are healing, if that's what you're asking."

"You know that's not what I'm—"

The dispatch voice echoed through the speakers. Multicar crash on the highway. They sprang into action, each heading for their lockers to get their equipment and head out. Jordan was already behind the wheel, cranking the big diesel engine when Laura hopped inside. He turned on the siren and they were off. A few minutes later, Laura could hear the blast of the fire engine behind them.

Jordan laid on the horn as they blew through every intersection, heading for the on-ramp to the highway. Other cars on the road tapped their brakes and moved to the side, parting like a suburban red sea.

The radio squawked with more information. Police were already on the scene. As if she had summoned her with her thoughts, Laura's phone buzzed with Ash's number flashing on the screen.

"You there?" Laura asked, skipping the hello.

"Not yet. Just hit the highway."

"We're ahead of you. Maybe one or two minutes out."

"Alright, see you there." Laura slid her phone away as Jordan pulled up alongside a crash with at least three cars smashed together on the road. One had spun into a ditch, the brown smoke rising from the woods just as Laura could make out the yellow of a taxi with a popped hood against a tree.

State police had beat them there and were directing traffic around the crash. Laura jumped out and saw a cop standing near the cab, waving them down. She grabbed her bag and ran across the grass, hearing the sounds of the fire engine in the distance.

The cab was open, the fire not a full blaze like it had been in Carter's crash.

"Driver was unresponsive when we pulled up and got him out," relayed one of the cops. She slid down to her knees, while the other cop continued chest compressions. With a nod he kept going, while yet another cop watched on standby, ready to jump in if the first one tired.

Jordan ran up behind her with the backboard in hand, and on the count of three, they loaded the man on to the board and made a break for the ambulance. Someone fell in step beside her.

"What can I do?"

Laura turned to see Megan with her helmet on but face shield up. Another fire engine from the next county had shown up, and the crew was spraying down the yellow cab's engine.

"How are the other drivers?" she asked, not breaking her stride across the grassy overgrowth.

"One may need transport just to get checked out for a concussion."

"Ash may have to transport if they consent."

Megan didn't need to be told twice. "I'll go let her know," she said, already peeling away toward Ash who had just pulled up near where all the cops were talking with the other drivers involved.

They placed the man on the stretcher and loaded him into the back of the ambulance.

Laura took a deep breath in through her nose, searching for the sense of calm she always needed. She slipped her gloves off and placed her palms over the man down by his feet, acting like she was checking his vitals, even though a trained eye would notice the cop had resumed chest compressions. She only needed five seconds, ten at the most.

With so many witnesses, she had learned how to be creative with her powers in the past. Laura wrapped her hands around his ankles and breathed, visualizing his heart beating again. The warmth tingled her palms, and she could feel the energy transfer from her body to his, but she could sense it hadn't gone far. With patients close to the edge, it was like throwing a stone down a deep cavern. She felt her energy piddle and fade, no matter how hard she tried to send it.

She nodded to the cop she was ready, then dug in a drawer to grab her tools. With a flick of her scissors, Laura cut through the striped-green golf shirt he wore, noticing he had a stain on his stomach that looked like mustard. She had to cut through his undershirt too and exposed a scar over his belly where his gallbladder probably had been removed. There was also a tattoo that looked like an Irish knot of some sort, right over the heart.

Praying it wasn't too late, she turned on the automated external defibrillator, ripped open the package, and pulled the backing off the pads. She slapped them onto his chest, attached the leads, and pressed the button for the machine to take over.

The older man had gray hair, and the lines of his face had relaxed along with his mouth where his lips were parted and losing color.

The AED ran through the cycle once, twice, walking them through the shocks and compressions.

"You good?" said the cop.

"Yeah, let's go," Laura said, before he jumped out and shut the doors. Jordan lurched the ambulance into drive and punched the siren on blast before bumping back on the road and into traffic.

The AED read ventricular fibrillation. Laura kept going with compressions in between shocks. She stopped to check vitals, taking a second to try to send another blast of healing energy to him. Like before, the energy never echoed back to her, but faded away into the man's body. She administered epinephrine and hoped like hell Jordan could get to the hospital fast.

She kept alternating the medicine and shocks with compressions until she felt the familiar jolt of the speed bump as they entered the hospital parking lot.

The doors opened and Mel was there with a team, pulling him out while Laura ran alongside the stretcher, filling Mel in.

"Do you know if the airbag deployed?" Mel asked, making notes as they jogged behind the ER nurses racing the man to the back.

"No, I don't know if it was the impact of the steering column or the shock to the system."

With a quick nod, Mel jogged off to the back, leaving Laura standing in a full sweat. She could hear the cardiac arrest team calling out to each other as they worked to revive the man with the tattoo.

Jordan walked in and put his hand on her shoulder. Jordan wasn't overly affectionate and didn't talk too much. Even though they had worked together almost the entire time Laura had been there, she didn't know much about him other than he was married, attended church, and liked to help people. She wasn't sure he even liked her, but either way, he drove fast and trusted Laura to be his second when they were short-staffed, which was most of the time, so she took that respect as a sign of approval. The gesture of his hand on her shoulder, a rare sign of emotion, touched Laura.

There were no words he could say. They had done this before. He'd pat her shoulder and walk off to give her some space. He, like everyone in the station, could see how much the patients weighed on her.

It was no secret she wanted to be a physician and hated giving up control, watching the doctors and nurses take the patients away from her. She wanted to be back there, scrubbed in, doing everything she could to help more people. Instead she did the best she could with what she had and passed them over to someone else. The lack of control and ownership ate at her, especially in tough cases. It was easy to hand over care for a patient who would make a full recovery, but with someone on the edge, she felt a certain ownership that she was always denied. Once they had the information they needed, the doctors and nurses no longer relied on the paramedic. Her role was finished, and she was no longer privy to what happened next.

"Hey, Laura," Ash said from behind her. "You okay?" she asked, looking unsure as Laura turned to her.

Laura pulled a hand over her face. "Yeah, I'll be alright. Sorry, did you give the other patient transport?"

"Yeah, I just dropped her off to check in. One of the nurses or volunteers got her a wheelchair, but she's waiting right now. They said they would come back with some paperwork in a minute. She's upright and talking. Looks like they're busy around here." Ash propped her hands on her belt and looked over Laura's shoulder.

Laura turned around to see Mel walk up, slowly, as if she were weighed down.

"They just called it," she said, meeting Laura's eyes. "I'm sorry."

CHAPTER 18

Carter could feel the energy shift when Laura followed Holden through the door. He practically bounced inside, while Laura sagged under an invisible weight.

"How was work today?" Carter said, getting up with his crutches.

Laura didn't meet his eyes, just put her purse down and kicked off her shoes. As if she realized she hadn't answered him, she flicked some hair out of her face and said, "Not great."

"I'm sorry. What happened?"

"Car crash. Cardiac arrest. Did everything I could."

"I'm sure you tried your best."

"Yeah," she said, walking away from him into the kitchen where she went through the motions of preparing a snack for Holden.

"That doesn't mean it doesn't hurt," Carter said, following her into the kitchen.

"I know. I guess I'm just tired."

Holden orbited her, singing the ABCs loudly and off-key while he did so.

"What do you want for a snack, honey? Goldfish or fruit snacks?"

"FRUIT SNACKS!" he said making a beeline for the seat he had claimed at the kitchen table.

"Don't worry about cooking tonight. I'll order in," Carter said, watching Laura open the little packet of gummies and turn on *Sesame Street*.

"No, you don't need to do that. We have food here," she said, but Laura looked like cooking was the last thing she wanted to do.

"Would cooking help take your mind off it?"

"I don't know." She walked over and put the food in front of Holden with a sippy cup of milk and planted a kiss on the top of his head. When she walked back toward Carter in the kitchen, she looked bone-tired.

"I don't know what to do here, Laura. I want to do something nice for you, but I don't know what that is."

She smiled in his direction, but the sadness seeped into her expression. "You don't need to do that for me, Carter. I'll be okay. I just need to change clothes and finish the plans for Holden's party. It's tomorrow, and all I've done today is send out the updated location. Thanks for letting us have it here."

Laura had brought up the subject that morning over breakfast, and Carter hadn't even thought twice.

"It's your home too."

"Yeah, but you know, I just really appreciate it."

"What does a birthday party for a four-year-old even look like?"

Laura blew out a breath and leaned against the counter. "I don't know. I feel like I'm making it up as I go. Usually I just do cake, balloons, and invite some kids from his class. Thank God, I can do that over email. All of the parents already responded yes."

"That seems easy enough," Carter said, glancing over at

Holden, who was chewing away on his fruit snacks, stopping to take a drink of milk.

"What can I help with?"

She waved her hand. "Don't worry about it. I'll just pick up some party food at the store when I get the cake and balloons. I looked at them a few weeks ago. They have Mickey Mouse, so that's a godsend."

She leaned her head back and stared at the ceiling while she rattled off a shopping list, more to herself than to him. Laura put her hands behind her neck and pulled on it, like she was trying to work out the kinks.

"Why don't you go get out of your work clothes? I'll keep an eye on Holden and order us some food."

Laura lowered her head and looked at him, taking a deep breath. "Are you sure? I feel like I'm relying on you too much."

"Nah, not at all. Go ahead, take a minute. You can even grab a shower if you want. We'll be okay. You've had a hard day."

Laura thought about it and headed upstairs. Carter went and sat next to Holden.

"All done?"

"Mhmmm."

"Want to go sit on the couch?"

"And color. You can help me," Holden said, looking up with a shrug.

Carter let out a laugh and followed him toward the living room.

Thirty minutes later, Laura walked downstairs to find them both coloring while talking about Oscar the Grouch. She had put on her blue robe over her gray sweatpants and wore her hair down, which was smooth, as if she had just brushed it.

Holden didn't look up, but Carter couldn't look away.

With her hair down, she looked softer, and knock-him-flat beautiful. The blue robe wrapped around her outlined her lithe body, hugging curves that he'd thought about all last night.

"What?" she said, looking at him, folding her arms in and hugging herself.

Carter didn't know what to say. The knee-jerk was some glib joke or comment about her, but nothing felt appropriate with Holden bobbing his head along to the Count on *Sesame Street* while he kept coloring. Even if they had been alone, none of those comments were worthy of Laura.

"I like your hair."

"Oh," she said, running her hands through it and tossing it behind her as if she didn't want him to see it. "Thanks," she added, not meeting his eyes. "I just washed it."

"You look nice."

Laura sat down on the other side of the couch from him. "Um…I have no makeup on and I'm in a robe. I should probably check you for a concussion."

Carter grinned at her. "No, I mean it."

"You're crazy."

"Is that a good thing?"

"Not usually."

"You used to like it in high school," he said, raising an eyebrow.

"Crazy looked a lot more exciting when I was sixteen."

"Are you saying I'm exciting?"

"No—"

"I could show you some excitement."

"No, thank you. At this point in my life, I don't need excitement."

"What do you need?" he asked, enjoying their little duel.

"At this point in my life? Stability with some peace and quiet thrown in for good measure."

"I'm very stable."

She rolled her eyes and pulled her mouth in a line like she had said, *as if*. "You have an order not to leave the state."

"A captive audience."

She rolled her eyes again but was laughing at him. Carter wanted to say he could make her do that again but demonstrated a considerable amount of restraint and maturity.

The doorbell rang at that moment.

Holden practically grew a foot with excitement when he stood on his tippy toes, lips forming a perfect O before he ran off with excited glee yelling, "Someone's here! Someone's here!"

"What did you order?" Laura asked, standing up. She reached out to hand Carter his crutches as he stood. "I can get it; you don't have to get up."

"No, I'm good. PT was pleased to see me moving around so much. Oh, and I got steak."

"What?" Laura turned around to face him. "You didn't need to do that."

"Yeah, those delivery apps have everything. I should've asked how you liked your steak cooked. I got one medium well and one medium rare. You can have what you want."

"Hello? HELLO?" Holden yelled while knocking on the door. "Mama, it's locked."

"Okay, sorry. We're coming," Laura said, unlocking the door and pulling him back.

"Yay! Food!" Holden said, seeing the bags and turning around to run back to the kitchen.

Laura reached out and took the food bags from the driver, while Carter slipped the guy a couple of bills for the tip.

"Alright, let's eat!"

"Do I need to get Holden something? I don't know what you ordered."

"Nah, I got him. Just a couple of plates and drinks. Holden, do you want to get the napkins?" Carter asked.

"Sure," he said with a shrug before walking over to the napkin holder on a low shelf at the end of the cabinets, grabbing a fistful, and slapping two or three down at each of their plates.

Carter turned around to catch Laura looking at him. She glanced away and started unwrapping the food, which included two steaks, loaded baked potatoes, a couple of side salads, a loaf of bread, and a plate of chicken tenders and fries with apple slices.

"Carter, this is too much. I'll give you some cash after we eat."

He waved her off and sat down at the table. Holden crawled up into his own chair and berated Carter through the prayer before they all started eating.

Laura had taken the medium-well steak, and he watched as she took the first bite, closing her eyes at the flavor. She opened them and wiped her mouth.

"Wow."

"Good, yeah? I'm glad. You deserve it."

"You're spoiling me," Laura said, and clipped her mouth shut as if she wanted to take the words back the moment they came out.

"What's spoiling?" Holden asked.

Carter looked at him and smiled. "It's when you like someone very much and you give them everything you can think of." He glanced back at Laura. "Everything they want."

"Oh." Holden shrugged again and plunged another French fry into a puddle of ketchup.

Laura glanced down and ate her food, not saying anything else to Carter for the rest of the meal, which didn't bother him at all because while she tried to hide it, he caught the glimmer of a small smile on her face.

They finished the rest of the meal and ran through the nighttime routine. While Laura bathed Holden and read him a story, Carter sat in his room, reviewing the emails from the day.

The board still wanted him to come back as soon as possible to discuss the possibility of the merger with a larger company. He wrote them back, laying out the reasons he didn't want to move in that direction, making sure to mention the other company's debt ratio as one of the many factors that gave him pause. He hoped the quick response time would calm things down and buy him more time. He didn't want to have to answer to the board as to why he couldn't come back to California personally. He'd schedule another video conference next week in an attempt to show them proof of life and possibly end all the discussion of a merger. Maybe in a few years, with the right opportunity, he would be open to a merger, but this certainly wasn't the right company or time.

"Goodnight, Carter!" Holden yelled down the hall.

"Goodnight!"

Laura shut Holden's door with a soft click and made her way down the hall to his room.

Carter had been looking forward to this all day. He had relived last night's kiss while he'd lain awake until early in the morning, thinking about Laura in the past and Laura now. He thought about his arms around her small frame in the apartment, committing everything she had said to memory.

Carter had thought he might fall for her again when he had called her, but after yesterday, he was officially a goner. Buying her a steak dinner had been planned before he knew about her day. He had wanted to take her out to dinner, do the whole thing up, but knew better than to even suggest leaving Holden with a babysitter. It just wasn't going to happen, and it didn't need to. A great meal at home after a shower had put a smile back on her face after a long day, and that was more than enough.

As much as her strength amazed him, Carter wished she would realize she didn't have to do any of this alone. He wished she would make space for him in her life.

Laura walked into the room, a vision in blue. In her robe, with her hair washed and down, she drew him to her like a beacon. There was something about the quiet comfort and unpretentious, natural beauty that made her stand above every other woman he had been with. Fake and phony could never hold a candle to natural, true beauty with a good heart. She was the real deal.

"Thank you for dinner," she said, walking in and retightening her robe. "You didn't need to do that. I left some money on the table to pay for my share."

"I meant what I said, Laura," Carter said, watching her walk toward the bandages as she shifted back into professional mode. "I like spoiling you."

Laura stopped and tilted her head to one side. "Carter—"

"Come sit here."

"But I need to change—"

"You can do that in a minute. Come here."

Laura eased down next to him on the couch, maintaining a respectable distance.

"I don't bite, unless you want me to."

"Uh-huh…Carter, we're both adults here—"

"Isn't that a wonderful thing? Don't need to sneak around anymore."

"That's not what I meant."

"Do you remember that night at the homecoming game?" Carter asked, sliding his eyes over to her.

Laura made a show of folding her arms.

"It was freezing," he reminded her.

"And we got the chili and hot chocolate from the conces-
sion stand."

"We had to snuggle together under that blanket you
brought."

Laura's smile grew with the memory. "My mom took one
look at the temperature and made me carry it in when she
dropped us off. I thought it was a dumb suggestion."

"You looked adorable hugging that blanket to your chest
when you found me by the ticket booth."

"It was the ugliest thing."

Carter shifted to fully face her on the couch. "Mustard
yellow."

"God, I know," Laura said, glancing over with a laugh. "I
still have it, you know."

"For real?"

She let out a laugh and went back to watching TV. "Yeah,
it's in my trunk."

"So do you make a habit of going out to games with your
blanket to entice others?"

"Pfft. Hardly."

"I don't know. The blanket was the only reason I got so
close," Carter said, shifting closer to her on the couch. Laura
didn't move away but rolled her eyes. "As I recall, we were
sitting with my arm around you the whole time."

"Because of the blanket, right?"

"I couldn't take my eyes off its satin edges," Carter said,
sliding his arm around her shoulders. Laura let out a sigh,
more resigned than relieved, but he'd take the win, and he
smiled when he felt her weight subtly shift into him.

His bandages could wait. This was exactly what he
needed.

CHAPTER 19

"**G**ood morning, Birthday Boy!" Laura said while Holden bounced up and down in his bed with one side of his hair standing on end.

Holden sprang off the bed and ran around, hopping in circles. "My party's today! My party's today!"

"Yes, yes!"

He stopped running and swung around to face her. "Now?"

"Happy Birthday, Holden!" Carter said from the doorway.

"Party?"

"Yes, but first breakfast. Do you want birthday pancakes?"

"CAKE!"

"Pancakes," Laura said, laughing.

Carter smiled, that same languid smile she had always dreamed of, especially after last night. Laura had changed his bandages like always after sitting there beside him, watching TV for a few minutes. Resting there against his side, with his arm around her, had taken her back to pleasant memories before everything had changed between them, ending with no closure or goodbye.

With her hand on his arm, she had tried again to heal him, only to be disappointed. There was no tingle, no echo, no warmth. It was as if she didn't have powers over him, a fact she would just need to accept. There was no manual for this. She had never told a soul besides her father and didn't understand it herself. Why she couldn't heal Carter made little sense. They weren't related like her mom or son. They had nothing together except a brief infatuation in high school that had shaped her idea of young love.

As she remembered, she hadn't been able to heal him then. She had tried once when he had jammed his finger in the door of his truck. Laura's hand closed now, remembering how she, at fifteen, had taken his hand in her own, folding it over and visualizing the pain leaving and the swelling going down. Nothing had come then, but now that she was a paramedic, Laura better knew how to target her ability. She hadn't remembered that moment where she had been unable to heal him until last night when he had started talking about the hideous blanket and the homecoming game. The game, the band, and the crowd in the stands had all made it a perfect memory, but sitting close to Carter, with his arm around her, had given Laura her first taste of love and wanting more.

When the commercial broke the magic, Laura had stood and changed Carter's bandages while trying not to overthink him watching her every move. When it was done, he had looked at her with a gaze that made her feel like a shy sixteen-year-old girl again.

Now Holden bounced around the room for another minute, then followed Carter out to go downstairs, both of them still wearing pajamas. Holden, in Mickey Mouse pj's of course, and Carter in athletic shorts and yesterday's button-down shirt, open at the neck. She knew he slept without a shirt on, as it was easier on his bandages, but every morning he made sure he covered himself before seeing her or Holden.

When they were all downstairs, Carter kept Holden company at the kitchen table, while Laura kept tradition by whipping up a batch of Funfetti pancakes, as she had for every one of Holden's birthdays. She stacked them up, opened the wax candle in the shape of the number four, and lit it before walking over.

"Happy Birthday to you…" she sang while Carter joined in, the two of them finishing the chorus while Holden vibrated with glee and a megawatt smile.

"Alright! Blow out the candles!"

Holden puffed out his cheeks and blasted the candle that never had a chance. Laura and Carter clapped and cheered. They all sat down and ate breakfast, talking about the party. Laura always scheduled it before lunch in case Holden got too tired. She had gotten up earlier to run and get a sandwich tray, some chips, the cake, balloons, and goody bags. Just like last year, after cake and presents, Laura planned on moving the party outside so Holden could run around with his friends.

She watched as Holden shoveled food into his mouth, syrup dripping down his chin. Her heart swelled. Every kid she had invited had said they would come, and a few of the parents had left kind messages, saying how excited their kids were to come and celebrate Holden's birthday with him. Maybe Carter was right about Holden being loved by friends and not necessarily being alone when the day came, but she wouldn't be a mom if she didn't worry.

A loud, shrill beeping echoed from outside.

"I told the movers to go to the storage unit. What is that?"

Laura said, looking at Carter. His lips slowly curved into a smug smile.

"Truck!" Holden yelled, running to smash his face against the front window. "Hey! Wait a second! They're driving on the grass." Standing on tippy-toe, his face an indignant snarl, he directed, "Trucks go on the road! Not the grass!" He glanced back toward Laura, his face growing into serious warning mode. "He's gonna be in trouble." Turning back around, Holden banged his little fist on the window. "YOU NEED A TIME OUT, TRUCK!"

"Carter?"

He grinned and blinked a few times to give the illusion of innocence. "I wanted to get Holden something for his birth-day, so I did."

Laura's mouth opened and shut. "Thank you, that's very kind, but you didn't need to do that." She looked back over at Holden, who was bouncing up and down and watching. "What did you get him?"

"OH MY GOSH!" Holden said. "Mama! Come see!"

Laura got up and hurried over to the window.

"It's a castle! A Mickey Castle!"

Holden was right. A crew of two guys were unfolding a giant inflatable castle. The turrets were already rising into the sky to the steady deafening beat of the compressor. On the entrance, Mickey's smiling face and big ears puffed up.

"Oh, this is perfect. Say thank you, Holden!"

"Thank you, Mr. Carterrrrrr!" Holden said as he ran back over to the kitchen table to slam into Carter with a big thank you hug.

"You're welcome, buddy!"

"I want to go outside!" Holden said, turning to her, his little feet tapping all over the place.

"We have to wait until it's ready and until all of your friends get here. Let's go get dressed."

Holden was so excited because of the castle, the cake, and the balloons that before she knew it, the first guests were arriving. While the parents hung out next to the castle and chatted about the daycare and summer plans, Holden and his buddies were tumbling around inside the bounce house, giggling constantly in a static-filled tangle of limbs.

Ash and Megan each pulled up and waved to Holden before they walked inside, carrying gifts.

"Hey! Thanks for coming! You guys really didn't need to get Holden anything," Laura said, giving them each a hug as they walked in.

Megan shrugged like Holden would. "I love parties, and Holden is so fun to shop for."

"Yeah, he's great," Ash said, passing over her own bag that had a police car on the side. "Mine has a police theme."

"I wouldn't expect anything else."

The two of them were such an unlikely pair. Megan looked like a sunflower. She wore a yellow sundress that showed off her freckles and flowed with the breeze along with her frizzed, red curls. She had on flip-flops and looked like she had lost a flower crown somewhere while singing with the birds.

Ash, on the other hand, looked like she had just come from the gym. She wore black Lycra pants and running shoes along with a sleek running jacket. Her short black hair swept over her eyes with a side part in her classic pixie cut. Ash had always kept her hair short, saying it was less work to deal with than the waist-length hair she had worn a long time ago. After one guy had used it as a takedown in a training exercise at the police academy, Ash had driven straight to the hair stylist and demanded the clippers. The only color she wore was on her shoes—which were bright green—and on the matching shirt that peeked out from underneath her jacket.

Due to their similar ages, the three of them had bonded almost immediately after they had met. Each of them brought the same level of confidence to their work. Laura had been tempted to tell them about her power more than once, and even though she never would dare share her secret, the temptation spoke to just how close they had grown.

"How's Mr. Green Eyes?" Megan asked, peering over her shoulder.

"Yeah, I was kinda surprised when Megan told me where you were living," Ash said.

"He's inside and he's good. No, it's not like that—"

"Uh-huh. Didn't you say you dated him before?" Ash said, narrowing her eyes.

"Yeah, but that was a long time ago. He's just here until the court date, and he's great with Holden. I was really reluctant, but it's worked out better than I would've hoped, actually."

Ash watched her again, and Laura felt a shiver over her arms. Ash could always tell when someone was lying. She followed due process to a tee, making sure to dot every i and cross every t, but Ash always knew the truth well beforehand. It was almost like she could read people. Laura must have passed inspection, because Ash smiled. "Well, as long as you're happy and Holden is too, and Mr. Price is following the conditions of his bail…"

"My ears are burning," Carter said, coming up from behind Laura. "Sergeant Myers. Megan, nice to see you again."

"Hi, Carter," Megan said with a smile.

Ash nodded once. No doubt it was awkward for her to stand at a four-year-old's birthday party with a person she had arrested a week ago.

To cut off any tension, Laura announced it was time for cake, and all the moms and dads started trying to coax the kids out of the bounce house, luring them with promises of cake.

"I love bounce houses," Megan said as they all walked inside. "You didn't tell me you would have one. Is it bad I want to get in later?" she asked with a laugh.

"Actually, that's Carter's contribution."

"Really?" both Megan and Ash asked in unison with raised eyebrows.

"Yeah, I know. I was surprised too."

"It's really nothing. Just a phone call."

"Well, it's a hit," Ash said with a small smile that Carter returned.

Laura lit the candle on the Mickey Mouse-themed cake once all the kids were sitting around the table with their parents behind them. Megan graciously offered to hold Laura's cell phone with her mom on a video call, so she could sing along and watch Holden blow out the candles.

Laura knew it crushed her mom to miss a birthday, but she had promised they would come and visit soon and that Holden understood. She also knew that the call was more for her mom than it was for Holden, who was too overwhelmed to converse with any of the adults beyond a sugar-fueled thank you.

"Alright, here it comes! Happy Birthday to you…" As they sang, Laura had to blink away tears as she crouched down next to Holden to smile so Ash could snap a picture. With a big puff of air that would've put the big bad wolf to shame, Holden blew out that candle. Everyone cheered, and the adults sprang into action. Ash and Megan kept acting as photographer and videographer respectively, while Laura cut the cake and Carter scooped ice cream into bowls for the kids who wanted some. The moms and dads went around helping the kids get drinks and other non-dessert snacks, and before long, everyone had food in front of them and fell into the happy silence of communal eating broken by bits of chitchat.

As with anything involving little kids, the silence didn't last long as Holden moved on to presents. He ripped through the paper of the first present from Laura and squealed in excited delight when he found a bunch of new Mickey Mouse pajamas and books, along with a Play-Doh set. Megan had gotten him a book about firetrucks that made noise when he pressed the buttons and walked him through how to press each one to make a sound. Ash's present was a remote-controlled police car, complete with siren and lights. Carter worked on installing the batteries Ash had thoughtfully provided, while Holden opened the gifts from his friends.

The huge house was a blessing when the kids took the toys around and tried them out before retiring to the bounce house again. Her kneejerk response was to follow them around to make sure they didn't mark the walls of the rental, but Carter just waved off her worry with a smile.

Laura took the phone from Megan, who followed them out to the bounce house with an impish grin in her eye that suggested she was so going in with them. Ash was talking with Carter about something, and the parents of the other kids milled about, snacking and chitchatting, each with one eye on their kids.

"Hey, Mom! Wish you were here, but I'm glad you got to see it."

Her mom's smile beamed back at her. "I know. I wish I could've been there too, but it looks like a great party. The house is beautiful!"

"Yeah, I know. It worked out perfectly."

Her mom beamed again and then gave her the explain-yourself-missy look. "I saw Carter Price in the background. You didn't tell me he was the one with a room to rent."

Busted. Laura hadn't mentioned that to her mom because

she didn't want her mom to get the wrong idea. The woman was a hopeless romantic.

"I know, I know. It's not like that."

Her mom smiled and lowered her voice to a whisper even though it was just the two of them in the kitchen now. "He looks almost the same as in high school. So handsome."

"Uh-huh. Don't get any ideas."

"I'm just saying, you two always looked good together. It was nice of him to come down and help out with Holden's party. Megan told me he rented Holden a bounce house. She brought me outside a little to see it. Looks like the boys are having a blast."

"Yeah, he did that as a surprise, just to be nice."

Laura's mom grinned again. "He was always good like that. I can't wait to hear more about him later."

"Mom—"

"I'll let you go. Give Holden a big kiss from me and tell Carter I said hello!"

Laura ended the call and went out in search of the other adults who had migrated outside. Carter was standing in the yard, watching and cheering Holden on from outside the mesh walls of the bounce house. Carter glanced over his shoulder with a slight frown like he was looking for someone. When his eyes met hers, he smiled. Laura smiled back despite herself. Maybe her mom was right about him after all.

CHAPTER 20

The birthday party had been a huge success, and the best part was that Carter had rented the bounce house for the weekend, which meant when everyone else left, Laura and Holden bounced around inside for an hour while Carter watched. He wanted to get in and tumble around too, but with his burns still healing, not to mention his leg, no one thought it was a great idea. Instead, he found a lawn chair in the garage and sat outside near the house, watching them.

Holden had dinner, another slice of cake, a bath, and was tucked into bed with new pajamas and Megan's book about fire trucks before eight that night. Carter knew because he could hear the sounds of the fire truck book blaring away down the hall until Holden had passed out twenty minutes later.

Laura walked into the room wearing her blue robe and sat down in the chair next to the couch he was on, as was their routine.

"I could fall asleep right here," she said.

"He had a great birthday."

"Thanks to you. The bounce house has really set the bar

for next year." Laura shifted to look at him. "Thank you again. You didn't need to do that for him."

"But I wanted to do it."

"Well, thank you."

"You're welcome. Watching the kids flip around in there made me feel young again, you know? Brought back a lot of memories I had forgotten about," he added when she nodded.

"That has been one of the biggest surprises since I became a mom. Just how much of it came back. Everything has meaning now. Before it meant something, but I was just floating from one goal to the next."

"No, I think I know what you're getting at. Sounds like you love it."

"Holden makes me happy."

Carter muted the news, which was talking about politics on the TV.

"You used to be happy all the time."

Laura didn't look at him, staring off into space at a past he couldn't see. "That was a long time ago, Carter."

"Are you talking about John?" he asked, not even liking to say the guy's name, but seeing no way around it.

Laura nodded.

"He didn't deserve you."

Laura's gaze flicked over to meet his, her deep brown eyes watching him in the dim light of the bedroom.

"I believe he's dead."

"What makes you say that?" Carter asked. He had already researched and read all of the newspaper articles on the man. John Burton had simply vanished and became one of the many people to walk away, never to be heard from again. A missing person report was filed with the police, and a social media post was shared, but weeks had gone by with no new information. Gradually, life went on for everyone, including Laura.

"I just know in my heart. I don't know where he is or what he did, but he changed. He wasn't like you to begin with."

"Like me?"

"Confident, funny, always the center of attention," she said with a smile.

"I'll take that as a compliment."

"You should. John was quiet. He was nice, kind, stable, or so I thought. We weren't together for very long. Dated, married, and then things started getting rough. We had talked about divorce, tried counseling, tried getting closer, but separation came up again. He told me he was going to run some errands." Laura stared off into space. "Then he never came back."

"There was no indication anything had changed?" Carter asked.

Laura shook her head. "We were together for two years total, including almost a year and a half being married. I thought I knew him, but six months is hardly enough time. Looking back, there were signs. I mean, he was funny at first and attentive. He was focused on his career and I was mostly still helping my mom take care of my dad, and he had always planned to support me in my dream to pursue medicine, with savings and everything. Honestly, it was my first real relationship after high school." No need to mention Carter, but she was sure he could put the pieces together. "He was quiet, but once we got married, in a very small, very low-key ceremony, he just kinda stopped talking to me."

"Stopped talking to you?"

"Yeah, like I'd ask him what he wanted for dinner and he wouldn't answer. It was like I wasn't even there. And then, I'd tell him I was leaving for work, and he wouldn't even look up from what he was doing on the computer."

"What did he do?"

"Remote tech support."

She continued, "We never merged finances, didn't take a honeymoon. Never took a vacation. It was like we were roommates. One day he went out and that was that. He was gone."

"That must have been hard."

"It was and it wasn't. It was hard because I couldn't grieve, couldn't have closure. I just don't know for sure. I think I do, but I have no proof. My confidence also took a beating. Megan has been after me to get back out there."

"Date again?" Carter didn't like the sound of that, or of any of this conversation.

"Yeah, she says it's time, but the last time I did any of that was with John. I would never say it was a mistake because Holden's the best thing to ever happen to me, but—"

"I'm sure you'd have your pick," Carter said, looking at her.

Laura let out a rueful laugh. "I wouldn't know. John seemed right, and he wasn't."

Carter wanted to ask if *he* had seemed right, felt compelled to prove himself time and time again, but forced himself to stay silent and listen.

"How did you two meet?"

"Friend of a friend whose boyfriend worked with him. That didn't work out, and well…I guess neither did we in the end. But again, I feel terrible saying that because of Holden."

"Everything that makes Holden good is because of you, Laura. You're allowed to comment on the relationship separately."

"I guess I just feel guilty. Like I wasn't enough for him. I tried to talk and be what he wanted, but I guess I never met expectations or knew where I fell short. I hadn't had a serious adult relationship before that, and part of me just figured that was as good as it was going to get. That's why, when he didn't want a big wedding or honeymoon, I didn't press the issue. I just figured that's what it was supposed to be like. You know, fairy tales aren't reality. I get that."

"I think every relationship has its flaws, but what you're describing doesn't sound like much of a relationship."

"I've learned that now. You're not the first to say it. Then I start to wonder if I even know what I'm doing or if I'm worthy of it."

Carter couldn't take it anymore. He moved closer to her chair. "Laura, I was in love with you from sixth grade through high school. I can promise you with my whole heart that you were worthy then and you're worthy now."

"Carter—"

"I'm not done. You are a beautiful, strong, funny, smart woman, and to top it all off, you're an excellent mother. I'm glad he's gone. I'm sad for Holden, but you both deserve so much more than a roommate who doesn't appreciate the treasure in front of his face."

"Treasure?"

"Laura, when I said I wanted to ask you to the prom, I meant it, but I thought I'd blown my chances with you. Now, hearing all of this, I wouldn't change Holden, but I wish you hadn't had to go through that. I wish you wouldn't for a second wonder if you have some kind of flaw. You deserve to be cherished, cared for, loved, and protected."

Laura searched his eyes and then looked at her hands in her blue robe-covered lap. "You make it sound so easy to think those things."

"You deserve all of that and more."

"Now you sound like Megan."

"She's right."

"Carter, no one wants to be with someone who's a single mom. I can't date when bedtime is at eight. I'm not interested in sleeping over or all that other stuff. Most people want to travel. All of that goes out the window when I'm the second most important person in my life. Holden's number one for me. He always will be. A guy isn't going to want to be with me when he knows he's automatically going to be second."

"You're wrong about that too."

"Oh yeah? Do you see a line of guys willing to sign on for that?"

"You're wrong about him being second. The right man would know he'd be third place, if not fourth after your mom. A good man is the least important person in the house and should view himself as such. If he even thinks that he's equal to you or Holden, he's dead wrong."

With that sentiment, Carter stood up—leg be damned—and leaned over and cupped her face and kissed her. He had wanted this for so long and wasn't about to lose any more time thinking about the past or what might've been. Laura tilted up, her lips meeting his own, until she pulled back.

"Carter?"

"What?" He braced himself up with his arms on either side of the arms of the chair she was sitting in. She looked so small and fragile beneath him. Tired of carrying all the weight for her past and Holden's future. She stared up at him with those big eyes and nearly undid him when she bit her pink bottom lip.

"I missed you."

Carter looked down at her, overwhelmed with emotions that swept through him. All of the wasted time without her crashed into him like a wave of regret. At least they had each other now. The emotions hadn't changed for either of them but had been lying dormant as they waited to see each other again.

"I missed you more," he said, leaning down and meeting her lips again.

The two of them entwined, shy at first, then picking up speed as they rekindled what had been there once upon a time.

CHAPTER 21

It had been so long since Laura had been with anyone. At first, she was anxious as she shed her robe while they kissed and moved toward the bed. Once there, even with her nightshirt on, she pulled the covers up to her shoulders to shield herself, trying to hide from his eyes. No one had seen her naked since John, and he had never offered any praise other than "fine" or "good." She'd since had a child, and any self-confidence had sailed right out the nearest window. Her stomach wasn't tight and neither were her thighs or breasts, but Carter's hands, gentle but firm, found them anyway, sliding over her skin, feeling, claiming. His lips left her mouth and trailed down her cheekbone toward her neck and then up to her ear where he whispered something she couldn't understand. His voice was low, husky, and almost reverent.

Laura wanted to know what he'd said but didn't dare stop to ask. What he was doing felt too good. Together in bed, his hands roaming under her thin nightshirt warmed her through to her heart. His hands slid out from under her nightshirt, and he wove them into her hair. He shifted in the bed now, partially covering her, his cast holding him back.

He murmured something again and went back to her neck, making her pulse pick up speed from a fast dance to an all-out sprint. Whatever spot he had found under her ear made her back arch up. Raw sexuality and primal need pushed past her inhibitions, as her body took control from her mind. She turned toward him then and met his gaze, brown eyes to his smoldering green.

He looked powerful, sexy, and focused on one thing in the dimly lit room.

"You're more beautiful than ever."

"That's not—"

His mouth cut her off, taking what he wanted without apology, just like everything else in high school—and apparently now in business. He scrambled her brain and cut off her argument.

"You're perfect, and lying here, this close to you, is killing me."

Laura ran a hand down his face, her fingertips following his dark hair. "I wouldn't want that. Thought the goal was to help you heal."

He smiled, and she watched the powerful muscles move under his shirt that really needed to be off already.

"I've wanted this for a long time," he said, his voice dry and strained with effort.

"I remember."

His brows dipped low. "The truck?"

Laura nodded, feeling a warmth come back to her cheeks at the memory. They had never gone any further than the kind of passionate kissing high schoolers specialized in.

"You know, things are different now," she said, resting her head on the pillow facing him, her hand still tracing his jaw, watching the muscles flicker under the tanned skin.

"Oh?"

"I can't have another child, by the way. Just in case you wanted to know." God, why did this feel awkward? Some women could just go for it, but Laura had years of practice being the good girl, which so did not help in these situations.

His smile deepened. "Is that an invitation?"

"Well, you know, in case you were feeling up to it."

He rose up on the bed and pulled the T-shirt off his head, not noticing where he tossed it. His muscular back was bigger than she remembered. He was stronger, and that was saying something, considering his height in high school. She had seen his chest in the ambulance and while treating his burns, but something about seeing him in bed made her body temperature climb and her heart kick back into gear.

"I'm always feeling up to you," he said, meeting her mouth again. "Don't be shy, you're not hurting me. In fact, you have me pinned with my leg. You have me right where you want me."

Laura still was shy. Their bodies tangled, his hands racing under her shirt again, hiking it up to explore every inch of her body. He dove at her neck, and Laura clung to his broad shoulders, feeling the heat rise between them, as she closed her eyes in the ecstasy that just having his mouth on her body could bring. His good leg swung over her own, pressing his erection against her and sending a thrill of energy up her spine. His breath was hot in her ear, as he panted with hunger like a starving man.

He tried to pull her shirt up farther and swore under his breath in relief when she took over.

Laura hadn't needed an invitation, sitting up to slide the shirt over her head and toss it off the bed. Carter was on her before it hit the floor. His mouth on her breasts was like gasoline on a fire, sending her into a frenzy of sensation and emotion. His hands kneaded and explored, teasing her body, which was already tight as a drum. Her back arched again, offering herself up to him for the taking, her body begging him to claim her with a primal need forged throughout history.

While his mouth worked her nipple, his hands moved south, finding her thighs and swiping up higher still, grazing her most tender part, sending a shockwave of excitement through her.

This was what she wanted. This was what she needed. This was what she had been missing all of these years.

A little sound escaped her as Carter kissed down her chest and over her stomach. Laura's nerves jangled when he reached the part of her stomach she had worried about. Carter stopped, his mouth hovering inches above her skin in the dim light, and she could see him studying her.

The shame she had feared started to curl into her chest, as she reached for the sheets and tried to shift away and hide the imperfections from his view.

But his strength held her still. He raised one hand and brought it down, tracing each of the faded white stretch marks from where she had carried Holden. Carter pressed his lips to each spot with such a gentle touch, it was like a puff of warm air on her exposed, still-sensitive body. He took his time, paying attention to each one, not rushing but acknowledging and praising each spot for its sacrifice. The tension melted out of her shoulders with each passing second as he saw her for what she was and elevated her with unspoken praise and gratitude. He continued like that for minutes, paying reverent respect to her body until he had reached the last spot and found no more.

Instead of shying away from the issue, he leaned back over to her head and cupped her face with both hands in the dark. His powerful shoulders and chest were still marred by burns in the shadows right in front of her, and he looked into her eyes with a depth she had always shied away from, afraid what people would see. But with Carter, he didn't judge. He saw her.

When he spoke, his voice was low and filled with rough emotion. The grip on her face was like everything else with him—gentle, tender, but supportive. If every muscle stopped working, she knew without a shadow of a doubt, he would catch her and hold her.

"Don't ever believe you are anything but beautiful."

She could just make out the intensity in his dark eyes.

He held her face and nodded his head as if begging her to do the same. "Promise me."

"Okay."

"No. I need you to believe it."

"I believe it," she lied.

"No. Believe me."

"Carter…"

"No." He lifted his hand and brushed the hair away from her face, pressing his lips to her temple. His eyes were closed when he pulled away. When the lids lifted, emotion shone through them like she hadn't seen before.

"You're too precious for me to ever let you think you're less than perfect."

The sincerity hit her right in the chest. She was precious to him.

Years of putting herself second rushed to the surface along with the raw gut instinct to consummate the love right here and now.

He kissed her, and she met him with every move, their mouths melding together as one. His hands swept down harder and faster, matching the pace and frenzy of her own as they tangled in his hair, urging him on. Enough time had been lost between them already.

Carter's hand pressed into the juncture at her thighs and

sent a jolt up through her body, now thrumming with heat and the desperate need to know more of him. He stroked her faster and harder, while she held on to his shoulders, burrowing her head into his neck, coiled tight until the wave crashed through her body, making her muscles spasm involuntarily and without any control. While her sated body twitched, radiating heat, Carter's hands ran over her body in the softest way, soothing her hot skin.

Laura watched him through slits in her eyes. "My turn." She propped herself up on her elbows and leveled a gaze in his direction before sitting up and meeting his eyes face-to-face.

Carter cocked a smile. "There's my girl."

"Down." She was going to show him a little bit about *his girl*. She shoved his strong shoulders back onto the pillow and peeled back the sheets. His body, even still on the mend, was magnificent. The burns were healing nicely, but underneath, the muscle was firm and strong. His abs rippled down toward shorts that were really inconvenient right now.

With a quick tug over the cast, and a prayer of thanks to whoever invented stretch, the shorts went flying to meet their friends on the floor. Laura looked back and found him big and ready, with a smoldering gaze that sent a thrill of anticipation right through her.

"No foreplay?" he asked with a tease that didn't fool her.

"No need, apparently."

She swung herself on top of him and leaned down to meet him before smiling right above him. His lips found hers, while his hands went right for her chest, kneading and claiming, while his mouth worked. He had always liked being in power, but tonight, Laura had him right where she wanted him, and he couldn't do a thing about it.

She moved her body like a cat, stretching and sliding over him until she saw the cords of muscle in his neck. His hands left her breasts to reach for her hips and pull her down, which she allowed for one second before pushing herself forward and filling his mouth with her breast. He sucked and made muffled moans from beneath her, while his legs pushed upwards, trying to come in contact with what he wanted.

His mouth was working her back up, and her defiant body once again had a mind of its own when she started panting with hot need. She had wanted to linger and make him beg, but one of his hands found her and made contact with her most sensitive spot. The steady friction made her legs tremble against all control, as if he had taken over her body with his quick rhythm. The swirling made her want to collapse onto his chest, knowing he would be there to catch her this time.

Carter found her neck again and nearly undid her thin veneer of control with the graze of his teeth and the stubble on his chin. Her pulse raced in her bloodstream, drowning out all sound except for the distant pant of Carter in her ears.

But she wanted him to beg. Needed to hear that he wanted her.

Emboldened by her line in the sand, Laura arched her back and grazed her teeth along his jaw line, finding his ear lobe, before giving it a gentle tug. In response, Carter's body tensed beneath her, and she smiled into his neck as a low moan escaped his lips. His hands went to her hips, squeezing her, holding on. He arched his pelvis up to press into her, his length reaching out to her and pushing into her stomach.

Laura's eyes closed with the sensation of him underneath her, sagging under the weight of her desire, almost ready to roll over and pull him on top, when he nuzzled toward her mouth and kissed her again. She leaned in, deepening the sensation, tasting, savoring, rediscovering him.

When they pulled away, Laura shifted again, pressing

down onto him, rocking against the hard ridge of him beneath her. The movement was almost enough to send her over the edge, but she stayed steady and slow, working them in a dance as if they had all the time in the world.

Carter's face was pulled into a tense exhaustion, when he looked at her through narrowed eyes and gave her what she had wanted in a hoarse and heavy voice.

"Baby, please. I need you."

It was what she wanted to hear, but her confidence faltered.

Suddenly, shy Laura tilted her head to one side.

"You know, I haven't...well, since Holden, I never..."

Carter's face took on a look of awe as his hands guided her toward him, cupping her face with the same gentle touch he had used before.

"Remember. You're perfect."

Laura smiled as he slipped his hands down her back, pressing into her skin to let her know he was there. Feeling the strength in his hands gave her comfort.

She went to slide off him, but his hands held her in place.

"This is about you, Laura. I want to watch you."

"But I don't—"

He shook his head. "I have you."

Laura let him guide her down, slowly over him. A gasp left her as she felt herself stretch around him as he pierced deeper. She rested her forearms on his shoulders and arched her back into the sensation of him filling her.

His face looked torn between deep satisfaction and desperation as she finished lowering herself, propped up on him, feeling full and at the same time as if they were always meant to fit together.

"With the light behind you, you look even more like an angel," Carter said, his voice tight. "Just like I always imagined."

Laura's eyes turned away and studied his chest, unsure how to handle the compliment and its implications, when Carter shifted his knees up, raising her with him. The movement pushed her forward enough to where he captured her breast in his mouth again, bringing one hand up to knead her, while the other kept her hips down. He moved his hips, amplifying her movements, slow at first, then faster, working her into a steady rhythm. Laura's breath came in quick spurts, and she lowered her head, shielding him with her hair that fell like a gentle curtain around where he lay beneath her.

He moaned and shifted his mouth to her right breast before picking up the pace of his movements, now riding her from below, hitting a spot in her that made her muscles quiver, breaking her pace. As it was, she was running out of steam, but Carter had her, pulling her hips in close as he kept going, giving her exactly what she needed. Her body tightened and clung to him as he sent her higher and higher until her senses couldn't handle any more.

A rush of passion flooded her, rocking her body as it clung to and convulsed around him. Carter was still moving but she didn't know how. Harder and faster and with one final thrust, he followed her over the edge.

They lay like that for minutes, or maybe it was hours— Laura didn't know. Her head was on his shoulder, right next to his jaw, their breathing in tandem. Neither had moved from the other's body. Her hand rested on his arm, while he stroked her exposed back, warming it against the chill of the air.

She went to slide off, but his hands stopped her and held her in place with that same gentle but firm touch she had come to know.

His voice was low, barely a whisper. "Don't go."

"I'll stay here, I just thought you might—"

A long breath shushed her, but she didn't take offense. "I've wanted this for so long. Please don't let it end yet."

Laura smiled to herself and stayed until the sounds of his breath stayed steady with the heavy sleep only healing could bring. Knowing he was at peace, she slid off him, overcome with an emptiness, her body immediately missing his inside her. She lay down on the cool pillow and pulled a sheet over her chilled skin.

Carter stirred, frowning. Laura reached out and put a hand on his waist, which he grasped and turned toward, pulling her in under his arms. Only when she was nestled close to him did he settle again, his breath resuming the steady pace, his forehead free of worries.

In the dim light, asleep and at peace, Carter's expression relaxed. She knew he was older, stronger, and a confident, successful businessman, but when his guard was down, sleep revealed the innocent boy Laura had always loved.

CHAPTER 22

Laura woke up in Carter's bed, stretching with the sun. He was still lying there, fast asleep with bandages visible on his naked chest. She had changed them late last night, which had led to more kissing and exploring each other. She had ended up snuggling in his bed, but fell asleep in the crook of his arm, feeling warm, but not hot from the pleasant firmness of him under her head. She had been hesitant to lie down because of his bandages, but a few minutes of readjusting had fixed that.

"Morning," Carter said, his eyes hooded with sleep, while his hair sprang away from his head, looking almost like Holden when he woke up.

"Sleep well?" Laura asked with a sly smile.

"Good night overall, but I could've slept better, if you catch my drift." He wrapped his arms around her and pulled her back into him, planting a series of kisses up the back of her bare arms over the skinny strap of her night shirt and onto her neck in the tender spot right under her ear.

The closeness of his body made her thrum with excitement in a way she hadn't in a long time. Never with John or the few guys she'd dated before. The last time she had felt this way had been with Carter, in his old truck. Back then, she had been so young that everything seemed exciting, but now with age and experience, she knew the difference between the physical act and a deep sense of belonging and craving more. She melted into him, letting his warmth encircle her, while he planted tender kisses along the column of her neck, murmuring sweet sentiments she couldn't quite make out.

She didn't want to walk away and wished she could lie back down into the pillows before getting all tangled up with him again in the soft, big bed, but it was already almost eight, and Holden would be up any minute.

"I'm going to go make coffee," she said, not moving away while his hands ran up and down her arms, warming her while also sending a wave of goosebumps over her flesh.

"In a minute," he said, his voice muffled against her hair. "I'm making up for lost time."

"We can pick up again later," she said, pulling away and reaching for her robe at the foot of the bed. She sat back down and threaded her arms through it before he pulled her against him again.

"I like the sound of that," his voice purred low in her ear, holding enough promise to send a shiver down her spine.

Laura smothered a laugh and stood up, giving him a coy smile. "What do you want for breakfast?"

Carter let his gaze run down her body in an unapologetic survey. "I can think of something."

Laura grabbed a pillow to throw at him, and he snatched it out of the air with one hand. He looked like a king sitting in the large bed, with the covers draped around him. The bandages didn't hide the strength he clearly possessed. He was, in a word, gorgeous.

"I like the way you're looking at me."

Laura glanced away, her cheeks warming at being caught.

"No, please…continue."

"Stop. I have to go downstairs. Holden will be up any minute."

"I have an idea. I want to make you breakfast."

Laura stopped and considered him. "You don't have to do that."

"I know, but I want to." He stood up with help from his crutches, which were propped up against the nightstand. "How does bacon and eggs sound?"

"Sounds great. I'm not used to such service," Laura said with a tease evident in her voice.

"Which is what makes doing it even more fun."

Laura smiled again, and they both went downstairs. She scooped the coffee into the machine, while Carter grabbed a few pans to set on the stove. Laura helped him get the eggs, bacon, and butter out of the fridge before he shooed her upstairs.

The sight of him in his loose shorts showed off the muscles in his leg, showing he had kept up with the running he had loved during senior year. Laura had no doubt the leg in the cast was just as impressive. He pulled up the sleeves of his wrinkled button-down, which had ended up on the floor last night, then cracked a few eggs into a bowl and grabbed a whisk. The steady sound of the looped metal hitting the sides of the bowl echoed throughout the kitchen. Even with crutches under his arms, he looked like a literal dream in the kitchen. This was what Laura had always envisioned for herself when she was younger. He was kind, funny, affectionate with her and Holden, and was now making her breakfast.

Yesterday had been one of the best days of her life, not only because the party had been a success, but having Carter next to her last night, cradling her with his body and words, had been a dream. Laura watched him lay the bacon in the pan, hearing the sizzle while the smells melded in the air with the coffee in the sunny kitchen.

She walked forward and wrapped her arms around his waist, laying her head on his back as he was at least a head taller than her.

"Thanks, beautiful," he murmured.

Holden's whimpers echoed through the house.

"I'll be right back," she said, planting a kiss on the back of his neck.

"Can't wait," he tossed over his shoulder with a million-dollar smile that made her sigh.

"Coming, Holden!" Laura bounded up the stairs, frowning when she heard him crying.

She pushed through the door and saw him sitting on the bed, looking green and sweaty.

"Hey, buddy bear. You feeling okay?"

His glassy eyes stared off into space, half-open as if he was still only half-awake. "My tummy hurts."

She put a hand to his head to confirm what she already knew. "Yeah, you're a little warm. Maybe too much fun at the party. I packed the thermometer. I'm going to take your temp and then we'll get you some Tylenol, okay?"

He didn't respond but swayed slightly from left to right.

"Holden?"

He burped. Before she could move away or duck, the second one came, and with it yesterday's dinner, spraying himself, the bed, and Laura's robe. She let out a squeal and lurched backwards, trying to find anything to use to wipe up. Holden burst into tears, his little arms outstretched, not wanting to touch any of the vomit around him.

Somewhere downstairs, a crutch clattered to the ground and Carter swore. "Laura! What's wrong?" he yelled up.

"Holden threw up," she called back, whipping off her robe

and using the inside to wipe Holden's face and arms. "It's okay, baby. It's okay."

She picked him up and headed for the hall bath. While he sat on the floor crying, Laura started the water and stripped him down, throwing his soiled clothes on top of her robe. "We're going to get you cleaned up. Don't you worry. Just a little bath will have you feeling right."

"Mickey?" Holden asked, his little voice coming out between sobs like a croak from a frog.

"Let me grab him. I'll be right back," she said, running out into the hall and back into the bedroom. The whole room stank with the thick stench of vomit. Mickey had been nailed. She threw him on the bed where there was a spray of vomit and gathered up the sheets from the bed into a makeshift sack she could carry downstairs to the washer.

"What do you need?" Carter called up to her.

"Can you get him a sippy cup of water? He needs to rinse out his mouth."

"On it!"

Laura rushed back to the bathroom, where Holden sat, looking glassy-eyed and pale. She threw the clothes in with the sheets and checked the water temperature. Perfect.

"Almost ready to get you in."

A few moments later, with much labored breathing and a sheen of sweat, Carter appeared with a cup. "Here's the water."

"Awesome," Laura said, taking the water and giving it to Holden, who took a sip and looked up at Carter with big sad eyes.

"I'm sick."

"It's okay, buddy. That happens." Laura could've wept when Holden nodded at Carter's encouragement and stood up to let her take his Pull-Up off before she put him in the bath.

"Can you sit with him? I need to clean you-know-who before his nap."

"Sure thing. Do what you gotta do," he said, using one crutch to move past her into the small bathroom.

"Thanks," Laura said, gathering up all of the laundry and taking it downstairs. She threw everything inside with a dose of detergent and hit the pre-wash and extra rinse buttons before heading back upstairs to Holden's room. The house didn't have another set of sheets that she knew of, so she pulled the sheets off the top bunk and made the bed. She stacked the stuffed animals that hadn't been in the line of fire against the wall of the newly made bed and threw open the curtains to let the sun in. Laura saw the latch, and cracked the window for good measure, before turning on the fan to help get the air flowing.

"The wheels on the bus go round and round. Round and round..." Laura came back around to see Carter sitting on the edge of the tub washing Holden's back with the gentlest touch, as if he was scared to mar Holden's baby skin.

Laura opened her mouth to speak when the deafening noise of the fire alarm blared above her.

"Oh shit!" Carter leapt up and grabbed his crutch to hobble out of the room.

Holden started crying again in the tub. Laura pulled him out, wrapped him in a towel and made a beeline for downstairs, following Carter as he limped his way toward the kitchen, now hazy with smoke.

Laura grabbed a dish towel and started flapping it with one arm at the ceiling while balancing Holden who was still crying. Carter cut off the burners and turned on the fan under the microwave before grabbing another towel and helping waft away the smoke, while the alarm still blared overhead, echoing through the whole house.

The doorbell rang just as the fire alarm stopped.

"What now?" Laura asked, hiking Holden back up onto her hip, patting his back while he rested his head.

"It's probably the neighbor. That alarm could've woken the dead. I'll get it, you take care of Holden."

"Alright, sounds good. Let's get you back in the bath—"

The doorbell rang again. Carter opened the door and froze.

A tall blonde in black leggings painted on long, thin legs, wearing bright red lipstick and oversized sunglasses broke into a wide smile before she threw herself at Carter, wrapping her arms around his neck and kissing him full on the lips while pressing her body against him for a few solid seconds. She pulled back and peeled herself off him.

"SURPRISE!"

Carter looked shocked and tried to step back and put more distance between them. "Ruby, why are you here? How did you get here?"

"I just *had* to see you! You've had me so worried since the accident, and I just couldn't wait. Once I had your address after you asked Janine to forward your mail, I started packing. The idea of you being here alone without anyone to nurse you back just *devastated* me. Besides, I figured it's about time you and I get away from the office again."

Laura's mouth fell open, as the woman's manicured nails raked through Carter's hair.

"Mama, I need to go potty."

Ruby and Carter both turned to see her there, standing in her pajamas, with trace amounts of vomit on her shirt, clutching Holden wrapped in a towel.

"Oh, hello," the woman named Ruby said with surprise. "Carter?" she asked, looking at him with a slight frown. "Who's this?"

Carter didn't look over at her but hung his head and sighed. "Ruby, this is Laura and Holden."

Ruby's eyes trailed down Laura's pajamas. "How nice." Undeterred, Ruby shifted her attention and bright smile back toward Carter, who didn't move away. "I came right from the airport. My bags are in the rental car. Where can I put them?"

"Let's go, Holden," Laura said, walking upstairs toward the bathroom, trying to figure out how she could let Holden rest and how she could escape another heartbreak.

CHAPTER 23

Carter watched Laura carry Holden up the stairs. The smell of the burnt breakfast hung in the air along with the look of betrayal she had just given him. Meanwhile, Ruby sashayed into the house and had the decency to pretend to look sad.

"I hope I wasn't interrupting anything," Ruby said when Laura's door had shut upstairs, far above them.

"This isn't a great time. I'm sorry to tell you this, but you can't stay here."

Ruby's perfect red lips formed a little o while her sculpted brows arched in question before she regrouped. "I had hoped we could use this time to ourselves. Be away from the office. Get reacquainted while you show me around this charming, little town. I traveled all the way here to check on you. I'm a little hurt you aren't excited to see me." She puffed out her lower lip and pouted in full-on flirt mode.

"Ruby, I told you not to come. I was fine."

"Well, *I* wanted to check on you. Do you know how terrible it was for me, wondering what might be wrong, knowing you were in some hospital miles away?" She eyed his cast and the gauze on his arms. "I had hoped you could come home with me, at least after a few days of alone time."

Alone time with Ruby was so not on his mind. Carter cursed the short-lived interest he'd expressed in her in the beginning. He wished he could go back and undo everything, right down to her hiring. She was smart, great at her job, and good with clients, but the headache and constant pressure was getting to be too much.

"Ruby, I'm sorry. I think you're great, but—"

"It'll be our little secret. I know you're worried about what the board will say."

Carter had nowhere else to look but in her big blue eyes as she pressed herself into him. She looked stunning. A total knockout who knew how to dress to impress, but one who wore too much makeup and was far too present for Carter's liking.

"Ruby…I'm sorry." Carter wasn't in the least bit sorry, but he still had to work with her, and it paid to be nice.

"Well, seeing as you're stuck on being so noble, that's not the only reason I came." She fluffed her bangs out of her face and back into line with her blonde updo. "We need to talk about the merger. How about we get some breakfast? I'm starved. There wasn't a juice bar at the airport this morning."

"Ruby, I can't drive." Carter motioned down to his leg.

"Don't worry about that. You head upstairs and get changed. I'll be in the car, waiting." She gave him a wink and nestled close to him. Her scent, a mix of hair care, lotion, and all of the other crap she carried with her in an oversized designer bag, could've smothered him.

"You know how I feel about you. I'd love the chance to show you what else I can do." She grinned while lowering her lids and studying his lips. "Just something to think about." Ruby backed away and picked up her bag before giving him a coy, little smile. "I'll be waiting for you."

Carter headed up the stairs, aware of a pounding in his head. The smell of the burnt bacon grease still permeated throughout the house, and as he climbed the stairs, the stench mixed with the remnants of vomit. All of it smelled better than Ruby had in his face.

She was nice to look at, he'd give her that, but Carter could not have been less interested. He had locked the door before climbing the stairs, and while she was his VP and had requested a formal meeting, she could wait until he was fully ready to discuss whatever business she had brought.

He knocked softly on Laura's closed door. Silence met him on the other side.

"Laura? Come on, we need to talk."

The door opened. Laura stood there in her pajamas. The warmth and familiarity of the woman who had grabbed him from behind this morning and slept in his arms last night was gone. In her place was the same disappointed stranger he had feared would be waiting for him.

"You don't need to explain anything to me."

"You're wrong," Carter said, walking in. "I didn't call her here. Instead I told her not to come."

"You told your girlfriend not to come?"

"She's not my girlfriend."

Laura folded her arms in front of her chest. The wall was back in place between them. "You have her lipstick on your face."

"It isn't what it looks like."

"I don't need to know what it is. I've seen everything I need to know."

Carter sat down on the window seat he hadn't taken much notice of before. The room was bathed in a yellow glow. He could see why she liked it so much. "No, you haven't. Ruby is my VP."

"It's not my place to say this, but it's usually not a good

idea to mix business with pleasure," Laura said, tilting her head to the side.

"Laura, I'm so sorry. I don't know why she's here, but she wants me to go to breakfast with her. Something about work stuff." He held his head in his hands and studied the carpet before scrubbing his face, trying to figure out what he could say to her to convince her of the truth. "This doesn't change anything between me and you."

"There is no me and you," Laura said, shaking her head. "You were always going to return to California. I'm not leaving here. That's it. Done."

"Laura—"

"No, I don't care. If you want to go, need to go, then go. Holden and I can find somewhere else to stay—"

"Absolutely not. I told her she cannot stay here, despite whatever she had in mind."

"Carter—"

"Where's Holden? Let's talk about something that actually matters."

Laura seemed to soften at that. She dropped her arms and massaged the back of her neck with the other. "He's asleep now. Resting. I'm going to check on him in a little bit."

"Okay, that's good. What do you think it is?"

"Probably just too much cake and bouncing yesterday, but I'm going to go easy on him today."

Carter nodded. "Good, that's good. Let me know if you want me to pick up something or bring something back with me."

The effect was immediate. "No, thanks. We have everything we need."

"Laura—" A beep from a car cut him off.

"Maybe it's best if we leave," Laura said again. "I can't get out today or tomorrow, but I'll start looking. You better go. Don't want to keep Ruby waiting."

Carter wanted to reach out to grab her and pull her to him. He wanted to press his lips to the column of her neck again and sweep her up and toss her in bed, but all of the progress he had made with her to prove he wasn't his past felt like it had just slipped through his fingers once again.

"Ruby can wait. I'm talking to you." Carter stood up with help from his crutches and moved toward her. "Everything I said last night is still true. No, this morning did not go as planned at all, and I hope you believe me when I say that I wish I could stay here with you, but I need to meet with her about a possible merger, so I can't."

Laura searched his eyes again and looked away, but not before he saw the pain in them.

"Nothing," he continued, "has changed between us or with how I feel about you. You need to know I'm going to be sitting at that breakfast, pissed off I'm not with you. I'll be counting down the minutes. As it is, I don't have much of an appetite right now, and if she blows that damn horn one more time I swear to God—" The horn cut him off. "Look, I'm coming home to you. I know we have a lot more talking to do about this, but I have to go or she's going to wake up Holden. You'll still be here when I come back?"

Laura didn't answer.

"Laura, tell me you'll still be here."

"Why?"

"I need to hear it from you."

Laura folded her arms again and looked out the window, blinking away tears she didn't want him to see. Carter stepped forward but stopped when she stepped back away from him. She swallowed once and met his eyes, so he could see her fighting to keep her composure. "Carter, I don't have any choice, so yes, I'll be here, but no, I don't think we need to talk. I think it's best if from now on, we just treat this as a roommate situation. Your burns have healed enough to function without the gauze."

"Laura..."

She sucked in a breath and looked away from him. "I also don't think it's a good idea for you to be around Holden anymore."

The news was like a gut punch that knocked the wind out of him. "What do you mean? Why?"

"I don't want him to get more attached than he already is. It'll just hurt and confuse him when you leave to go back to California."

Carter opened and shut his mouth, trying to find the words.

"You need to go. Please," she said, turning away from him. "I want to be alone."

"Laura—"

"Just...go."

Carter left, even though everything in his body was screaming for him to march right back into the room and not leave her side. He made it to his bedroom down the hall and heard the soft click of her door like a nail right through his heart.

The anger replaced the hurt. He stripped and tugged on fresh clothes, not giving a damn which ones they were. He grabbed his wallet, and with a last look toward her shut bedroom door, he headed out to meet Ruby.

Outside, she sat in a black Mercedes with the driver's side sunshade pulled down where she was applying more makeup using the mirror. Carter opened the door and climbed inside as she leaned over to smile at him. "Took you forever!"

"Ruby, lay off it."

She sat back in her seat and pouted, then threw the car in gear. "I'm the one who flew all the way here and drove myself to this little town three hours from the airport. You should appreciate me more."

"I asked you not to come. What business could be so pressing that you had to see me in person?"

"Why does it always have to be about business with you?"

Carter's voice was like a razor's edge. "Ruby, you're really pushing me. I'm not interested. I appreciate you coming out here, but I would've preferred you not suddenly show up unannounced like this."

"So you can be with your little *friend*?" she said, making air quotes while they sat at the stoplight. "I don't understand you. You're the one who left and never came back. Now you don't want to leave."

"Well, Laura is an old friend and happens to be the one who pulled me out of the crash."

Ruby made a condescending awww sound that made Carter want to commit murder on the spot. "That's so sweet! Remind me to thank her when we get back later. It's nice of you to take her in when she so obviously needs the help."

"What does that mean?" Carter said, looking over at her.

"Single mom? I didn't see a ring on that finger. No wonder you don't want me around. I mean, I'd hate to make her feel bad. I'd just drop dead if anyone saw me dressed in that, with breakfast burnt, and a naked baby. God, I can't imagine."

"No, you can't. And if you must know, she's not the one who burned breakfast. I did. I was making breakfast for her because she's a friend and I care about her."

"You're so kind, but she's not around, Carter. You don't have to put on a show for me."

"I'm not putting on a show. She knows a lot more about strength and grit than you would ever understand."

"Than *I* would understand?" Ruby's shrill voice made Carter's head pound harder. "Do you have any idea how hard

I work to make you look good? Everything I do is for you and that company, but do you appreciate me? No. I come all the way out here to the middle of nowhere and this is the thanks I get while you play house with some tired EMT? You're lucky to have me. And to think that I throw myself at you and you just throw me away like some piece of trash. You prefer that woman to me?"

"Ruby, take me home. I don't want to do this right now."

"No. I will not." She gave him a sly grin that made his muscles knot together with tension. "Because we need to have a little chat."

"Is this about the merger?"

She grinned again like a cat. "Not exactly. It's about what you can do for me—to make sure the board doesn't find out about your little DUI."

CHAPTER 24

Laura sat on the couch watching a movie with Holden tucked into the crook of her arm while he nursed a Pedialyte in his favorite sippy cup. He had taken a morning nap, woken up hungry, and after demolishing a few crackers while doing every puzzle they owned, had finally nestled on the couch to rest for the afternoon.

Sitting there had also given Laura a chance to think about everything that had gone on between her and Carter. She had revisited the past, the present, and Ruby's arrival. All of it had left her with a giant headache and a plan. He might have said what he wanted to do, but actions always spoke louder than words for Laura. Her dad had passed away. Her husband had left. Carter had lied to her in the past and when he got caught, hadn't spoken to her again for fifteen years— not until he learned she had brought him, reeking of alcohol, to the hospital. Now, some blonde woman had appeared, and the second she had, Laura and Holden were on their own once more. If anything, all of her thinking had reaffirmed her decision to let him go before he could do it again to her. The problem was how.

Laura had spent the rest of the morning searching for apartments online. If Holden felt up to it in the evening, Laura had even considered going on a drive to see a few of the models—that was, until she saw the prices. She had some money saved, but spending it would take her account down to a point she wasn't comfortable with, so none of the ones she had seen were really an option.

Her phone buzzed on the coffee table, displaying her mom's number on the screen. Laura answered the video call.

"Hi, Gramma!" Holden crawled over her to stick his face in front of the phone.

"Hey, Holden! Having fun with all your birthday toys?"

He gave her a signature shrug that didn't match his wide smile. "Yes! We're watching *Winnie The Pooh*."

"That's great! I always liked Rabbit," Laura's mom said with a grin.

"That sounds about right," Laura said.

"Everything calming down from the party?"

"Yeah," Laura said. Holden snuggled back in to watch the TV with his big brown eyes, blinking slowly. Maybe he would take a little nap after all.

"What's wrong?"

"Nothing."

"You shouldn't lie to your mother."

Laura drew in a slow breath. "I think we'll need to move again."

"But what about that big, beautiful house? It's not working out? I thought it was perfect," Laura's mom said with a frown.

"It's just not a good fit anymore. I've looked around but can't find anything for the next three months. Nothing reasonably priced is available."

"Is it just three months?"

"Yeah, until we can move back into the apartment."

"You could always move out here, you know. I'd love to see you both more often."

Laura sighed and tucked her legs under her. "I'd love that, but I can't leave my job. Besides, Holden loves his school."

"You could find another one here. I'm sure they're always looking for paramedics."

"I don't know, Mom. I really don't want to start over."

"Well, it was just a thought. You're overdue for a visit at least. You could come here to think it over."

"Yeah, that's true. I'll figure something out."

"Are you sure you can't work it out with Carter?"

Laura tucked one corner of her mouth up into her cheek. "Too many memories."

"I'm sorry, sweetie."

Laura shrugged again, brushing off the apology. "It was a nice idea. Gave me a spot for the birthday party at least."

"Yeah, that's something."

"So anyway," Laura said to get off the subject. "How's therapy?"

The shadow that crossed her mom's face told her everything she needed to know. Her speech was still slurred, and while she could very well make herself understood, the whole idea had shaken Laura to the core. She had already lost so many people. She could remember her parents being the strongest people she knew, convinced as a child that so much of her life would never change, but of course time moved on. She remembered seeing her dad's body wither away with the cancer, and now, seeing her mom sitting up in a medical bed brought all of the memories back.

"It's okay, Mom," Laura said, her voice soft. "It takes time. That's understandable."

"I don't know what more they can do for me, and"—her mom looked away and swiped under her eyes with one hand —"I'm...I'm just so damn mad. I don't know what all of this therapy is doing. I don't feel any better. I can't even make a pot of coffee!" She frowned and shook her head, fighting back tears before drawing in a shaky breath. "I've made coffee every morning since I was eighteen years old, and I can't even raise my arm to do that now. I can't clip my own bra. I can't even wash my own hair." She propped the phone up again with her good arm and touched her soft auburn hair that had streaks of gray showing at the roots. "I can't even put in an earring."

Her mom shook her head and pulled in her shaking lip to compose herself. Candice had always looked like Julie Andrews and had managed to be just as graceful, at least in Laura's eyes. That her mom refused to cry spoke to her strength, but that she was so close to tears told Laura just how bad it had gotten.

"Mom—"

"Your father gave me the most beautiful earrings. I've worn my hair short since I turned thirty-two. I wanted to look chic and sophisticated, and I was tired of putting in all that effort every morning. Your dad had to get used to it, but I always loved to show off my earrings. My favorites are the pearls. You know the ones?"

"I do." Laura shifted again on the couch as Holden snuggled close and leaned back against her, watching Rabbit fuss out in the garden and fix something in the kitchen.

"They're real. All the way from Japan." Her mom sniffed again. "I want you to have them, Laura."

"Mom, you just said those are your favorites—"

"I can't put them in anymore. I just can't. I try and I try and I just get so damn frustrated that I can't even look at them anymore. I've already lost your father, had to sell the house, and now I can't even wear what he bought me."

Laura's heart broke. "Mom...you'll get there. It'll come back."

"You don't know that," she snapped.

Laura knew it wasn't personal, but more than anything she wished she could heal her mom. She had tried with her dad over and over, but nothing had come of it. The guilt of being able to heal strangers but not loved ones bubbled up to the surface again. Laura would give anything to be able to lift all of this burden from her mom's mind and bring back the muscle strength she was missing so much.

"No, I don't know that," Laura said. "And neither do you, but we're not doctors."

"I keep trying and no matter what, I can't put them in. My fingers won't do it. I can see it in my mind like it's nothing, but my body is failing me. I used to make beautiful pottery. I loved making that piggy bank for Holden. I'm glad I did because it's the last thing I'll ever make for him."

"Mom, don't upset yourself. You have to keep hope. It'll pass, and once we're back together, I can help you put in Dad's earrings. It'll just be a new normal. I know it's hard now, but with time it will get better."

"And if it doesn't? What if I'm stuck like this?"

"We'll make it work. We'll make a new normal together." Laura waited and watched her mom draw in another shaky breath, while she tried to remember something from her brief stint in therapy back when John had gone missing.

"You have to focus on what you have, Mom. Right now, you and I are talking. There are a lot of people who don't have that."

"That's true."

"And you know, there are a lot of people who don't have an adorable grandson," Laura said, shifting the phone to Holden, who giggled.

"Hi, Gramma!"

Her mom sniffed and smiled. "Hi, sweet boy!"

"I threw up!"

His sweet smile turned to a sad puppy frown only a grandmother could love. "You what? Laura, you didn't tell me he was sick!"

The way to Candice Purcell's heart was through her Holden. The weight of the entire conversation vanished in an instant as she shifted into Mother Hen mode.

"I don't think he's sick—probably too much cake and ice cream while tumbling around."

"Gramma, today the fire alarm went off and a lady came to the house," Holden said, his brown eyes big as he ratted out Laura like any good toddler.

"What? There was a fire?!"

"No—"

"Yeah, Gramma! It was stinky."

Before her mom could get all excited, Laura jumped in. "It was just a little bacon grease. Just got smoky. Nothing an air freshener couldn't fix."

"Who was the woman?"

Now this, Laura really hadn't wanted to discuss, but her mom was like a dog with a bone when it came to information. Laura didn't know what to think herself. Carter had tried to explain, but again, actions spoke louder than words, and he still hadn't come back from his *meeting* with Ruby. No girlfriends, he said? As if. She wasn't stupid and if actions did speak louder than words, then she had certainly gotten the message.

God, the sight of her wrapping her thin, toned limbs around him was enough to make Laura's stomach churn and heart hurt. To be honest with herself, it was like prom all over again. There was that pain and humiliation of knowing there was no way she could compare. Despite whatever Carter told her, the truth was, he hadn't asked her to the prom then, and he wasn't with Laura now.

"Carter's friend from California."

Laura's mom's eyebrows disappeared under her bangs. One lagged a little, but the stroke hadn't affected her facial movements like her arm, which was the main reason her speech wasn't all that affected. Her mouth formed an o before pursing into a thin line of contemplation mixed with disapproval and disappointment.

"I have a mind to call his mother."

"Mom, please no. Stay out of it."

"I think she should know. Besides, I just want to reach out and say that I saw him and he was well and that I'm thinking of him in my prayers."

"Mom—"

"I used to talk with her all the time when we were in the PTA together. She remarried and moved to Florida, you know."

"Mom, please. I just don't want to deal with it. It was his VP apparently, here to talk about some merger."

"Laura, if that was all she was, you wouldn't look like you do right now."

Laura frowned. "Like what? This is my face. I always look like this."

"Don't lie. You look like one sad puppy, just like you did when the police brought you home that August night after Carter had been arrested and his friend was in that horrible accident."

"Mom, if you know all this about him then why did you say you liked him so much? Remember? You're the one who said he was always so nice."

"He was nice."

"Was."

"He's letting you stay there now."

"Not anymore."

"Laura, I refuse to believe Carter Price would kick you and my sweet grandbaby out."

Laura glanced at the TV so she wouldn't have to meet her mom's eyes. "He's not. I just don't need to be around him anymore."

"Have you told him how you feel?"

Laura let out a rueful laugh. "Mom, this isn't a fairy tale. What does he care? We're both adults. If his model of a VP wants to walk up in here and throw her arms around him, that's none of my business."

"Are you sure?"

"Mom, I don't want to hear it."

"I think you need to tell him how you feel before you go moving my grandson all over creation again."

"Alright, Mom."

"Well, I'll let you go, but promise me you'll tell him."

"Yeah," she lied.

"You shouldn't lie to your mother."

"I love you, Mom."

"Love you too, sweetie. I'll call tomorrow to check on Holden."

"Alright, sounds good."

"Bye, Gramma!"

Laura ended the call and snuggled close to Holden, smelling his soft brown hair. Her mom had always wanted to think the best of people Laura was involved with, but Laura had been the one to face the heartbreak. Laura had been left hanging so many times, she had no choice but to learn how to be independent. She had Holden to think about, and when he was born, she had promised him she would do everything she could to protect him from the hurt she had known.

As she patted Holden and rested her head on his, Laura weighed her options and what she had to lose. Regardless of her mom's fantasy, Laura's reality was very different. She had learned a long time ago that the only thing she could control was herself.

CHAPTER 25

C arter climbed out of Ruby's rental and made his way up the front walk, not looking back. She had held him hostage for the entire morning and the better part of the afternoon. She had finally agreed to bring him home so she could check in at the hotel she had booked at breakfast, after drumming up some fake tears when he'd made it clear she would not be staying with him under any circumstances. The tears had been short-lived and vanished with an ice-cold smile before the waitress had even dropped off the coffee and waters.

The whole thing had turned into a nightmare. He knew that Ruby had always liked him and wanted more of a relationship, but before, he had assumed she was just lovesick. Now, he could clearly see her for what she was—power hungry.

Throughout her breakfast, which consisted of the closest thing to health food the diner could deliver—whole grain toast and a yogurt parfait, served with scrambled egg whites that she still managed to complain about—she claimed the board was on her side regarding the so-called merger. What she really was suggesting was more akin to selling off the company he'd built to a competitor that—surprise, surprise—she had a connection with. It now made complete sense why she had been pushing for the whole thing.

While he had been stuck out here, Ruby had been busy. She had used the opportunity to convince the board of the benefits and install herself as acting CEO when she knew he wouldn't be there to know what she was doing. When Carter had reached out to the board, ruining her plans, Ruby had wasted no time getting on a plane and digging to find out where the head of the company had run off to.

He had sat there, watching his coffee grow cold, refusing to eat and give her one ounce of comfort after seeing what she was up to. She had probably wanted him to yell at her, so she could cause a scene and go running back to the board or the police. Once she had mentioned the DUI, Carter had shut his mouth, giving away nothing that she could twist and use as ammo.

The only time he had spoken up was when she had tried—and she had tried hard—to dig at Laura and Holden. It had taken every ounce of strength Coach had instilled in him to keep control when, before he got out of her car, Ruby's parting words had been, "Say hi to your whore and her brat for me."

There were no words that would take the place of a car door slamming in her Botox-filled face. Carter wished he could fire her, but with going public and having a board, every move was scrutinized. Still, as much as Ruby was trying to get under his skin, it was still his company. He would call a board meeting tonight and get everything straightened out. He would also explain the DUI and the events that led up to it, knowing how well the board members appreciated a good *mea culpa*.

Ruby thought she had it all figured out, but she had made

a critical mistake in misjudging his kindness for weakness. He couldn't wait to get revenge, but first, he needed to talk to Laura.

He opened the door and walked inside to silence. The effect was eerie. The living room was immaculate, and the TV was dark. A bubble of panic rose in his chest. He hadn't seen her car when they pulled up, but she had moved it to the garage the other day. Was it still there now? She couldn't have left without saying goodbye.

Carter swung himself into the kitchen and relaxed a little when he saw the birthday party decorations were still up, but all of the evidence of the breakfast he had been trying so hard to make for her was gone. A creak upstairs made him sigh with relief, announcing Laura's arrival as she came down the stairs.

She was still just as stunning as she had been last night. The quiet beauty of her chestnut hair pulled back away from her face in a bun showed off the slim column of her neck. The shirt she wore was a blue and white tunic that hit below her hip and flowed around her as she padded toward him in bare feet and black stretchy cropped pants that outlined her toned legs.

"Laura, I'm so sorry."

Her face didn't move. Fresh and free from the heavy makeup that Ruby was so obsessed with, Laura's brown eyes held a professionalism that walled off the familiarity he had worked so hard to rebuild. The trust was gone again, and Carter's heart filled with worry it might not come back.

"Did you have a nice breakfast?"

"I didn't eat," he said.

"It's three o'clock."

"Yeah, I know."

"You didn't have lunch? You must be starving."

"I haven't really thought about it. Ruby insisted we go to

the diner and then a coffee shop."

Laura sniffed and shifted to walk toward the cabinet. She reached up inside and grabbed a glass and poured herself some water. Carter followed her as she walked to the kitchen table.

"I'm surprised you didn't eat."

"It doesn't matter. Where's Holden?"

"He's upstairs, taking a nap."

"How is he?"

"He'll be okay," she said, sipping the water. "Just too much fun."

"What did you guys do?" Carter wanted to beg her to meet his eyes, but she wouldn't. Her dark eyelashes rested on her cheeks as she looked down at her plain, trimmed nails. There was nothing fake about her.

"We just watched a movie and snuggled on the couch."

"Sounds perfect."

Laura met his eyes with a frown. "Does it? You got in her car pretty quick."

"Laura, I'm sorry. It's not like that."

She sucked in a breath and took another sip. "Just like the captain of the cheerleading team?"

"God, you have no idea how much I wanted to come back here."

"Carter, you've been gone for almost eight hours. Do you really expect me to believe you didn't want to be with someone who was hanging off of you after just flying here from California? You're a rich man now, not bad looking, and own your own company. A thin, pretty woman shows up and kisses you on the mouth, and you want me to believe she's not your girlfriend."

"That was a long time ago."

"Oh, so you do have a history? Let me get out my surprised face."

"Laura, she has me over a barrel. She knows about the DUI and wants to get the board to agree to a merger I don't want. If that happens then—"

"Carter," Laura said, with a strange look on her face. "You can stop there, because none of what you're saying is my business."

"Laura, that's not—"

"I don't think this arrangement is working out anymore, so I'm going to leave tomorrow. I'll pay you for the time we were here and for the bounce house from yesterday."

Carter sat, dumbstruck. "No, you're not leaving. I just got you back."

"Got me back?" Laura said, the line between her brows deepening. "You think you have me back?"

"Yes, and I'm so—"

"You don't have me. You don't mean anything to me. In two months, you're going to go back to California with Ruby and leave Holden and my life forever. There is nothing between us."

"Laura, I was hoping—"

"I'm done with hoping, Carter. I'm not sixteen anymore. You've proven time and time again that you say one thing and do another. I've been left a lot, and you don't know what that feels like. You think you do, but you have no idea what it's like to walk in my shoes. The only person I can rely on is myself. If I fail, I'm failing Holden. This isn't about me or you, it's about him. I gave this a try, but we were doing fine on our own until you showed up."

"You need a place to live. Don't storm out because Ruby showed up. I didn't call her."

"Why should I believe you? And why does it matter if you did or didn't? The only reason we needed a place to stay is because my apartment is being renovated. I can find another one."

Carter drew in a breath and made a fist on the table. "We're both adults here. I know you don't make a lot."

Laura stood up. Her hands were clenched into fists, and she snatched the glass off the table and walked it over to the sink. Carter scrambled to stand up and face her.

"I make people feel better, and that's a helluva lot more than you."

"C'mon, you know I didn't mean it like that," Carter said, reaching out, but she evaded him and walked upstairs.

"We're leaving tomorrow."

"Laura, please don't. Stop, no, don't go upstairs. Stop, please. Listen to me." She didn't turn around. "You'll wake up Holden if we go up there."

Laura halted and slowly spun around. "What?"

"Let me help you."

"I don't need your help. I'm everything I need to be on my own."

"You don't have to do this all by yourself."

"Yes. I. Do. Today proved that."

Carter hung his head and stared at the floor. "I wanted to do something nice for you."

"And the second Ruby walked in, you left, while I stayed to clean up your mess and continue my average life. You know, Carter, I don't have a sports car I can just crash into a tree, I don't have a lot in the bank, and I may never get to see California, but everything I have means more to me than you could ever understand."

"I'm sorry for how this looks. I really am. I didn't think it would be a reflection on how I feel about you or Holden. I was wrong."

"Yep, but it's okay. I'm used to being left."

"Laura—"

"No. I don't want to hear any more. I have to work tomorrow, but after that, Holden and I are leaving."

Laura turned on her heel again and marched upstairs, leaving Carter in silence. He heard her door close from downstairs and slowly followed in her wake, climbing the staircase of the large rental house.

Yesterday, it had felt full of life and normalcy, with kids running around and people leaning against the kitchen counter, chatting with cups in hand. But now, as he stood there alone, the weight of his reality dropped around him like a silent blanket.

By now, everyone knew he had been in an accident. A ton of people had reached out via email and on social media, and a few had texted, but Ruby was the only one who had come out personally, and it wasn't about him. Carter's mom had been ready to come, but other than her, the only person who had stayed real was Laura.

After fifteen years, she was still the quiet, steady friend. Out of all of the people he knew, she was the only one he could rely on to do what she said. Everyone else had their own motives, and now that he had so many zeros in his bank account, he might have more friends, but they were around for the wrong reasons, if they were around at all. Hell, even his dad had miraculously shown up, and after all the publicity about his net worth, it certainly was convenient timing.

Carter had become so obsessed with being something else, he hadn't looked behind or around him for a long time. There were plenty of photos with him in a large group of people, each entitled, "the best night ever," but where were they now? Nowhere to be found.

The realest person he knew was upstairs. And to her, he was just another unreliable disappointment who had hurt her again. Carter knew in his gut, he had to change her mind. He had to show her how much he had changed.

CHAPTER 26

Laura had avoided Carter like the plague the following morning, which was difficult because every time she turned around, he was there, looking like a sad puppy, giving compliments, and wanting to be involved in every breath she took. The whole effect was maddening, and the more annoyed she got, the more persistent he became.

Holden, of course, hadn't known anything was wrong and so he engaged with Carter, talking about everything from dinosaurs to the weather to the one time he threw up in the car. Throughout it all, Carter nodded along, smiling and asking follow-up questions. It was cute, but Laura knew he was just using her kid as a way to get back into her good graces.

Laura did her best to give him as little information as possible without being rude. She wasn't looking for a fight, and she was moving out, though she hadn't figured out where to yet, but it still paid to be civil. When they left the house, Carter had even followed them out to the car and waved to them both as she had pulled out of the garage and down the driveway.

Laura refused to let any of it change her mind. Carter hadn't said anything when she pointed out he was just going to pack up shop and head back to California the second he could. He hadn't mentioned Ruby again, but Laura suspected she was still in town and would no doubt be back at the house today.

She closed her eyes against the visual she really didn't want in her head and turned off the car before heading into the station for her shift.

"Morning, Laura! How's Holden?" Megan asked when she came inside to put her stuff into her locker.

Laura had texted Megan last night to thank her again for coming to the party but also to give an update on Holden, in case he got sick again and she needed to leave work. Megan was an EMT, which required less training than a paramedic, but in a pinch, Megan could fill in for her at work. The woman had no fear.

Laura slammed the locker shut. "He's better. Thanks for asking. Probably too much excitement. We just kind of chilled yesterday."

"With Mr. Green Eyes? I'm jealous."

Laura sighed. "Mr. Green Eyes's girlfriend showed up yesterday when I was covered in vomit and the smoke alarm was going off, so not much to report on that front."

Megan's big blue eyes practically popped out of her freckled face. "Shut up. For real?"

"For real."

"He never said he had a girlfriend before."

Laura folded her arms and leaned against the lockers, letting her head fall back with a metallic thud. "Yeah, convenient, huh?"

"Are you sure?"

"She threw her arms around him the second she saw him and kissed him on the lips."

Megan's mouth fell open. "Is she pretty?"

Laura shrugged. "It doesn't matter."

"So that pretty, huh?"

"Seriously, no, it doesn't matter. We were together in high school for a very brief time. He's going back to California. There was nothing between us."

Megan studied Laura and narrowed her eyes.

She opened her mouth to speak when dispatch cut her off.

They both sprang into action, each heading for their own equipment and vehicle. Jordan wasn't in today. Instead, Mike, a young guy in the Army Reserves, hopped up inside and put the ambulance in gear, punching the siren and horn to stop the traffic as they pulled out onto the main road.

"Any info?" Laura asked Mike, checking her phone to see if Ash had texted.

His face was set in a grim line. "Unconscious, suspected drug overdose."

She nodded even though he couldn't see her and held on while he drove through red lights down the road. Mike drove like a champ and faster than Jordan. They had seen more and more overdoses and had even treated the same patient more than once. Very rarely did someone seek treatment for addiction after leaving the hospital, creating a heartbreaking cycle that impacted more than just the victims, but their families and friends too.

Laura had never experimented with anything—seeing Carter put into the back of a police car when he was sixteen had left an impression—but her heart went out to people who turned to drugs as a way to cope with their lives. Many were good people who struggled with a trauma and didn't know how to find their way out.

The opioid crisis was strong in rural America. People from all walks of life had suffered and died from their addictions, but poorer communities were hit harder. She watched outside as Mike turned onto a side street. They had been in this neighborhood before, where the houses were older, smaller, and needed a large dose of TLC. Within five minutes, they were there.

A police vehicle was on the scene in front of a single-family home that had seen better days but had flowers in the front. Laura hopped out when Mike stopped near the curb. There were a few officers rushing to the back of the house. Laura followed them down to a basement where, in the corner, Ash was crouched down over a woman in faded yellow flip-flops.

"What do we have?" Laura said, bending down. She didn't even need to ask because the pin pricks on the inside of the arms told a story. The woman was pale, and the purple bruising around where the veins had been punctured by a needle in an unskilled hand matched the blue tint to her lips.

Ash glanced up at Laura and then nodded to an older man who was wiping his eyes, talking with another officer. "Dad left to pick up a sandwich nearby. Gone maybe half an hour. Came home and found her unconscious. Said she'd had problems before with heroin, but they sent her to rehab, thought she was clean."

"Vitals look okay," Laura said, administering Narcan, an overdose reversal drug, by squirting it into her nose. "She's breathing about six times a minute. Mike, let's do a ventilator just in case."

Ash stood and moved out of the way so Laura could work, prepping a hypodermic needle with more medicine in case she needed it. Mike slapped the vent on the girl's face, sealing it around her lips.

She was a pretty girl wearing a yellow top, looked to be in her late teens, probably still in high school. Her phone had landed a few inches away from her when she fell. Laura noticed the screen was cracked. Laura listened to her dad cry and talk with Ash and the other officers from the other side of the basement. Her back was turned to them all.

The minutes ticked by. Narcan would wake up a patient so they could breathe on their own, but Laura's hands itched to help.

"Hey, Mike, will you go grab the backboard?"

He nodded and walked away, leaving Laura a few seconds. She closed her eyes and placed her hands on the girl's stomach, which was bare thanks to the cut off T-shirt that exposed her midriff. She closed her eyes and visualized the girl waking up and taking a breath. Her hands warmed under her and started to tingle. Almost immediately, an echo of her energy came back to her as Laura felt the girl's health and will to live. Her heartbeat thrummed through her body while her lungs filled with breath. She was going to be okay.

Laura opened her eyes and looked around. There still wasn't anyone focused on her as everyone was prepping for transport or talking to the dad. She had tried before to help with addiction, but never knew what happened to the patients afterwards, so she couldn't be sure she was actually doing anything, but at least in her case, thoughts could really count.

She closed her eyes again and pressed her hands into the girl's stomach, feeling her diaphragm inflate. Laura sent waves of love and peace throughout the body, hoping to fight off whatever trauma or mental illness had taken root in the girl beneath her hands. Her palms warmed again to the point they were almost hot, and the tingling sensation got stronger as if the girl was vibrating beneath her.

Laura sat back in time to see the girl's eyelids flutter open, then she turned to her horror to see Megan sitting next to her with her big blue eyes, wide in stunned disbelief.

"Laura—what did you just do?"

A hot wave of panic swept down her body from her head. A series of worst-case scenarios flashed through her mind while she tried to come up with something to say. No one had ever seen her do this before. What did it look like? What might Megan have seen? The look on her face told Laura that Megan had seen the exact thing she had tried to hide from everyone and was now grappling with the implications.

"I don't know what you mean."

"Your hands…"

Laura pulled the gloves back on right as Mike came back with the backboard. They didn't need it, though, because the girl's eyes fluttered again and she took a breath on her own.

They pulled off the ventilator and examined her while her dad rushed over.

"Hey…Dad. I was just taking a nap," said the girl, trying to pull together a sentence. The dad had tears in his eyes and tried to blink them away, but they still fell down his red face, sliding past his mustache.

"You said you were better. I know what happened."

The girl's head fell back on the ground as she turned away from him, pain etched on her face. "I'm sorry, Dad."

He held her hand and gripped it hard. "We're going to get through this together. I wish you had told me, but we *are* going to get through this together."

"Let's get you to the hospital," Laura said, helping her sit up and walk through the basement to the outside where the ambulance was parked.

While Mike and the girl's dad helped her to make sure she wouldn't fall, Laura walked behind, carrying the backboard, aware of Megan's eyes on her.

"You did something to her."

Laura tried to stay calm and not react, but inside she felt like she was on fire. "What do you mean? I was just checking vitals. It was the Narcan."

Megan jogged up and closed the gap so they were walking in step. Her voice was a low hiss. "I know you were doing something."

"What are you talking about?" Laura said, trying to remember how her voice sounded when she was confused. She had always been a terrible liar.

"I saw your hands."

Laura loaded the backboard into the ambulance. "What do you mean? These? Of course you saw them. You see them every day."

Megan glanced from side to side and pulled her in close. "They glowed."

Now Laura's heart went into panic mode. Megan was one of her two closest friends, but Laura could never tell them anything because who would believe her? She didn't need more people leaving her. She'd had her fill of that. And if they found out, they'd call her crazy, probably stop speaking to her, and try to have her fired. None of that was an option.

Laura drew in a breath and turned to face her friend. "I don't know what you thought you saw. It was probably nothing or a trick of the light. I don't know what you're talking about."

"But Laura—" Megan said, her arms reaching out to stop her.

"Look, we have to go. The dad's all loaded up front with Mike. I'll see you later," Laura said, hopping inside the back with the girl and shutting the door.

She watched as Megan stood there in the weed-covered yard, rooted to the spot, watching the ambulance drive away.

"I don't need to go to the hospital. I just took a nap," said the girl from behind her.

CHAPTER 27

The minute Laura and Mike pulled into the station, she made a beeline for the exit, avoiding Megan like the plague. She ducked into the locker room and pulled out her purse. She made some excuse about Holden to Mike, told him to tell Megan she would text her later, knowing it was a complete lie and hating herself for it.

She had to get out.

As she slammed the car door shut, she pulled out of the parking lot without looking behind her. Her hands were trembling on the wheel. Without taking her eyes off the road, she reached over and cranked the A/C up to full blast. Her heart hadn't stopped racing since Megan had confronted her. Maybe it made her look guilty to run, but no one could know her secret. This was the only thing she had left to her name. The only constant in her life. Her dad was gone. Her husband was gone. Her mom was still here but limited and needing care hours away. Holden was growing up, and all the while, time was slipping through her fingers. She couldn't even stay in her own apartment right now, let alone try to get back into school.

No one could know her secret, and she knew Megan. That red-haired flower power girl would stop at nothing. As much as she hated it, she had no choice but to leave.

Laura glanced down at her watch. The time was right. She had left about two hours early, which meant she had just enough time to run by the house and pack before she had to grab Holden.

She stopped herself midthought. Pack? She had nowhere to go. She couldn't think of another place in town she could afford. Laura sat at a stoplight and watched it change to green but didn't move. She had literally run out of options. Everything she had tried to make work had fallen apart. There was no other place she could go in Goldvein that was within her budget, no other station to work out of, meaning Megan would always be there, watching to see her hands. Until today, Laura hadn't even known they glowed. She had never seen it before.

Laura clenched her eyes tight as a fresh wave of heartache tore her apart. How could she leave Megan and Ash? God, it was going to devastate Holden and destroy her.

A horn blared somewhere behind her before a car sped around her. She came to her senses and drove forward with a plan. She had hit rock bottom before and knew from experience that the only way out was to take one step at a time. Only this time, it was going to take her away from so much love and friendship, but she had no choice. No one could know her secret.

Laura hit the gas and pulled into the driveway at the rental house a few minutes later. The front door opened, and Carter waved from his crutches, wearing a gray T-shirt and black shorts. She didn't return the gesture, just threw the car in park and got out of it, her mind racing, trying to come up with possible options. Since Holden's birth, the only other place she had driven to was Missoula to visit her mom. At least it was a start.

"Hey, I didn't expect you home this early," Carter said as she walked up the steps.

Laura stepped inside and threw her purse on the table by the door. "Why? Ruby here?"

Carter frowned and looked confused. "No, that's not it at all. I just got off the phone. Talked the board off the ledge so she can head home. The merger she wanted isn't going to happen. And just so you know, I have no intention of seeing her again. No reason to."

Laura shrugged, not really listening to what he had to say. She couldn't care less about his business right now.

Carter followed her inside to the kitchen. "I'm just glad to see you. I figured you and I could talk about what happened."

Laura pulled open the garage door to grab a few of the boxes she had broken down a few days ago. Had it even been a week yet? She dug around in a kitchen drawer looking for scissors and packing tape.

"Hey, hold up. What are you doing?"

"Packing." Where in the hell was the tape?

"What? Why? Listen, I shouldn't have gone with Ruby. I'm sorry. I said I was sorry. There's nothing between us."

Laura found the tape in the drawer next to the phone, of course, and grabbed scissors out of a crock.

"Laura…stop, talk to me."

She looked up into his eyes and saw earnest concern.

"I don't want you to go," he continued. "I'd like for you to stay. Being with you and Holden has really shown me how much my life is lacking. Please don't go. We'll talk it over. I'll stay out of your way."

Laura tilted her head to one side. "Carter, I'm leaving tonight." She walked around him, evading when he tried to grab her hand. She took the stairs two at a time and made it to Holden's door just in time to lock the door behind her.

She could hear him climbing up the stairs, calling her name, and even though it wasn't menacing, the sound of it scared her for some reason.

"Laura!" Carter rattled the locked knob. "Laura, open this damn door."

Her heart beat faster, which was ridiculous. She wasn't a child, and she wasn't afraid of him, but still, the feeling of being trapped had always been unwelcome.

She took the time to throw some things in a box, starting with the piggy bank her mom had given Holden. She hadn't brought a lot of clothes with them, just stuff for this season, his favorite books, and stuffed animals. What she hadn't accounted for were the extra birthday presents.

"Laura." Carter's voice was muffled through the door. "I don't like this. Please don't shut me out. I just want to talk to you."

She looked around the room. One more box would do it, and she had to go back to the garage anyway. With a sigh, she opened the door.

"What is going on?"

"I already told you. I'm leaving tonight."

Carter looked at her for a full three seconds. "Why? What about your job? Where are you going to stay?"

Laura drew in a slow breath and looked at him. "I don't know. I just know I can't stay here anymore." The thought of Megan coming to the house had occurred to her, and if Megan caught Laura before she could get on the road, she wouldn't be able to get out without another round of questions that she couldn't and shouldn't answer.

"Laura, please don't go. I feel like this time with you has been some of the happiest I've had in a long while. I can't

help but feel like we're supposed to be together. Be honest—
did you hate the idea of sharing that bed?"

No, she hadn't. Laura closed her eyes, feeling another
wave of sadness wash over her. Before she could respond,
Carter continued.

"I never should've left. I think we were supposed to be
together. I have felt that since I first met you in sixth grade. I
let you down, and I would give anything to turn back the
clock. If I had, I would've made sure you were never with
someone who would just walk out on you—"

"I'm never going to regret John because of Holden."

"I know, I'm not saying you should, but I'm sorry you had
to go through what you did. I'm sorry you've had to be on
your own for so long. I love you, Laura."

The words hit her like a thud in the chest.

"I always have, ever since sixth grade."

"Carter—"

"Please don't go." He reached out and took her hand. "I
can help you. I want to be with you. I want to burn pancakes
with you and Holden for the rest of my life."

Laura drew in another breath, tearing her eyes away from
his stunning face. He hadn't shaved in a while, and instead of
a dark stubble, he had the makings of a full-grown beard. He
had the same handsome face she had always watched from
across the classroom, the one with the big wide smile that
always made her laugh. She had wanted to hear these words
ever since middle school and had even practiced writing her
name with his. The great irony was that now it was too late.

"I have to go."

He blinked again and propped his hand up against the
door, the fingers curling into a fist. "But why? I told you
Ruby doesn't matter."

"You think this is about Ruby? Carter, this has nothing to
do with her. You have your own life and so do I. We aren't

kids anymore! Wake up! This isn't high school. I can't just hop in your truck and ride away from my problems. You have a business to run when you get back to California, and I have real problems right now."

"What problems?" He frowned.

"Nothing you can help me with, believe me."

Laura tried to duck around him.

"What's wrong?"

"I can't tell you. I just need to go."

"But I want to know. Maybe I can help?"

"No." Laura threw the box down behind her before ducking under his arm and marching past him to get a few more boxes for her own things. She checked the time on her phone. She had already lost an hour.

"Laura, seriously. What's this all about?"

"It's none of your concern," she said over her shoulder. Damn he was persistent, standing at the top of the stairs. She grabbed another few boxes from the garage and did the climb to the top again, knowing full well that he would be standing in her way when she got there.

Part of her wanted to tell him everything, just break down, but what good would that do? He belonged in California, surrounded by beautiful women and men who talked about technology and money. She belonged here, taking care of Holden and keeping up with her mom for whenever she came out of the facility. She needed to work and to heal, and without that, she basically had nothing to show for her thirty-one years on the planet. She couldn't take another chance on him or anyone else who might knock down the house of cards she had so carefully built herself.

Sure enough, at the top of the stairs, there was Carter looking deeply worried.

"I don't like this. Why all of a sudden? What happened today?"

"Nothing."

"You're lying."

Laura rolled her eyes, and this time, walked toward what had been her beautiful bedroom for all of five nights. The night before last had been spent in bed with Carter, and though she hated to admit it to herself, that was one of the best memories she would take with her on the drive tonight. It probably was the last time she would ever let someone get that close to her again. She closed her eyes to savor the memory and brace herself for the pain that leaving would bring. Being lonely was better than being left.

Carter followed her into the yellow and white room. "Laura. Laura, talk to me. What are you running from?"

She didn't answer, just kept throwing her clothes into a box before going to grab her toiletries.

"Is your mom okay?"

"Yes, she's fine. Thankfully."

"Okay, then what is it?" He lowered his voice. "Is this about John?"

Laura looked back at him over her shoulder. "You've been watching too many movies. Real life isn't like that."

"Well, I don't know what to think, since you won't let me help you."

"I don't need your help."

"Laura, please just stop this. I've already told you how much you mean to me. The idea of you running from something and me not even knowing what it is..."

His voice trailed off as she taped a box shut. "Carter, I'm sorry. I don't think you're in love with me."

He jerked back like she'd slapped him. "What?" His voice was a whisper.

Laura stood slowly and faced him, squaring her shoulders with his, even though he was at least a head taller than she was. With her still in her uniform, the stiff, dark blue fabric compared to his T-shirt, shorts, and bare feet marked yet another difference between them.

"You almost died. You feel guilt. You got scared. What you're feeling isn't love for me. It's a love for life."

He blinked a few times, furrowing his brow while trying to process what she had just said. "That's not true though. I know what I feel."

"You think you do. You've been through a trauma. It's natural to latch on to something familiar and stable."

"Laura, stop. No—that's not it at all."

"Didn't you tell me you were coming from a funeral? Remember you said that the other night? Coach? The father you never had?"

"Yeah, but—"

"Carter, don't you see what's happening? You got scared. You don't feel anything for me. The second Ruby—and no, hear me out—the second she came here, I don't know. I just felt like everything went back to how it was before. Back before this. You're not home, you're recovering, and you're scared. We don't actually share anything. You're not in love with me."

Laura picked up boxes and turned away from him, heading down the hall and out to the car. When she returned, Carter had seated himself on the bench watching her as she took six boxes' worth of her and Holden's life out the door.

She came back in for last looks and to pack Holden a snack in the kitchen. The sound of the sack of Goldfish being thrown into a brown paper bag echoed throughout the massive room. She grabbed all of his sippy cups and plates and spoons. The tap of Carter's crutches on the tile floor told her he was behind her.

"I wish you would reconsider."

"Carter, I can't. I have to go." Time was ticking. The idea of Megan talking to Ash and them both coming to the house made Laura's heart race. The feeling of being trapped came back.

"I want to know why. I have lawyers who can help with whatever is going on."

"I don't have that kind of problem yet, but if you keep standing in my way, I might," Laura said, leveling a gaze at him.

"At least let me give you some money."

"Absolutely not," Laura said on instinct, wondering how much was in her account. She knew it wasn't more than a couple hundred because she hadn't gotten paid yet, and the grocery runs for the new house and the party had tapped out her rainy-day fund. What little money she had stashed away for college wasn't liquid, and she wouldn't dream of touching it anyway.

Laura hoped she had enough for dinner and a couple of nights in a hotel until she got paid, but still she wouldn't dream of taking money from Carter. Doing so would be proof she couldn't do this alone, and she was determined to never rely on another person again. She might be a single mom, but she was employed and didn't need charity from Carter. What she needed now was space. She just needed to clear her head from everything and get some time to herself.

She dug in her pocket and slapped the brass key he had given her when she arrived on the counter, picked up the grocery bags and pushing past him.

"Is this what it feels like?" Carter asked.

"What?"

"Being left behind?"

Laura slung her purse over her shoulder. She had already checked the upstairs for everything in every place she could think of.

"We've been living together for six days, Carter. You have no idea what being left behind feels like."

While he stared at her, Laura took the last of the bags and the rest of her pride and walked out the door, shutting it behind her.

As she pulled out of the driveway, just like when Carter was arrested all those years ago, Laura felt her heart break and didn't turn to wave goodbye.

CHAPTER 28

L aura drove in the dark. Holden had finally fallen asleep in his car seat. It was too dim to make out his little face slouched against the side, clutching Mickey Mouse, and she didn't dare turn on the light to check. Just knowing he was there was enough.

She'd been driving for almost three hours now. They had left school in a rush, stopped to get Holden some dinner and change him into a Pull-Up, then she called to reserve a hotel room by putting it on her credit card.

In the quiet of the night, she had time to think through it all. She didn't feel as hunted and exposed in the quiet car, with the air conditioner on low. The quiet thrum of the highway outside, lit only by the occasional other car or a passing truck, gave her a feeling of safety. Out here no one knew her. No one knew about her or the secret she carried with her. How she was different.

God, the look in Megan's eyes. The horror and recognition mixed with a little shock was Laura's worst nightmare. By now, Megan had probably told Ash what had happened. Laura wondered if Ash would believe Megan for a second.

Ash was so much more grounded and down to earth, but the pair of them got along fine. She imagined Ash's look with those almost purple eyes narrowing to slits whenever she was trying to figure out if someone was telling the truth or not. Ash could always tell—it was just in her nature.

Laura's chest ached, and she gripped the wheel with one hand while holding her head in the other, propping her elbow up against the door of the car. Her coworkers and closest friends were left behind without so much as a goodbye.

The last face floated to the surface of her mind. She hadn't wanted to think about him. Didn't dare pick up the phone. But Carter had called every thirty minutes, sometimes leaving voicemails, sometimes texting. He had finally said the words she had always dreamed of hearing since she'd been a girl in middle school. He had always been the one for her, but now, just like everything else in her life, the timing was all wrong and she just wasn't meant to have what others did.

A warm tingle rose in her chest as she thought about how he had held her the night before last in his bed, cradling her and whispering everything she had never thought she'd hear from anyone, let alone him. He had been the one for her. The one she'd always wanted. The one she'd dreamed about and probably always would. Everything in her wanted to cave and fall into his arms, to sob like she had at her apartment. She wanted to let him smooth away all her worries and fears. She had been on her own for so long now, trying to carve out a life for Holden that was stable and consistent, but she was still a person too. Sure, she was a mom first. Always and forever. But Carter had shined a light on a part of her that she had ignored for so long. He made her feel special and wanted and unique. She wasn't just Holden's mom to him, but someone special.

Driving away from him felt wrong, but staying scared her more than anything. She couldn't take another rejection. The pain she had felt when Ruby walked in had been the same kind of devastating as when John left and when she'd seen Carter in the back of the cop car.

She couldn't do it again. He was going to go back to California, and cutting him off now might be painful, but it would save her a lot in the long run.

Had it not been for Megan seeing what had happened when she'd healed that girl, Laura might've actually stayed. Gone back inside and talked it out, told him how she felt. But she was a mom first. If any wind of this got out, she could lose her job, or worse—Holden. And that was not a risk she could even imagine taking. Nothing was worth that.

A soft ping from the dash welcomed the orange gas light. Perfect. Low gas. At least she was almost halfway there. A quick fill-up would take them the rest of the way and be one less thing to worry about when they got there.

Laura hit the blinker and eased off the highway, wondering if she would catch back up to the truck she had been following for an hour. It had been a game she liked to play when she was little, making up stories about the people in the other cars on long road trips, but then she always felt sad when they turned down a different path.

Thankfully, there was a gas station with bright lights right off the road. A few cars were there, but it looked clean and safe.

Laura pulled up to pump five. There was no one else around them except for one car with a guy standing next to it, smoking a cigarette like an idiot. Mercifully, he ambled away toward an empty parking spot. He wasn't doing anything, but the sight of him made her nervous. She grabbed her purse and dug out her card so she'd be ready.

A quick peek behind her let her know Holden was totally

out, fast asleep. He was so pretty, she could watch him all night. Getting him into the hotel was going to be a beast. He was always so cranky when woken up halfway through sleeping.

She got out of the car. The wind pushed against the car door and threw her hair all around. She stuck her card in the reader and typed in her zip code while waiting.

The guy with the cigarette hadn't moved back over toward the pumps, which made her feel a little better, but the feeling vanished when the screen read: *card declined*.

"Okay, don't panic," she whispered to herself, trying it again and holding her breath through the loading screen until it read, *card declined*, again.

She tried to add up everything she had spent and didn't see a problem. Laura dug out her phone and dialed the number on the back of her card. She hated doing this outside but couldn't wake up Holden.

The automated message sounded pleasant and took forever to get to the part she needed where she could put in the numbers and her pin. She almost jumped when a voice came on the line.

"Hello, my name is Nick. May I have your first and last name, please?"

"Laura Burton," she said with a quick glance toward the man, who was now leaning on his car. The attendant inside hadn't seemed to notice.

"Alright, Ms. Burton, let me pull up your account here and take a look. Please give me one moment."

"Okay," she said. While she waited, listening to scratchy classical music, punctured with a friendly reminder about her value as a customer and the benefits of a loan, she thought of what other options she had.

She was due to be paid in two days, but she could use the money now. This was literally the worst time. When she had paid for a cheeseburger on the way out of town, her bank had sent her an alert letting her know she had overdrawn the account. They had covered her fine without a fee this time thanks to her credit, but she had no money in her account.

She hadn't worried too much because any day her paycheck would come through, and until then she had her credit card. She focused on her breathing. Maybe it was a glitch.

"Hello, ma'am?"

"Yes? Can you tell me why my card has been declined?" she asked, clutching the phone. The man who had been smoking finally sat in his car, which made her breathe a lot easier.

"Yes, ma'am. It looks like your last transaction was with a hotel company? Is this correct?"

"Yes, it is. It's in another zip code, but I've traveled there before. I'm sorry I didn't call to verify beforehand. Are you able to unlock my account?"

"I'm sorry, ma'am, I will not be able to do that."

"What? But it's a place I've traveled to before. I don't understand." Laura tried to breathe slowly while her heart pounded in her chest.

"Yes, ma'am. I understand that, but sometimes hotels take the full payment upon reservation depending on the brand and when the reservation has been made. They have put a hold on the account for the total amount due."

"The total amount due?"

"Yes, ma'am, so they have charged your account for six hundred seventy-two dollars and thirty-seven cents. That has put you over your limit, and as a result, we have placed a hold on your account."

Laura started pacing next to her car over the cracked concrete spotted with darkened gum. "So wait, is there anything you can do? How am I supposed to use my card? I have a line of credit."

"Yes, ma'am, I understand your concern. You can contact the hotel and try to get the amount refunded—"

"That will take days. I need something now."

"I am sorry, ma'am, there is nothing I can do on this end of things. May I suggest raising your credit limit? If you share your updated income with us, you may be eligible for—"

"How does that help me now?" Laura said louder than she should.

"I'm sorry, ma'am. I am unable to delete this hold now without authorization from the hotel or a payment to bring down the balance. At that time, you may call us again and we will unfreeze—"

Laura cut him off and didn't care. "I am at a gas station with my son asleep in the car and my card is not working."

"I am sorry, ma'am, perhaps you would like to take our survey—"

"I don't want to take your survey! I want my card to work! I need to put gas in my car!"

"Alright ma'am, I have noted you do not want to take the survey. Is there anything else I can help you with today?"

Laura stopped and looked out toward the highway at cars passing by. The only light in the night was the red and white lights with occasional flecks of amber from passing eighteen-wheelers. She tried to calm her breath.

"Ma'am, is there anything else I can do for you?"

"No."

"Okay, well, thank you for using—"

She ended the call and dug in her purse for any cash, knowing full well the last of her cash had been left behind for Carter as a rent payment and contribution toward all of the takeout he had ordered. Still, she searched, dumping out the contents onto the top of the hood, finding nothing but a few Lifesavers, a hair tie, and a few broken crayons.

She swept it all back inside the bag with her arm and went to the passenger side, taking out a giant box of toys from the front seat to excavate whatever was in the glovebox, hoping for any kind of emergency money.

Laura sat back on her heels by the open passenger door with papers scattered all over the floorboards, fluttering in the breeze.

There was only one place in the car with money. She knew it had at least a twenty inside along with two handfuls of coins and maybe a five. It'd be enough to take her the rest of the way until she could figure out her card and get paid. She'd put the money back eventually, and she had heard of other moms having to steal from the piggy bank to play tooth fairy because they were strapped for cash.

She turned to the toy box next to her and dug around inside, throwing Mickey and all of his pals right onto the scattered paperwork in the car. At the bottom of the box was Holden's piggy bank.

It was pink with oversized ears that were a little lopsided, and the whole thing was uneven and tilted back and forth because her mom hadn't been able to get the legs right.

Laura breathed through the memory of her mom's once capable hands making it and tried to steady herself when she turned the piggy upside down and froze.

There was no hole.

Her mom had forgotten to put the hole at the bottom. Laura twisted it all around looking for anywhere to get the contents out without harming the little piglet, but there was no way. She squinted through the slot and saw the edge of a crumpled bill just out of reach, mocking her in the bright overhead lights.

She cradled it in her hands and thought through all her

other options. She only had one credit card, and it wasn't working. Her ATM card wouldn't work because her account was already overdrawn. She had no cash. She was in the middle of nowhere, hours from the hotel room, and needed to buy gas. She couldn't even make it back to Goldvein.

There was no alternative.

Tears flooded her vision as she thought of her mom's hands shaping the piglet as a gift for Holden. If she broke it, he wouldn't get another one like it. Laura swiped at her eyes. She could glue it. Whatever it took, she'd make it right. What would her mom want more? Them to get back onto the highway or Holden to have his bank?

She closed the car door and walked to the edge of the concrete pad underneath the pump. The curb was perfect.

With the remains of her heart already breaking, and holding back a choked sob, Laura raised up the piggy bank with both hands and started to bring it down hard when a hand grabbed her arm.

She shrieked and pulled away, clutching the bank to her chest.

"Laura! Laura! It's me."

Carter.

She started sobbing even more, feeling the hot, fat tears run down her face. She sat on the curb and held the bank with relief. Her breaths came in quick spurts. She tried to slow them but couldn't.

"Hey, hey, hey." He dropped his crutches and sat back on the curb, pulling her in close to his chest. He was wearing the same black T-shirt he had been wearing when she'd left him. "It's okay. It's okay." He made a shushing sound and smoothed the back of her hair, letting his hand run down her back before repeating the process.

"How...did...you?"

"We spotted your car from the highway. It was the only

silver sedan we had seen for an hour. Dad called Jordan. He told us you were probably going to Missoula."

Her eyes tracked over to the truck a few pumps away. She could see Carter's dad standing outside by the wheel well with his hands in his pockets, watching from afar. She wondered how they'd met up, let alone were in the car together for three hours, but it didn't seem to matter.

"I also talked to Megan. You don't have to be scared anymore. It's okay."

Laura's eyes flew up to search his face. She tried to shift away, but he held her tight.

"I know it's hard that you lost your OD tonight, but it's not your fault. You know that, right?"

Laura looked at him and blinked a few times trying to understand. "Not my...fault?"

"Yeah, Megan told me what happened. How hard you take it when they die. It's okay. No one blames you."

Laura searched his eyes but found only sincerity. "Megan told you that?"

"Yeah." He nodded and held her shoulders and searched her eyes, taking one thumb and rubbing it under her eyes to wipe away the tears. "She also wanted me to tell you it's okay —she understands how you feel."

"She does?" Laura said, frowning. How could that be possible? Why was Megan covering for her? Maybe her secret was safe after all.

"Yeah, she was really upset you were leaving. Said she felt like it was her fault."

Carter looked at the piggy bank in her hands and frowned, taking it from her and studying it in the harsh light of the gas station. He turned it over, studying it from all angles, and sighed.

"Is this how much you hate me? You would rather destroy something of Holden's than let me help you?"

Laura closed her eyes and turned away. There was a smear of gum on the stained concrete that looked like one of Holden's dinosaurs.

"I didn't mean for it to be like this. I…." Words failed her. She looked at the ground and shook her head.

"I don't like that it turned out this way. I can't have you doing this to yourself. I know you don't love me back, but I do love you, and whether or not you like it, I'll do whatever it takes to take care of you and Holden." He held up the piggy bank. "And this little bacon bit too."

Laura let out a hollow laugh that was more a breath than anything.

Carter gave her another squeeze and planted a kiss on her head. "C'mon, let's fill up that tank and go home."

CHAPTER 29

C arter woke up late to the sound of Holden down the hall and the smell of coffee brewing. He smiled to himself through the exhaustion. That was exactly what he wanted to wake up to.

He turned over and checked the clock, then sat up and scrubbed his face. He had slept late, but not nearly enough. Still, no amount of sleep could balance out the emotional weight of last night. They hadn't gotten home until the early hours of the morning. He hadn't liked the idea of her driving alone, but she insisted, saying she was fine and with Holden asleep, it was better the car was quiet. So Carter had ridden home separately, watching the back of her car like a hawk the whole way in case something happened. He didn't want to lose her again. He had also called the hotel and canceled the room on her behalf, alarmed at the quality of hotel she was willing to sleep in.

He stood and headed to the bathroom on his crutches, where he splashed some water on his face before watching it cycle down the drain. The sight of her on the curb of a gas station in the middle of the night, alone, about to smash a piggy bank, was seared into his brain. The heights of desperation she was willing to go to for survival was on a level he had long forgotten about. He was sure his mom had to do things like that and would never tell him. Why would she? Once his dad had left, it was just her.

That had come up last night too. Not riding with Laura meant Carter, who had never known his father, had just spent six hours in the car with him, catching up man-to-man.

Frank—he still wasn't so sure about calling him Dad—had cried, apologized, and filled in the gaps with answers to questions Carter had always had. His grandparents had lived in the south and had passed away from heart disease and cancer before Carter had been born. Frank had settled in Montana after getting out of the Marines when he was looking for something different.

Frank had met his mom on his first day in town and fell head over heels with her, and still claimed she was the only woman he ever loved. They had spent two blissful years together before the alcoholism started to take root. His first arrest, before he had met her, had been by the MPs on some base in California. His first arrest as a civilian had been a drunk and disorderly charge that involved a late night at a bar and a political discussion that had gone bad. After that, he had lost his job at the lumberyard and things went downhill from there. He kept drinking and one thing led to another.

Throughout the story, Carter sat fascinated and saddened. The anger he held toward his dad faded and softened. Frank had gotten himself locked up for a while after a few DUIs and a run-in with drugs that he claimed was a case of being in the wrong place at the wrong time. To hear Frank tell the story, Carter's mom cut him off one day. Said he was a bad influence and he wasn't welcome back until he cleaned up his act. That's how it had ended.

Unbeknownst to Carter, his dad knew about his mom's new life and that she was living in Florida. Apparently, he even had her phone number, and they spoke from time to time so she could keep him up to date on what was new with Carter.

The real gut punch was when his dad—still felt weird to say and not be angry— told him his mom had been the one to tell him he'd been in the accident. Both of them had agreed it was finally time. Frank had been clean and sober for almost nine years and had picked up a job installing cabinets and floors for a general contractor. Mom was the one to give him the address and the news.

Carter had a lot of questions for her.

He wiped his face off with the towel and heard the telltale sign of fast little feet running down the hall.

"BOO!" Holden hopped out from behind the wall, covered in a blanket with his arms outstretched.

"Ahhh! It's a ghost!" he said, clutching his toothbrush to his chest.

Holden pulled it off and threw his head back laughing. "I scared you!"

"Yeah, you did. Where's your mom?"

"Right here," Laura said, coming into the room. The circles under her eyes were dark and confirmed she also needed more sleep.

"Do you work today?"

She shook her head no, while Holden danced around the room with the blanket on his head. "No, Megan wants to come over and talk to me."

He studied her. "Are you okay with that?"

"I don't know. I love her to death. I mean, I don't know where I'd be without her and Ash, but—"

"It's okay. Just tell her you're free tomorrow. You need to rest."

Laura nodded and swallowed.

"I'm going to make you breakfast, okay? I owe you that," Carter vowed.

Laura started to shake her head, but Carter kept going.

"And then I think you need to have some chill time." He turned to the bouncing ghost. "Holden, what would you like for breakfast?"

Holden stopped midbounce and pulled off the blanket before thinking. "Ummm…pancakes." He added a shrug for good measure and nodded. "Yeah, pancakes."

"Have you ever made pancakes before?" Laura asked with a doubting smile.

"Nope, and I welcome the challenge."

"Oh boy," she said, leading them down the stairs.

Carter pulled out a pan and his phone, looking up a few recipes while getting a bowl. He hadn't made pancakes but figured it couldn't be that hard.

Fifteen minutes later, he'd been proven wrong. The kitchen was covered in flour and splatters of batter. Three blackened pancakes were in the trash, and he was watching number four like a hawk just in case it decided to get an attitude and burn on him the second he turned his back like the others.

"Want some help?" Laura said from behind him. He turned to look at her.

"I think this one is going to be it."

"Usually the first one is a sacrifice, but I never throw it away and always eat it myself," she said with a shrug.

"That sounds about right." He turned around and grabbed the spatula to prepare for the flip. "Oh, you've got to be kidding me! How is it raw in the middle and black underneath?"

"Um…your heat is too high? Have you really never made these before?"

"Nope," he said, throwing it into the trash. Carter was getting good at that part at least.

"Well, why did you want to make them?" Laura said with a laugh.

"Holden wanted them, so"—he gestured around him—"I make pancakes."

"That's very sweet. Will you let me help you?" Laura said, stepping up to the stove.

"Absolutely not."

She jerked her head toward him with a frown. "Well, I hate to tell you this, but if you keep it up, at this rate, we'll be eating breakfast for dinner."

"If you help me, they won't be pancakes I made for Holden. I need to do it all by myself for it to count."

"Don't be ridiculous. How is me helping you… Oh, right. Well played, Carter. Okay, you made your point, now let me take over." She reached for the spatula and he held it away.

"Why should I let you help me?"

Laura threw back her head and looked at the ceiling. "Are we really going to do this?" She rolled her head back down, then stared at him sideways.

"Why should I let you help me?" he repeated.

Laura sighed. "Because we need to eat, and this way Holden can have better pancakes. Okay, you've made your point."

"Do we need to unpack this further?" he said, adjusting the grip on his one crutch so he could better face her.

"No. I think you proved that last night."

"Here you are, madam," he said, passing over the spatula.

Laura accepted it. "Okay…did you actually want to learn or was this just a lesson in humiliation?"

"I'm all ears."

"Alright, so first you need to drop this heat down because your butter is starting to smoke. Pass me a paper towel. We need to wipe this out."

Carter passed it over and with a flick of her wrist, she sopped up the black butter and then, after throwing away the paper towel, lifted the pan. "Let's cool this sucker down. Holden, you okay?"

"Yeah!" he called back from the living room. Today he had been tracing shapes and numbers in front of another Mickey Mouse cartoon.

"So, okay, now the pan's cool. Let's put it back on the burner and get some fresh butter." Carter passed it over and watched as she sliced a pat off the stick of butter and slapped it in the pan where it sizzled into a light foam.

"Time for a dollop right in the middle. You have a ladle?"

Carter handed it over, and when Laura grabbed it, he didn't let go, holding it until she met his eyes.

"What?"

"I just want you to know you're beautiful."

Laura smiled and looked away. "We're going to miss our moment. The pan's ready."

"I don't think we've missed our moment," he said, his voice low, letting go of the ladle.

Laura dipped the ladle into the batter bowl and poured it into the glistening butter.

"Maybe not, but I don't know what that looks like. I mean, we can't exactly go to prom."

"If you want to, I'll make it happen." That should be easy. Hell, she could ask for the building to be cleared and the same DJ and he would do everything in his power to try and make it happen.

"No, God, the last thing I need is to try to fit into a dress."

"I bet you'd look great."

"Pfft. Anyway, what I meant was, I'm not the same person

I was before. I have Holden and don't own any nice clothes. I haven't been out in...God, longer than I had realized." She took the spatula and ran it under the edge of the pancakes, which had little bubbles forming on the edge. "I mean, how does anyone in their thirties date?"

Carter stepped closer and slipped his arm around her waist, feeling the smooth cotton robe under his palm. Laura didn't pull away, so he pressed her to him and watched as she did a perfect flip, revealing a golden pancake.

"That's the best part. We're older and we don't give a damn what anyone else thinks." He planted a kiss on her hair. "It can be whatever we want."

Laura let her head rest under his chin and leaned into him while the pancake rose in the pan and the sounds of *Sesame Street* echoed from the living room.

"First pancake is finished," Laura said, lifting it from one side with the spatula to show off the golden-brown color underneath.

"We'll let Holden have it," Carter said, passing over a Mickey Mouse plate.

Laura slid it onto the plate and turned to him, setting the plate down on the counter. She looked up and smiled. Carter bent down and hovered above her, giving her the control she needed.

Laura's smile widened before she closed the gap and they kissed.

CHAPTER 30

L aura set the plate on the stove and loaded it up with cashew chicken. Neither of them had been up for cooking and had agreed on an early dinner of Chinese food. Carter and Holden had been sitting in the living room for most of the day, playing, coloring, reading, and watching TV. All of it made Laura's heart swell with joy. It was perfect, and she started to feel like she had dropped her guard and was starting to relax, which admittedly scared her.

The last time Laura had let her guard down she'd been hurt in so many ways. Every time she got attached, something happened, and at the end of it all, she was left alone with zero closure. She had been through it twice, and while she didn't think Carter would do it again—at least she didn't want to believe he would—she wanted more than anything to protect Holden from the same loss. As it was, she and Carter hadn't talked about "missing their moment"—at least not yet. Laura figured all of the talking would happen later, after Holden was asleep.

Last night had shown her how much he cared, but it had

also given her a chance to sort out her own feelings on the way home, knowing he was in the car behind her.

Carter had come for her.

Laura closed her eyes and let the fork rest on the counter while she took in a breath and savored the moment again. She was embarrassed and still scared about Megan finding out her secret—and about her weirdly covering for her with Carter, who still had no idea. She wasn't ready to call Megan yet—maybe tomorrow—but having Carter with her again warmed every cell in her body.

If she was honest with herself, she had dreamed of him off and on for years. Ever since the last time they were together, an idealized version of Carter popped up in her dreams and every time, she ran up to hug him, only to wake feeling like a guilty fool in the morning. Holding onto those childish fantasies and dreams had given her so much comfort in the middle of the night when she would lie awake and play "What if?" until sleep pulled her attention away from the memory of his dark green eyes.

She had always wanted him but had been too afraid to admit it to anyone.

Now they were seemingly together. Her dreams had come true. Laura was still worried about what would happen in a couple of months when he went home, but all Carter had said about it was, "Don't worry." Clearly, he didn't understand that's what moms did twenty-four, seven.

"Alright you two. Supper is ready!" she said, carrying the plates of food to the table. Holden's little feet ran in fast, followed by Carter on his crutches. Together, the sound worked somehow, and seemed to sum up all the good in her life right now.

Holden picked a bite of food off his plate after he climbed up into his seat, then shrugged at something Carter had asked before he explained who the character was on the show they'd been watching.

Looking at the two of them sitting next to each other while still talking about whatever had happened on TV made her heart swell. She didn't want to think about what might happen in the next few years, instead trying to savor the moment in front of her and commit it to memory.

She poured drinks, placed the egg rolls and wontons on the table, and led them through the prayer, with Holden correcting her all the way through.

"There's something about Chinese that always hits the spot," Carter said.

"I know. I'm boring though. I always order the same thing."

"Yeah, you got to change it up. See what's good."

"Sooo good," said Holden, shoveling in a bite of something on his plate, chewing with his little cherub-like cheeks.

"Are you working tomorrow?" Carter asked before taking a sip of Coke.

"Yeah, I'm scheduled to, anyway, and I guess I'll need to see Megan sooner or later. God…"

"It'll be okay. Everyone will be glad to see you."

Holden reached for a fortune cookie, but the chair slipped and clattered to the floor, followed by a loud thud as Holden's head hit the tile.

Carter and Laura both jumped out of their chairs. He wasn't moving.

"Call 911!" Laura was running her hands over him checking for broken bones. Her blood turned cold when his little limp body didn't respond to her touch.

"Is he bleeding?" Carter said, crouching down.

Someone kept saying, "Oh God, oh God, oh God," while Laura tried to wake him, and she realized it was her.

Training. She had training for this. Oh God, not Holden though. She didn't have her kit.

"They're on the way," Carter said from behind her. She couldn't turn to look at him. He was probably still on the phone anyway.

On the way was not here and that was not good enough.

She tugged up his Mickey shirt and pressed her palms to his tiny chest where she had given him so many tickles, closed her eyes, and sent every ounce of her energy into him.

It had never worked before, but she didn't have much else right now.

"Please God, please God, please God" she chanted through tears, pouring everything she had into him. She closed her eyes and tried to imagine his perfect little body pulsing with life. A flash of heat swept through her arms, down to her hands as a blast of the energy within her surged into her arms, radiating from her. Her arms trembled and shook as she gritted her teeth and dug in deeper, trying to send every ounce of her into her son's body. If it killed her, so be it.

She could see in her mind blood rushing to the head, but also felt something else. A hairline fracture in his skull.

When the well was dry and there was nothing left to give, her arms gave way.

She opened her eyes to see three things. A golden glow around her hands, Holden still on the ground, and Carter, across from her with a phone up to his ear, his mouth hung open in shock.

"Oh God, no, no, no, no!" She fell across Holden's chest, sobbing and pleading with whomever might be listening to bring him back to her.

Carter didn't wait for an answer. "Try again. Whatever you just did, try it again."

Carter tucked the phone into his shoulder and pressed his hands to Holden's head, matching her form perfectly.

"Come on, come on, come on," she said, pressing her hands to Holden's cheeks and digging deep. Another blast of energy almost pushed her off him, rocking her back on her heels. She pictured his skull and pressed her palms into his face as hard as she dared without hurting him and endured the searing heat in her palms until she couldn't bear it any longer and had to let go, to get a breath herself.

Once again, when she opened her eyes, there was a golden fog fading from her hands, though not as powerful as the first one.

"What is that?" Carter asked, his eyes wide as he watched her hands while he crouched over Holden's chest.

Laura was heaving now with sobs. Holden had been unconscious for too long already. There was a siren in the distance. She felt so hopeless without her kit, tools, or ability to heal. Her words came out in a rush while she pressed her hands to him just to have something to do. "I can heal people, but not Holden and not you. God, just this *one* time! I need this. Please God, no." She glanced up at Carter's face. "He has a skull fracture. I can't explain it, but I can feel it."

Whatever remaining color there was in Carter's face drained out, but his focus never wavered, while he relayed the statement to the dispatcher on the other end of the phone, never taking his eyes off of her.

"They're coming."

Sure enough, the fire engine and ambulance pulled up right before Jordan and Megan ran into the living room. Both were laser-focused on Holden, for which Laura was grateful. Carter must have had the foresight to open the door while on the phone with 911, and he rattled off what happened to Jordan, who nodded without speaking.

Laura had to hold herself from ripping the backboard out

of Jordan's hands. Megan came around and held her while she shook. She folded her arms under her elbows to hide the shaking she couldn't seem to stop.

The sight of Holden strapped to a backboard and being carried out and into the back of her ambulance seemed like a surreal nightmare. There wasn't room for Carter, whom she watched through the back window. He turned to Megan, who nodded and led him back toward the fire engine.

Jordan was in the back with her, while Mike took the wheel. Laura watched from the seat as the siren blared from outside and trained her face on Holden's perfect lips, as Jordan popped in the nasal prongs and started an IV. She hadn't stopped holding Holden's hand since they had moved him into the back of the ambulance. Megan had given her a quick hug and Holden a kiss on the head, but when Jordan, who had never shown much emotion, reached over and squeezed her shoulder, Laura started sobbing.

CHAPTER 31

Carter wanted the fire engine to drive faster, which was ridiculous because they were right behind the ambulance the whole way to the hospital. He hadn't needed to think twice when Megan offered him a lift. The whole way there, he had leaned forward in his seat, willing himself closer to Laura and Holden. Being away from them was torture.

He racked his brain, replaying the moment Holden fell, wishing he could pay God himself to turn back the clock.

"He has a good shot," Megan said, when Carter had updated her. "Jordan and Mike have everything he needs on that ambulance, and they'll make sure he gets it."

"That's good." Carter wanted to ask what the odds were but didn't have the courage to do it in case he didn't get the answer he wanted. He couldn't even bear to think of what life would look like without Holden's smiling face. His heart had been in high gear since dinner, but even considering the possibilities made it lurch into his chest.

"He's young too. Kids are pretty resilient."

He didn't know if she was talking more to herself or to

him, but either way, her voice was reassuring in a soft kind of way that made him wonder how in the world she ended up being a firefighter.

They finally arrived, and he clambered out of the truck, not giving a shit if his leg hurt in the process.

"Hey, Carter?"

"Yeah?" he said, trying to walk backwards while turning to see Megan. He failed miserably and stumbled over the curb. The ambulance's engine rumbled awake and headed out of the parking lot with its siren echoing off the building.

Megan glanced behind her and looked back at him. Her blue eyes shimmered with tears and worry. "I have to go. Besides I don't think me coming in there will help Laura right now, but give her a hug from me."

Carter nodded once. "She'd love to see you later."

A pained look crossed Megan's face, making him wonder what had happened between them. Perhaps they had a falling-out, but then again, it had been Megan's message that had finally gotten through to Laura last night at the gas station.

"We'll see." She gave a half-hearted smile. "Thanks for going after her and Holden. Give him a squeeze."

"I'll text you updates," he said, moving toward the doors of the emergency room.

"Thanks. I'll pass them on to Ash and everyone else. I think she's on her way here now."

"Sounds great."

Carter walked inside the oversized sliding glass doors while the fire engine followed in the ambulance's wake. A blast of air conditioning welcomed him into a cool waiting room with abstract art on the walls and a large welcome desk with a TV behind it. The ladies at the front must have seen him come from the fire truck, because they hit a button to open the double doors and waved him through.

It was the same place where he had woken up after the crash and seen Laura's face for the first time in far too long, at least while not in a haze in the ambulance after the accident.

Carter frowned when he heard Laura's voice getting louder and more upset. Like a wolf seeking his mate, he swiveled to see her squaring off with some skinny, tall guy in scrubs. He narrowed his eyes and maneuvered his crutches toward his target, who was standing between Laura and the door to a room down the hall.

"Ma'am, I understand you're upset."

"I am not upset. I am his mother and I am a licensed paramedic. You can ask anyone here. I have years of experience and I know he has a fractured—"

"Ma'am, I am a doctor—"

"I understand that, but please look for it when the X-rays come in. I'm telling you, it's not just a concussion. He needs to be seen by a neurologist—"

"Ma'am—"

"Would you just *listen* to me?" Laura threw out her hands, exasperated. The panic had turned into rage, and hot angry tears were coming back.

The doctor had the audacity to smile and nod before speaking. "I know I'm new here and we just met, but I'm going to take good care of him. You may find it useful to calm down. He's starting to wake up, and we'll be sure to monitor him."

"HE IS FOUR YEARS OLD AND HAS A FRACTURED SKULL."

"As I said before, there is no sign of a fracture on the—"

"What the hell is going on here?" Carter asked, standing shoulder to shoulder with Laura before nudging her out of the way. "Where's Holden?"

The doctor slid his impatient smile and thinly veiled

annoyance toward Carter. "Hello, I'm Dr. Bray. I'm treating Holden." The stick with legs held out his hand, which was thin and bony with veins sticking out everywhere. The fingernails were flat and club-like, as if they had been smashed. His glasses were too small for his features, and his dark hair looked greasy next to his pale, sallow face, which was wearing a fake smile. Carter hated him immediately.

"If you're treating him, why the fuck are we out here in the hallway?"

Dr. Bray's mouth opened and snapped shut, before he opened again. "Well, I just wanted to explain the treatment options—"

Laura swerved back in front of Carter. "They're not what's best for him! He has a skull fracture and needs to be evaluated immediately."

"Ma'am, I've heard your concerns. I'm sure you see a lot of trauma as a paramedic, but I can assure you, I've looked at the X-rays and found no sign of any fracture. I suspect it's a mild concussion."

Laura's voice went shrill again. "Why aren't you listening to me? I know he needs treatment. Can we request a second opinion?"

The doctor glanced behind him to a woman in scrubs at the nurses' station. "Um…can you put in a code gray?"

"Security?" Laura shrieked. "You're calling *security* on me? I know all of the nurses in here. I'm in here every other day!"

Carter edged past Laura again and got close enough to the doctor's face to have the smug bastard take a step back. It took controlling every fiber in his body not to grab the know-it-all and pin him to the wall. "I know you're not about to have a mother escorted away from her child who has just endured a scary event and is waking up in a new place alone."

The pale doctor looked like an eel, and his mouth worked like a fish while he tried to process the obvious threat in

Carter's eyes. He took another step back, and Carter closed the gap, glaring into the man's eyes. "Laura, go inside the room," he said in a low voice that he hoped communicated the level of violence he intended to rain down from on high.

Laura looked from him to the doctor and back again before pushing through the door behind them. A nurse looked up from Holden's bedside and waved at Laura, who ran inside and started talking in hushed tones. Holden was starting to wake up.

Carter turned back to face the good doctor. "I haven't heard one explanation about your treatment plan that's worth a damn. I have a team of lawyers itching for something to do, and if that child does not receive exemplary care, I promise you I will go after you for everything you have. You better be damn sure those X-rays are right and that you read them correctly."

A man in a dark uniform walked in through the oversized doors to the lobby.

"Everything okay in here?"

"Yes, sir, just wrapping up," Carter said, beating the doctor to the question. The tone in his voice had the security guard stopping but staying nearby just in case.

"You said you're new, so a word of advice from someone who knows business." Carter leaned in again, so close that the doctor's beady eyes flicked over to the security guard, who started walking toward them both. "You're only as good as the people you listen to, and you just ignored one of the best paramedics in this city, who will save a lot of people's lives before they even get to your doors. Maybe you should think about how many people do the work you take credit for."

The doctor's brows furrowed as he thought about what Carter said, while an almost indiscernible tremble ripped over him. "Security!"

A thick meaty hand cut through the tension between Carter and the doctor. "Sir, I'm going to have to ask you to come with me."

Carter's stare bored right into the doctor. He wasn't worth hitting, and that probably wouldn't thrill the judge. After all, he was still awaiting his court date. "Fine, but if anything, and I mean anything, happens to that little boy, I'll be placing a call from the lobby."

He let that sink in, and though the doctor put on a good show of standing tall and trying to act indifferent in front of the other staff members, his eyes looked wary and cautious.

Good. That's just how Carter liked his doctors. Nice and on edge.

CHAPTER 32

Laura stepped out into the hall outside Holden's new hospital room in the pediatric wing. He had woken up, eaten dinner, watched TV in bed—which he thought was a real treat—and had fallen asleep in his hospital bed. He was going to be fine, but did have a minor, hairline fracture that had originally been missed in the doctor's haste. The doctors and she agreed he needed to be kept overnight and most of the following day for observation, just to make sure he didn't have any complications before going home. Most children with mild skull fractures were able to heal on their own, and lucky for Holden, his fracture was in a positive spot, if you could call any skull fracture positive.

It had been a day, and Laura's shoulders ached with the tension she had been holding.

Ash had stopped in to see if they needed anything, carrying well wishes from Megan. Laura had practically dived into her friend's arms for a hug before the sobs came again. After about an hour of telling Ash there wasn't anything she could do, she left with strict orders to be called if the situation changed.

Carter had been by several times, checking in on Holden and her, asking the nurses questions, and holding her when she kept breaking down from the stress of the day. He had even brought her a candy bar from the vending machine because that's what Jordan had told him she liked.

Really, the man was perfect.

Dr. Bray on the other hand—God, she didn't even want to think of him. Most doctors were good and caring, but there were some who got into the profession and let it all go to their head, believing themselves to be infallible. In the end, she had been right, but he didn't want to listen to her because she was *just* a paramedic.

Laura's shoulders crept up toward her ears as the familiar feeling seeped into her soul. She cringed as always with the shame. She wasn't good enough. She didn't know enough. She wasn't a doctor, wasn't a nurse, and wasn't even in classes to make her dream a reality. She might know her stuff and have a magical ability with her hands, but in the eyes of Dr. Bray and the rest of the medical field, she just needed to quiet down and stand aside to let the real medical professionals do the work.

But he had been wrong, and she had been right. If he hadn't listened to her...she couldn't even think about it. Holden might've been sent home without treatment from a pediatric neurologist.

The only reason Dr. Bray had listened was Carter. She never thought she was the damsel in distress type, but she had never been in a situation where she needed backup like that. Dr. Bray was an elitist or a sexist, but either way, in that moment, Carter came to her rescue and cleared the way for her to speak without being interrupted. She hadn't even minded when he had ordered her into Holden's hospital room.

In thirty seconds, Carter had spoken his mind and gotten

himself escorted away by security, but when Dr. Bray had come into the room, he had an attitude adjustment, and with a subtle clearing of his throat, had asked her to repeat her concerns.

Laura checked the clock on the wall. Carter should be back any minute. She wasn't heading home tonight but hadn't brought anything with her to the hospital other than her purse. Of course, emergencies with young children never happened at convenient times, so she desperately needed a change of clothes. Carter had been asking what else she needed and what he could do. The second she had given him marching orders to go pack a bag of toiletries and clothes for herself and Holden, he had planted a kiss on her lips and was out the door.

"If you'd like to step outside for some air, I'm happy to keep an eye on him," said a nurse from the station. Laura didn't recognize her but knew the charge nurse well. It was quiet in the department, as the hospital wasn't very big and it was getting late.

She glanced at Holden, who was sleeping peacefully. All of the monitors showed normal numbers, and he had just had some medicine to help with the pain.

"I'll just run down to walk around and I'll be right back."

"Take your time. I'll find you if anything changes."

Laura thanked her and pushed the button to leave the department through the oversized double doors. She had been in that chair for hours, and it felt good to move her stiff legs. Carter had texted her, saying he was a few minutes out and had brought her something to eat. The dinner from the cafeteria had been fine—she was used to it—but her stomach had growled with the idea of more food to eat. Stress always made her hungry. Laura didn't have many vices, but she could eat the hell out of her feelings.

She walked through the hallways and did a few laps

around the main entrance. The quiet, clean linoleum gave her comfort as she tracked her pacing and made it down to the lobby. Carter would be pulling up soon. A few people milled about, but mostly it was silent. The quiet calmed her like a smooth balm over the hard edges she had been carrying for the day, the week—hell, for years.

Laura stopped to study a painting—abstract, of course, why always abstract?—of a mother and child on the wall. She tried to imagine what her life with Holden would continue to look like without Carter. Could she do it by herself? Of course. Plenty of strong women raised wonderful children all by themselves. Would it be as easy or convenient? Absolutely not.

"Hey, you," Carter's deep voice said from behind her. She turned to see him standing there in fresh clothes with one of her bags stuffed full and a shopping bag of snacks, along with a takeout bag of what looked to be Styrofoam containers. How he'd managed to carry that with his crutches was beyond her, but he had gotten pretty good at getting around places.

"You don't need to keep buying me food."

He gave her a lopsided grin, revealing white, gleaming teeth.

"I'm comfortable. I have a few extra bucks in the bank this month." He passed the bag over to her. "I grabbed everything you asked for. Toothbrush, shampoo, some fresh clothes, and your robe. What? Why are you making that face?"

Laura pulled a hand over her face. "I just can't believe a billionaire went through my underwear drawer."

"I was very entertained."

"You lie like a rug. There's nothing fancy in there."

"Not yet. Gotta have a growth mindset."

"Ha-ha. I like to be comfortable. I'm not buying anything fancy anytime soon."

Carter sent her a coy smile like he wanted to make a wisecrack, but she saw the tired lines around his eyes. This was the second time he was up in the middle of the night, saving her and Holden.

"Let's go sit in the lobby. The nurse is watching over Holden. He's asleep anyway. We can take a few minutes to eat."

Carter nodded and followed her lead toward the empty waiting area. They opened the Italian food, which, incredibly, was still piping hot, and sat down to eat.

"So about what happened today..." Carter said, looking at her over a garlic knot. "Care to elaborate?"

Oh shit. She had forgotten about that. She should've panicked and lied, but exhaustion won out. "I guess you pretty much saw it all."

"I saw a..."—he looked around to make sure they were alone. She could've kissed him right there for that alone—"glow," he finished.

"Yep," she said, eating more spaghetti.

"How?"

Laura shrugged. "No idea."

"No, I mean how does it work?"

She chewed and swallowed. "I touch someone and visualize them healing." She tilted one palm up and studied the ordinary-looking hand. "My hand tingles and starts to glow. It gets warm too."

Carter's eyes narrowed. "It works."

Laura glanced over at him. She couldn't bring herself to nod but just met his eyes with a solemn confirmation.

"How?"

"I thought we just covered that."

Carter shook his head. "I know, sorry. I mean...why?"

"No clue."

Carter nodded and kept staring at her while holding the garlic knot he'd apparently forgotten about. She thought she would've felt uncomfortable with the conversation, but at least with him, it felt natural, or maybe she was finally too tired to care.

"When did you realize?"

"I was little."

"You knew in high school?" If his eyes went any wider, they would pop out of his head.

Laura nodded while she chewed.

"But not Holden," he recalled.

"Nope. Or mom. Or you."

"Why me?"

Laura shrugged and ate some more food. "I kept trying, but nothing. Remember when I kept touching your leg?"

"Of course I do." His voice took on a husky tone that sent a shiver down her spine.

"I was trying to do it where you wouldn't notice."

"I notice everything about you."

Laura looked up and met his dark green eyes, which zeroed in on her as if she was the only thing in the world worth focusing on. She felt a little awkward at the attention, not because he had done anything wrong, but because she wasn't used to it.

"Well, yeah, I kept trying. I don't know why it doesn't work on you. It's worked on everyone else other than family." A thought occurred to her and she looked over at him with a worried look. "You don't think...somewhere in the gene pool?"

He shook his head. "Absolutely not."

Laura let out a sigh. "Well, at least that's a relief. Didn't sleep with my cousin. Big win for the day."

Carter laughed. "We can scratch that one off the list."

"Yeah, thank God," she said, taking another bite of her food. She probably should've ordered something she could eat a little more gracefully. Carter kept glancing over at her. It would've given her a complex, but hey, turns out there were some real perks to being too tired to care.

"You said you had this ability in high school."

Laura nodded. "Forever, really."

"Is that why you ran out of the car when I told you to stay behind?"

Laura frowned and took a sip of the bottle of water he had thrown in the bag. "Told me to stay behind? You never did that."

"*That* night."

Realization dawned. Back when their relationship had changed forever, when the accident had happened after the bonfire, Laura had raced into the night to try to get to the girl thrown from the car. When she hadn't been able to revive her, she had been the first to dial 911.

"Does that mean you...you know, tried to heal her?" Carter asked, looking into his stuffed shells.

"I did. I didn't even hear you, and if I had, I wouldn't have listened."

Carter nodded again. "I guess that's why you're a paramedic."

"Yep. I don't understand this, and every time I do it, I'm nervous that it will be the last time—or that the time before had been. That this is when it all stops and everyone knows I'm fake."

"You're not fake."

"I'm more confident than I should be. I can take risks others can't. I walk around feeling fake. I can't imagine doing the job without it." She bit her lip and turned to him. "You're the first person I've ever told other than my dad. He always said to keep it a secret. Wanted to protect me. You know, a lot of people don't understand these things. I'm not even sure I do. It's just how I am."

Carter reached out and held her hands. His touch was warm, firm, reassuring. "Hey, look at me." He gave her hand a little shake until she met his emerald eyes. "I'm so honored you've given me that gift. I respect the hell out of you and, with or without an…ability, you're a damn good paramedic, an incredible mother, and you'll outshine all the other doctors when you graduate. You're beautiful and sexy and smart, and while we're at it, I have to tell you…"—he sighed and squeezed her hand again—"I am sorry for everything. The way it all ended. I've told you that before, but the truth is, I never stopped loving you. Always did, always had. No one else ever came close to you."

Laura's heart leapt up into her throat. He had said it before, but she hadn't believed it. After the past twenty-four hours, though, he had left her with no choice.

"Funny thing about that," she said, leaning over until her face was inches from his, "I was just thinking the same thing before you showed up."

"Because I brought food?"

"Not just that, but it's a perk." Laura leaned over and kissed him, which he readily returned, pressing himself into her before his tongue snaked out to taste hers.

"This probably isn't the right time or place, and I'm really scared to say this out loud, but I love you too, Carter. I always have and I always will, even when you go back to California." Tears flooded her vision, whether they were from exhaustion or fear or worry or the stress of the day, it didn't matter. She swiped at them too late and they fell.

"Hey, hey, hey. Come here." He wrapped her in his arms and rocked her back and forth, pressing her head into him where she found a perfect nook to nestle her head against his shoulder.

He took a breath and shook a little. Laura opened her eyes but didn't shift to look at him, instead staring out at the empty lobby while she tracked his movements that jerked with every intake of breath. Was he…crying?

Carter inhaled and murmured something into her hair, while he clung to her.

"I love you. God, I love you. I never thought I'd get the chance to say it again," Laura said, squeezing him tighter. "I've been so focused on trying to be there for Holden and Mom that I didn't realize I needed support too. I didn't think about how letting you in could help me. Thought taking any help would make me weak, but if you hadn't been with me today, I…" She couldn't bring herself even to finish the thought. "I don't know what would've happened to Holden. I'm scared you'll leave and it'll hurt again, but I don't care because I love you. I have since I had a crush on you in middle school."

"I love you more. You have no idea how much more. I'm not going anywhere."

Laura pulled back and looked up at him, searching his eyes for the true answer to her next question. They were red-rimmed as if he'd been crying. "Really? What about your business?"

Carter shrugged. "You know, I was thinking, in tech a lot of people work remotely, and with video conferencing apps, we don't need to be in California anymore. It might be nice to give my employees more affordable housing options and maybe settle in a place that could use another employer. I think my tax accountants would love me for it."

"You'd be okay changing your whole life for me?"

"It only bothers me when I think of you hurting. I love you, and I love Holden already."

Laura let out a silent, choked sob. "I was so scared today. I can't heal people I love." She stopped and replayed that again in her mind.

"What?"

"I can't heal people I love. I should've realized the connection. That's why I couldn't heal you."

Carter smiled before he wrapped her up in his arms again and held her.

They stayed like that, each clinging to the other, whispering sentiments about lost time and trading kisses that held the promise of more in a more private, appropriate setting.

"Let's head upstairs and check on Holden," Carter said. "I brought Mickey too."

Laura beamed at him and gathered up the empty takeout containers to throw away in a nearby trash can. "Thank you, for everything."

"You're welcome. You know, you're a tough woman to woo," he said as they headed toward the elevators.

"What do you mean?" she asked, turning to face him after hitting the button for the pediatric floor.

"I just want to take you out to a nice dinner or weekend away, but instead I spilled my guts in the lobby of a hospital."

"Well, when you consider its connection to the moment we first met again, that does make it sound more romantic."

"Good try," Carter said with a sly smile. "Don't worry. I owe you a lot more than one prom. I have ideas."

CHAPTER 33

The next morning, Holden had been released after much paperwork and an appointment made with the pediatrician to follow up on his healing and make sure nothing had been missed. By the time they left the hospital, it had almost been time for lunch and Laura was exhausted.

They had stayed at the hospital overnight, her asleep on the bench the hospital execs had the gall to market as a bed. Carter was prepared to sleep in the waiting room on a chair, but Laura felt better with him closer, and though they couldn't snuggle, she asked him to sleep in the chair in Holden's room. Getting comfortable wasn't going to happen, but she slept on her side on the thin pad covering the cinderblock window seat just so that when she opened her eyes, she could see Holden and Carter sleeping peacefully in one glance. That alone gave her enough comfort that after the five hundredth time checking, she fell asleep, only to be awakened at six in the morning by an over-enthusiastic pediatrician with a flair for singing while popping the lights on full blast. Bless him, Holden didn't budge but kept sleeping like an angel. Laura was still groggy from the night and tried to scrub her face with her hands to catch up with the good doctor's caffeine-fueled introduction and exam. Either Carter had already been up, or he came awake on a dime and stood, nodding politely and asking pointed questions, while Laura tried to smooth her hair down and eye where her bra had landed in her bag.

Thank God for Carter. It was a sentiment she had said throughout the morning. He not only was present and aware with every doctor and nurse, but he'd also made a coffee and breakfast run, got Holden a balloon from the gift shop, and arranged for an SUV with a car seat to pick them up, even making sure to tip the attendants who brought them to the door.

With him there, entertaining Holden with his phone, Laura was almost able to relax and enjoy the ride. There was a feeling of trust and reliance she hadn't known before. There was love.

When they got home, Holden bounced off toward his room to show his balloon to his stuffed animal friends, and Carter shooed Laura into the shower, promising her he would watch Holden like a hawk. She could hear them now in his bedroom, talking to all of the stuffed friends and reading *Olivia* over and over.

Satisfied there would be no crisis for a little while, Laura crept into her bedroom and sat on the white chair, taking a moment to admire the sunny white and yellow room. She slipped out her phone and dialed.

"Hello?" her mom answered. Laura could've wept at the sound. So much had happened, yet there was no way to dump all of the past days' events on her.

"Hey, Mom!"

"There you are, stranger. I was wondering when I would hear from you. Want to video chat?"

"Sure," Laura said, hitting the button for the phone to do its thing.

Her mom's face flashed on the screen. The sight always made her smile with—

"Mom, are you wearing makeup?"

"Why, yes, I am. I'm glad you noticed."

Her mom hadn't worn any makeup since before the stroke. "What's the occasion? And you know, you could've called me too. I was starting to worry because I hadn't heard from you."

"Well, I wanted to surprise you."

"Surprise me?" Laura studied her mom a little closer.

"Your earrings!"

"Aren't they fabulous?" Her mom turned her head and fluffed her hair with her bad arm, the movement jerky and unnatural, but great progress from where she had been even just a week ago. "I feel like a woman again. Even got the highlights with my new color."

"They look great. You look..." Laura couldn't find the word.

"Like my old self?"

"Well, um, yeah, actually you do. So tell me about this surprise."

"Well, I've done some thinking, and there's a place near Goldvein that has apartments for people my age that look very nice. I'm going to take the tour, and I'd like you to come with me. They're in my budget, too, and I have my eye on the two-bedroom, so I can have Holden sometimes."

Laura blinked a few times. This was not the woman she had spoken with a few days ago. Had it only been a few days? Hair color, earrings, apartments, Holden?

"Mom, this is all great news, but what did the doctor say?"

"That's the best part! The doctor agrees that I'm ready to move to a different setting, and as long as I keep up physical therapy and ask for help when I need it from a nurse that will come in, I'm good to go!"

"Wow, that's amazing. I mean, I didn't think...you know, after our last conversation..."

"You were right. I had let it get me down, and then I reminded myself I'm still here! I still have a daughter and an adorable grandson, so why give up hope?"

Laura blinked away tears, not wanting to get her own hopes up, but still feeling the shift in the universe as her luck changed for the better.

"Where is my sweet little boy?"

"He's playing with Carter."

Her mom gave her a very sly smile and raised an eyebrow.

"It's not like that."

"You shouldn't lie to your mother."

Laura smiled. "Okay, it is like that."

Her mom's grin flashed like a Cheshire cat with a big bowl of cream. "I know."

"What do you mean you know?"

"I already talked with Carter's mom, who talked with his dad. You know he really was a nice man. It's good to see that he got cleaned up after all this time. Anyway, they both told me what happened. You know, you should've just listened to me."

Laura listened to her mom go on and on about all of the behind-the-scenes matchmaking and smiled. Holden was happy and healthy, and since everything was handled, Laura didn't want to ruin her mom's good mood. She'd tell her about Holden later.

"Well, anyway, since you know everything—tell me about this apartment."

"Oh, it's gorgeous. South-facing, natural light, and you know, it even has granite. Can you imagine? Me. I would have granite. I always said I didn't want it, but God, did I. Just never wanted to spend the money."

"Sounds nice."

"I can't wait to have you over for coffee once I move in."

"So I guess you've already made up your mind then. Wait, did you say coffee?"

The smile that spread across her mom's face could've powered the city for a month.

"That's right. The nurse, Lynette, may have helped me with my earrings, but guess who made her first cup of coffee?"

CHAPTER 34

The next afternoon, Laura sat at the tea shop in town and fussed with her blouse, which was one she hadn't worn in ages, having fallen into the trap of wearing the same three shirts. It was a pretty blue button-down she had loved but avoided for fear Holden would spill something on it. As beautiful as it was, it demanded ironing with extra starch, and that just was not in the cards for her with a limited amount of time, money, and patience.

Still, every time she wore it, she felt confident and put together. She would need that boost today.

Megan had called Carter asking if she was okay, and as much as Laura wanted to chicken out and fake that she was too busy and couldn't leave Holden, the fact that one of her best friends had called Carter instead of her was a bridge too far. She had a choice to make, and she wasn't the type to run from a tough situation just because it was a little uncomfortable.

Carter had coached her over lunch while Holden ate his sandwich, which Laura had even taken the time to cut into a dinosaur shape with a cookie cutter she found at the store.

Mom guilt brought out the best in her. As far as Holden was concerned, he was having the best day a kid could, getting to eat almost whatever he wanted, snuggle, and watch TV. He had gone down for another nap, which was when she had made her escape.

While Holden was living his best day ever, Carter had listened as Laura explained exactly what Megan might've seen, and he pointed out that Laura didn't truly know what Megan thought about it.

"Let her speak first. You don't know what you're dealing with. Once she talks, then you can defend what you need to. Don't overshare. Deflect, and relax," Carter had said, making it all seem so much easier than it felt. She wasn't cut out for this type of intensity.

"Can I take your order while you wait?" the young waitress in a yellow apron asked.

"I'm sorry, I haven't had a chance to finish the menu. There are so many choices."

"I'll bring you a water while you pick something out. The most popular teas are at the top. Let me know if you have any questions."

Laura thanked her and tried to read the menu again, but every time she reached the second line, her thoughts kept looping and cycling with everything that could go wrong.

Megan would know what to order anyway. Laura had picked the sunny little tea shop downtown because of its cute, rustic charm and artsy, feminine flare, which fit Megan to a—well no pun intended—tee. Everything from the little cakes to the mismatched china cups was perfect. The bakery case was full, and they even had gluten-free and organic and locally-sourced, sustainably-produced products as well as a bunch of other things that Megan had talked about too many times to count.

Laura kept clenching and unclenching her hands under

the table and tried to bring her shoulders down from her ears, but the more she thought about it, the more they kept creeping up.

Laura took a few deep breaths and was studying the little yellow flower in the vase on the table when the sound of bells tinkling from the door to the tea shop announced Megan's arrival. Her shoulders hiked back up, and she didn't know whether or not to stand and greet her friend or keep it chill. What did she do before? Would she be rude? Laura played it safe and clambered out of her seat.

Megan walked over in a pink sundress and flip-flops that were so her. Her shy smile and frazzled red hair completed the look along with a little crossbody bag she had bought at the secondhand store in town.

Megan's lips turned up into a shy, nervous smile. "Can I ask for a hug?"

"Come here, you," Laura said, pulling her in tight. Megan smelled of good shampoo and lotion like always. The two of them stayed like that, rocking back and forth like the best of friends do.

"I'm so glad to see you. How's Holden?" Megan said, not letting go.

Laura pulled back and faced her freckled friend. "Better. Happy. God, it was awful."

"I know. You've had a rough few days," Megan said, putting a toe in the water. "I'm glad he's okay."

"You and Jordan made it to the house in record time."

"You must not have been keeping track of time," Megan said, sitting down. "The traffic downtown slowed us up. That's why I'm late, by the way. You know I can't park."

"Parallel parking isn't that bad. I could teach you."

"I know how to do it, but it stresses me out. All of those people behind me just give me anxiety. I'll just walk farther."

The waitress came over then and took their orders for

tea. Laura followed Megan's lead; she ordered something Laura had never heard of and recommended the oolong for her. They also agreed to split a tiered tea service with all the usual goods because as Megan told the waitress, "We need to eat our feelings," which was totally accurate.

"I'll slip you an extra couple of eclairs."

Megan thanked her and took a sip of water.

"Where's Ash?" Laura asked. "Working again?"

"Yeah, she picked up an extra shift. Said she would swing by later to check on Holden, but she'll call first to make sure it's a good time."

"She's always so good about that," Laura said. Megan nodded.

"I didn't tell her."

"About what?" Laura said, feigning ignorance, while privately letting out a sigh of relief. Ash wouldn't have believed it for a second, but still, she had been worried.

"You know...the OD."

"It was pretty intense."

"Yeah, I know." Megan spun her cup on the polished table between them. Oh God, what if Carter was wrong and she did have to lead? She hated awkward silences and couldn't handle letting her best friend hang out in the wind.

"I'm sorry," Megan said. "I'm really sorry for making you feel like you had to run."

"What do you mean?" Laura said, trying to play it off like she and Carter had practiced.

Megan's big blue eyes rolled so hard they almost bounced out onto the table. "I thought we were better than that. The whole Missoula thing?"

"Yeah, you're right. I'm sorry. And it wasn't you, by the way. I just...I don't know. I've had a lot going on, and I'm not in my right mind."

"Mr. Green Eyes?"

Laura wanted to lie and hide the truth, but Megan would know. She let herself smile and indulged in a small shrug. "Yeah, he's okay."

"He's a good one. Was determined to find you."

"I know, and he arrived in the nick of time too."

Laura told her about the frantic packing and the near-death of the piggy bank. It felt good to get it all out, and saying it aloud made her realize how good Carter had been and how much of an idiot she had looked like. She was sitting across from Megan right now. This had been her biggest fear and yet it didn't seem like a big deal at all.

The waitress came with the teapots and then returned with the elaborate tea service, including little brown sugar cubes Lara had never seen before and a tea strainer, which looked like a colander for a Smurf. Megan poured with expert hands, while the waitress came back with the three-tiered array of confections and sandwiches, all artfully piled with ramekins of clotted cream and house-made huckleberry jam. Sure enough, there were four eclairs instead of two.

Everything tasted incredible, and Laura was grateful the waitress had given them instructions to start on the bottom and work their way up. Her favorites were the egg salad sandwiches, while Megan liked the cucumber. They then moved on to the little macarons and bite-sized tarts with a spoonful of custard, single raspberry, and a dollop of cream, all in the tiniest pie crust ever. Laura had worried she would leave hungry, but now she was starting to hit the wall and wondered if she would be able to eat the dinner she had planned.

The tea was exceptional as well. Megan talked about flavor palates and finishing notes, but all Laura knew was that she liked it.

"So, we're to the desserts and I'd like to ask something," Megan said, putting her cup down without making a noise, which was an apparent art form that Laura had not mastered. Her own landed with a loud clatter.

"Okay." She tried to relax, but her shoulders kept creeping up toward her ears. The shoe was going to drop. This was it.

"Do you know anything about what happened that day?" Megan asked point-blank.

There wasn't anything she could do. She couldn't—wouldn't—lie to one of her best friends. Megan knew everything else about her. Why was this different? Carter found out and the world had kept spinning.

"I don't, except that I've had the ability for a long time. I feel it. Like, not literally, but I imagine things…well, healing, and then I feel warm and tingly and then I feel a warmth back in my hands." She paused and looked at the table. "Oh, and I can't heal Holden, Mom, or, apparently, Carter. I thought it was a family thing, but I guess not."

Laura risked a glance in Megan's direction to see how her declaration had landed. She was still sitting at the table and hadn't leapt up for the door, which was a great sign.

"That's cool."

Laura sat and waited. When nothing came other than Megan taking a sip of tea, she looked around her, a little disappointed there wasn't a bigger response, not that she wanted one. But that couldn't be it, could it?

"I haven't told anyone—until recently, when I told Carter."

"That makes sense."

"You don't seem too shocked."

"I've thought about it. Figured that's what it was. Makes sense now about you being a paramedic. You know…how you always wanted to do this."

Laura nodded, still wondering how and why Megan was taking this so well. Normally, she'd be all wide eyes and questions, but she was like some quiet, demure lady in a historical novel.

"So…you're not surprised?" Laura asked.

"I mean, I was, sure…but also, I believe in magic."

"I've never called it that."

Megan looked at her. "That's what it is though, isn't it? Or do you call it a superpower?"

"I definitely don't call it that. I'm kind of scared to call it anything other than an ability. Like, if I think too much about it, someone will know what I'm thinking and then I'll get caught and maybe it won't come back."

"I understand."

"Like I said, you're taking this really well."

Megan poured another cup of tea and shrugged, looking down. "Like I said, I believe in magic."

That didn't surprise Laura in the least. Megan believed in everything from horoscopes to meditation to most major religions, arguing that all of them told people to be good. This was the first time she had ever mentioned magic though. "What kind?"

"People having abilities, like you said."

"Have you heard of anyone else?" Laura said, her voice more hushed than it had been. The tea house had music, which thankfully masked their conversation. The few other people were scattered throughout the dining room, and their table was far from the kitchen.

"I've never met anyone before. Just read stuff online. A lot of it is people claiming they can do stuff. There are a lot of party tricks too, so it's always hard to know."

"Sounds like you've researched it."

Megan nodded and didn't say anything, but when she met Laura's eyes, she squirmed.

"What did you learn?" Laura asked.

"Nothing concrete, just myths. Legends. And like I said, party tricks."

Laura kept watching Megan, who was doing anything but what Laura had expected. "Before, you said you wanted to talk to me, and now you're not saying anything."

"Well, I don't want you to run off again."

"No, no. I won't. I'm just surprised. When exactly did you start looking this up?"

"When I was thirteen."

"That's specific."

"Yeah."

Laura picked another pastry, if only to break the tension. "Why thirteen?"

Megan took a breath and pulled her pink lips tight. "I went to a summer camp."

"Too many stories around the fire?" Laura teased, not sure why she was pursuing this. She was the one with the secret after all.

"Not exactly."

"What was it?"

Megan met her eyes, dead-on, with a seriousness Laura didn't see outside of work. There was a mix of grief, guilt, and sadness in those normally bright happy eyes. "I learned I was different. Laura, I think we have more in common than we first realized."

CHAPTER 35

C arter looked up when Laura came into the house. She had chosen her outfit so carefully and had worried about the way the conversation would go, only to stay three hours longer than she had said she would before finally texting him that she was running late but would be home with dinner she had picked up along the way. He had texted back, but the phone had stayed silent, which was a sign the conversation had gotten intense.

"Mama!" Holden said, running up to her with his arms outstretched. Laura let her purse slide off her arm and put down the bag of takeout just in time before he launched himself into her arms.

"Hey, boo boo!" She smacked three big kisses on his cheeks. "Did you have a good day?"

"Yeah! We did puzzles and watched a Halloween Mickey Mouse."

"I see you found out about his favorite holiday," Laura said, letting Holden slide down her to skip back to his puzzles.

"Yep," Carter said, standing up and grabbing his crutches.

KATHRYN K. MURPHY

"Can I finish this one? Pleeeeeeeeease?"

Laura glanced at the TV and the puzzle, both of which were almost finished.

"That's fine, but after that, dinner. That's it."

"That's it!" he echoed.

"Oh yeah, he explained every monster to me. I can tell he's seen this episode before."

"It's his favorite. Thanks for hanging out with him. He wasn't too much?"

"Nah, he was good. We had fun. Kept it chill. He ate all of the apple slices and an orange too."

"That's good!" Laura said over her shoulder, pulling down plates. Tonight, it looked like she had grabbed their meal from the diner which was near to where she and Megan had met. He could smell the meatloaf and was so down with that choice.

"So, how did it go?" he asked.

"Really well."

"Oh yeah?"

"Yeah." Laura pulled out plates and started filling glasses with ice.

"That's nice. I don't get to know any of the details? You got me curious."

"There's not much to tell, really."

"Um…I beg to differ. You had a conversation about how your best friend discovered you have magical powers. That doesn't happen every day."

Laura let out a laugh while she plated the food. "No, you're right. It was good. I was nervous about seeing her, you know, wondering if this would make it weird between us, but it didn't. Not even a little bit. It was actually really nice just to be able to talk about everything that's happened."

"You've had a lot going on."

"Yeah, and of course, she wanted all of the details on you."

Carter raised an eyebrow in her direction and smiled. "You like to kiss and tell?"

Laura grinned at him while filling the glasses with ice. "Stop. Gave her just enough to get her going."

"Okay, so then what happened?"

"Well, we had tea, which was delicious. They had all of the little treats, and the sandwiches were so good."

"That's nice."

"Yeah, I had never had a true afternoon or high tea. I'm not sure which is which. Thought I would leave hungry, but we had a hard time finishing it all. I brought home two eclairs for you and Holden. Anyway, we started talking about, you know, the incident, and then me, and I used your tricks but she called me on it."

"That's surprising."

"I know, I thought so too, but I guess with this, she was paying close attention. Anyway, we ended up talking about it for a long, long time."

"What did she say?"

"You know, just questions, that sort of stuff, but it was weird. I could tell she was holding back."

"Well you can't fault her. It's not an everyday thing."

"I'm just grateful you both don't think I'm crazy."

"Why would we?"

Laura turned away from the meatloaf and faced him. The worry and fear came back into her face, pulling at her delicate features as clouds of concern rolled in from past memories. Carter wanted to reach out and smooth the worry away, shielding her from ever feeling like that again, but he stood rooted to the spot, waiting for her to speak.

"Carter, for so long I kept it hidden. I'm not even used to talking about it out loud. I was worried that if anyone ever found out, I'd lose my job or worse—custody. I couldn't risk it, so when she saw me, I just had to leave, and I know that seems silly, but I didn't know who I could trust. It's not about her or you, it's just that the stakes were too high. Failure wasn't an option."

Carter closed the gap then and wrapped his arms around her, resting his chin on her head. When he breathed in, he could smell her shampoo, which was the best intoxication he could ask for.

"Did John know?"

"Oh God, no. I could never tell him."

"Why not?"

"He didn't believe in that sort of thing. Never would have. Half the time he would talk to me like I was crazy and the other half of the time he would treat me as if I wasn't there. It was always about him. Still was when he left."

"Sounds like a terrible person."

Laura nestled her head in his shoulder so he could hear her better. "I hate to think that, you know, because of Holden, but I look back sometimes and wonder why. I mean I know I was lonely, and I figured he was good enough, so I guess I settled. Wanted to make it work. He seemed intelligent and funny at the time. Our differences were never a problem and we never fought, but I later realized we didn't have anything to fight over. Really, we were just two different people. Roommates. He didn't involve himself in my life more than was necessary and well, he didn't want me in his."

"I'm sorry. You deserve so much better."

"I was always scared he would find out. I don't know what I was scared he would do. He never hurt me or anything like that, but I just had a feeling that if he ever found out, something would happen."

"Does your mom know?"

He felt Laura's head shake against his chest. "No, I was too scared to even tell her."

Carter rubbed her back and pressed his lips to her hair. "You don't have to be scared anymore."

"I know that, but it's going to take me some time."

"I know."

They stood like that a moment longer, until Holden came bounding in. They all sat down, ate dinner, cleaned up, and then did the bath and bedtime routine together, which was a first for Carter. It was new, but somewhat familiar probably because he had remembered more than he realized about his own childhood. Even some of the books were the same, which was great because other than the odd story he'd read to Holden during the day, he hadn't read anything other than domestic thrillers and nonfiction in years.

The best part about the whole thing was the moment Holden snuggled in and looked at the pages of *Goodnight Moon*, then leaned his little head against Carter's chest. He stole a quick glance at Laura who was sitting on a chair across the room, smiling. After the book had ended, they tucked Holden into bed and shut out the lights before making the journey down the hall toward Carter's bedroom.

His burns hadn't needed bandages for days and were fast on the way to healing, but out of routine or habit, he sat on the couch, and Laura took the spot next to him. He reached for the remote and turned on a documentary, but lowered the volume to be barely audible, so they could talk.

"You've been quiet. What else did Megan say?"

Laura chewed her lip and looked at him. "Just stuff."

Carter blinked and watched her sort through her thoughts and feelings, her eyes glued to the screen across from them in the oversized bedroom.

"Just stuff?"

"I don't know if I can tell you."

He held up his hands in his defense. "I understand. I just want to make sure you're okay. You seem a little out of it."

"I guess I'm just thinking it all over. I'm probably a little tired too. Have you talked to your dad?" she asked, turning to face him.

"Yeah, actually he texted and asked how you were doing. I don't yet know if I see much of a close relationship between us, but it's nice to have another person to talk with."

"I'm sure it'll come in time," Laura said, nodding and letting her eyes wander back to the screen while she tucked her legs under her.

"How's your mom?"

"I haven't talked to her today. She called when I was out, but I'll call her back tomorrow. It wasn't pressing, because she always calls twice if it is. She's actually moving back here soon."

"That's great!" Carter wanted to push for more details, and figured now that she had rested, tonight would be the night to swoop in, but Laura was still preoccupied with whatever she'd discussed with Megan. She had to work tomorrow, so getting some more good rest was more important for her to get back into the routine.

He was about to open his mouth when she spoke.

"Megan offered to watch Holden later this week."

"Really?"

"Yeah, he adores her and she's stepped in before. She's an EMT, so if anything were to happen, she's prepared, but just thought I'd mention it." Her brown eyes met his and bored into them. She was wearing her blue robe, which made her skin look like porcelain in the dim light of the bedroom. Her dark hair was piled up on top of her head and she looked like a Grecian, like a goddess.

"What day?"

"Sunday."

That was three days away, which would give him plenty of time.

Carter smiled in the dim light and leaned closer to her. "Are you asking me out on a date?"

Laura shifted her head a little higher as a small smile touched her lips. "Just thought it was information you should know."

"Did you accept?"

"I said I would let her know."

Perfect. "Text her now and"—he leaned over and closed the gap between them, pressing a soft kiss to her lips—"consider it a date."

CHAPTER 36

Three days later, Laura eyed her closet with disdain. She had nothing to wear, hated everything she owned, needed to lose fifteen pounds, was starving, and already in a bad mood.

She hadn't been on a date in years, and the last few she'd gone on hadn't been great— they'd been disasters.

Over the past few days, Laura had talked with her mom, with Megan, and with Ash, all of whom had agreed that this was *the* date.

Not only had the truth come out that her feelings for Carter had never gone away, but everyone had been quick to point out how great he was with Holden, not to mention the little fact that his net worth had almost twice as many zeros as the mileage on her car.

Laura had tried to tell them Carter didn't act like that around her. He had been nothing but a nice, average guy, who hung out in a T-shirt and shorts and made sounds like Donald Duck while eating leftover takeout. That point hadn't stopped her friends from making a big deal about his billion-aire status, which of course made her freak out in front of her closet. The last time she'd done this, the stakes hadn't seemed all that high. She had thrown on some clothes, run a brush through her hair, swiped on mascara, and hadn't thought twice about it.

Now though, Laura wanted this to work. She didn't like herself for it, but she *needed* to look good tonight. She didn't want to be one of those women standing in front of her closet, but here she was, with her discarded clothes piled around her in heaps.

Up until now, she had been so focused on Holden and herself that Carter, while nice, had remained in the background. Tonight, however, thanks to Megan, it would be just him and her. Alone.

All of the talk of Carter being a billionaire who had dated his fair share of models—models for God's sake—had put her on edge. She wasn't proud of it, but she had finally looked him up on the Internet and subjected herself to pages of pictures of him looking fine in a tux with some twig in glitter on his arm. Of course that meant she was up half the night, looking up all of the twigs in glitter, only to find that they were lingerie models and actresses who had appeared on the covers of magazines.

Perfect, just frigging perfect. He was used to a tanned body, women who worked out and put effort into their looks, and she hadn't even been clothes shopping since she was buying maternity wear. All of her insecurities from high school were just begging to jump back into her mind. It was the captain of the cheerleading squad at prom all over again.

Being a ponytail girl who had grown into a ponytail woman meant she settled on brushing her hair and hoping for the best. A quick smear of her only lipstick and a few dabs of concealer did most of the heavy lifting, but a couple of quick swipes of mascara jumpstarted her confidence.

Laura stood back to admire herself. She didn't look half

bad. Who was she kidding? She wasn't a model or actress and no agent was calling her, but she didn't have any gray, and thanks to her mom's insistence, her sunscreen habit as a kid meant her skin looked alright too. She wasn't the most striking knockout, but for a mom of an awesome little boy and a woman who had saved more lives than she could count, Laura thought she looked alright.

The doorbell announced Megan's arrival. Laura pulled on her heels and grabbed her purse. She didn't have an evening bag, but she at least had a black bag.

Holden's little feet pounded toward the door, the hollow sound echoing off of the hardwood floors and up to the second floor. From where she was coming down the stairs, Laura saw Megan open the unlocked door just in time for Holden to launch himself at her knees like a tiny linebacker with a personal space problem.

"Hey, buddy! Ready to have fun tonight?"

"Yeah, yeah! I have puzzles!"

"Oooh, that's fun! I love puzzles, but I have a surprise for you too."

Holden bounced up and down on his feet. "A prize?" he asked with reverence in his voice as he mispronounced the word like always. "What is it?"

Megan slid her hand in her bag for dramatic effect. Her red hair was coiled up on her head, and she looked perfectly comfortable in an old hoodie and some loose jeans.

"I...brought...PAINT!" She yanked out a watercolor palette and a new coloring book.

Holden exploded with joy. "Thank you! Thank you! Let's do it now! In the kitchen, come on!"

"Hey, Laura, you look awesome!" Megan said as Laura came down.

"Thanks. The dress would've looked better fifteen pounds ago."

Megan waved her hand, while Holden came back to grab her leg, trying to tug her in the direction of crafts.

"Not so fast, buddy. We have to be gentle because of your head, remember? I'm coming, hang on. I need to talk to your mom. Go take the coloring book and pick out a page."

Already rifling through the book, Holden made his way back to the kitchen.

"Thanks again for watching him. I'm still not entirely sure about this. I have the doctor's numbers on the kitchen counter, and you can text me if anything gets weird."

"Not Bray's number, right?"

"God, no. The neurologist gave me her cell."

Megan nodded and plugged it into her phone right then and there, which made Laura feel slightly better.

"Ash is going to stop by later for pizza too, since she's off. Said she would take the night shift if you guys want to make it an overnight."

"Yeah, she texted me. You guys are the best, but I don't know about an overnight."

A door closed upstairs and Carter came down, fixing his cufflink. He was freshly shaved and in a dark sport coat over a crisp white shirt and dark jeans that he had folded up on one leg to fit his new cast, which had been adjusted so he could bear some weight on his leg. He still needed the crutches handy but was stubborn enough to go without them for short distances.

His eyes met hers and did a quick glance down her dress, which sent a shiver of anticipation over her. The heat in his green eyes told her exactly what he thought of her outfit.

Megan let out a breath and said, "I'd go for the overnight."

Laura shook her head. "Uh-huh. Not going to happen. You're lucky I'm wearing the good bra."

Megan shrugged.

"Getting faster on the stairs every day. Hi, Megan," Carter said when he reached them. "Thanks for watching Holden. Tell Ash we really appreciate her staying the night."

"Of course—"

"Wait, you know about that?" Laura said, staring at Carter.

He smiled and nodded. "Yeah, Megan texted me last night, and I thought it was a great idea."

"Uh-huh," Megan said with a grin.

Laura slowly turned to face her guilty, traitorous friend, who smiled sweetly and batted her eyelashes.

"Well, I'm off to do watercolors! Have fun, you two!" Megan walked behind Carter and spun around to wiggle her eyebrows behind his back before flashing two thumbs-up.

"How is it I get no say in this?"

Carter grinned at her. "They're just trying to help." He gave her another appreciative glance and cocked his head to one side. "Hey, gorgeous." His voice was low and simmering.

"Stop trying to distract me. I haven't packed anything. I didn't think we were doing that."

"Don't worry about it. I got you covered."

That's what he thought. There was packing and then there was packing for an *overnight* getaway with a man she had been in love with for most of her life, whose ex-girl-friends just happened to all be models. She tried to remember how many undies matched her one good bra and if they were clean. Maybe she could duck upstairs—

"You okay? You look a little nervous."

"What if I just run upstairs and grab some stuff?"

He shook his head and smiled at her. "Nope. Not necessary."

Laura tried to look calm and relaxed. Sure, no big deal. At least she had shaved and thrown a stick of deodorant in her purse to get her through wherever they were going. Still, she had doubts.

"Okaaaaaaay. Let me just give Holden a quick kiss goodbye."

"Sure, the car's already here, but take your time."

Laura ducked back into the kitchen, shooting daggers at Megan. "You are going pay for this," she hissed before planting a kiss on her son's cheek. He was focused on his creation with the intensity of a Dutch Master. "Bye, sweetie. Be good."

Megan leaned forward in her chair. "You need this. And you are going to be thanking me for a long time. Ask him if he has any single friends."

The joke took her by surprise and broke the tension. Laura let out a bark of laughter while Megan giggled.

"Seriously? *You* ask me this *now*?" Laura asked, incredulous.

Megan gave a little shrug, a tinge of pink hitting her pale cheeks. "Yeah, well, maybe I can work up to the idea of dating his friend if they're like him."

"I bet he does have friends like him, and I'm going to tell them you snort through your nose when you laugh."

Megan made a face. "Don't be ugly. And that's not entirely true."

"First impressions are tough."

Megan rolled her eyes. "I bet you'll be in a better mood tomorrow," she added with a sly grin.

Laura didn't have a response so she rolled her eyes and planted another kiss on Holden's cheek before walking away, hearing Megan laugh behind her.

Megan was right, but Laura didn't have to like it. Besides, it was easier to be mad at her than to be nervous about the date, which was childish, but hey, it had been a while and they were close enough that Megan could handle the abuse.

"Ready to go?" Carter said when she reached the foyer. He held the door for her and looked every bit as handsome as Megan had made him out to be. He had been one of the best-looking guys in their class at school, but now he was older, more accomplished, and all of that lean youth had grown into toned muscle with maturity, which was far more attractive.

"Yeah, I think so, but you still haven't told me where we're going. I thought it was just dinner."

"I have ideas. I've had a lot of time to think about them, which I'm not used to."

They walked outside to where a sleek black luxury sedan sat idling. A man hopped out and held open the back, passenger door. "Your chariot, miss."

Laura thanked him and sat down on the supple, cool leather. Soft jazz music was playing, and the cup holders had glass bottles of sparkling water that were icy to the touch. There was a magazine in the back seat pocket in front of her and a few of the expensive snack bars Megan was always raving about.

The thump of the trunk was followed by Carter angling himself inside, without his crutches, which he must have stowed away. Clearly, the driver was in the know because once he shut Carter's door and climbed back in, he drove away from the house without a single word.

Laura looked in the rearview, trying to settle herself.

"He'll be fine," Carter said, taking her hand in his.

"I know, I know. I trust Megan with my life, but it's just hard. I'm out of practice, I guess."

Carter's green eyes met hers with a warmth and kind understanding. "You've never left him?"

"Well, there's daycare, of course, and I have to go to the doctor and run errands. Mom could take him up until her stroke, but I only leave him for work and I hate it then too." Her voice trailed off. She wasn't sure what to say.

"Sounds like this is the first time you haven't *had* to leave him."

"Yeah, I guess that's it. This is my first fun trip, I guess. God, that makes me sound terrible."

He squeezed her hand until she met his eyes again. "No, it doesn't. It makes you sound like a good mom who puts your kid above yourself. It also means you're a woman who knows how to save her money."

"Yeah, I'm always thinking about what I don't need so I can put it in his account. I know I should be better about it, but it's hard to get out of that habit."

"I know, but you've earned it, so no mom guilt, okay?"

Saying it was one thing. "I'll try, but I'm new to this, so go easy on me."

He pulled one corner of his perfect lips up into his cheek. "You sure that's what you want?"

And *that* made her almost break out in a sweat. "I don't know."

"Well, we'll have plenty of time to figure it out."

"Where are we going?"

"You don't like surprises?"

"I'm not used to surprises."

"We'll have to change that."

"Uh-huh. So do I get to know?"

He smiled. "Well, this is a date, so I figured we would start with dinner."

CHAPTER 37

Dinner had been exceptional and educational. Carter had arranged for them to go to the nicest place in town, which was a Japanese steak house with hibachi. Everything from the wine pairing to the dessert was beyond expectation. As opposed to her usual fried rice, Carter had apparently called in ahead of time and arranged for something called Kobe Beef, which she hadn't heard of until tonight.

That had led to them talking, actually talking, without being interrupted by a loving and adorable four-year-old every other sentence. She had found out more about his personal life. He had gone to Stanford, launched a start-up with a few guys in his fraternity, and proceeded to live off ramen noodles for months before hitting it big and going public. He loved to travel, but had spent more time doing adventure tourism, which meant mountain climbing in Canada, hiking in Patagonia, and joining in on a trans-Pacific sailing excursion with a bunch of friends who had sold everything to buy a boat.

The conversation had been intriguing and funny, and

Carter had taken special care to avoid making her feel any less than because she hadn't checked anything off her list, which seemed mundane compared to his. It had taken some convincing on his part, but Laura shared her dreams of going to New York to see a Broadway show, to Hawaii, and to Washington, DC. It was surreal to watch the man nod as if making a mental list of where and when. Nothing seemed to faze him, which is why she brought out her big dream at the end of the meal when they had been wrapping up dessert.

"I know you're going to say this is me just being a mom, but I can't help it. My number one thing is to take Holden to Disney World and make it the best trip possible."

They talked about that for a while. Carter apparently had studied Walt Disney from an entrepreneurial standpoint and had read his memoirs but had never visited the parks.

"See? Our lists have something in common," he'd said when they were wrapping up at the restaurant.

"Yeah, but I'm not sure it's quite as exciting as Victoria Falls or Everest."

He had paid without even checking the bill. She had thanked him and even gave him a kiss before they walked to the car, which proved that with the right time and circumstances, she could be bold. Maybe the overnight wasn't a bad idea after all.

"I'm going to be dreaming about that steak for a long time," Laura said when she slid back into the back seat of the sedan.

Carter took her hand in his in the dark and gave it another squeeze. "You can have it as often as you'd like."

"I'm not used to that."

"I know." She couldn't see the details of his face in the dim light but could tell he was smiling. "And that's why it's going to be so much more fun spoiling you."

"No, you don't need to do that. I wouldn't know what to do in a fancy restaurant. What fork to use."

"You know, I don't either, but I've learned when I'm paying the bill, no one seems to judge me."

Laura laughed and leaned into him. Carter put his arm around her, which sent a thrill down her spine that warmed her chest. All of it reminded her of when they were kids. The dark car, the nervousness, and even the road.

"I'm getting some déjà vu."

"Me too," he agreed.

"I bet you don't think about high school that much with your job and everything."

"Nah, not too much. Sometimes people will pop up online, and every now and then I catch an old picture or hear a song that'll bring back a lot of memories."

"I know what you mean. Well, it's easier for me, being in town," Laura said, starting to relax even more. It was kind of nice having a driver. Before, she hadn't seen the appeal, but now she could lean into him. Hell, they could get all tangled up and still make it to their destination. She slid her hand up his leg and rested it on his chest. She shifted and pressed into him, leaning up to face him and find his mouth with hers.

The wine had helped, and knowing everyone else was safe and secure was a bonus too. Megan was right, of course —she hadn't had any fun in a long time. They were both adults. They could make up the rules as they wanted.

"Hey now," Carter said, his voice like a low purr. "We have a few more stops planned, but I'm tempted to just have him drive around in circles."

Laura kissed him again and pulled back. "Depends on what the other stops are."

"Funny you say that because we're here."

Laura looked outside, knowing full well where they were, but not exactly why.

"Allow me to get your door."

Carter stepped out of the car and used his crutches to get around and opened the door to their old high school a moment later. Why were the lights on?

"What are we doing?"

"I think you know."

They walked into the building that should've been dark. The familiarity of the walls and hallway were a testament to how some things didn't change. Laura and Carter had changed since being kids, but to walk inside the hallway tonight made her feel like she was late for math class. The speckled floor and fluorescent lighting hadn't changed a bit.

"How did you get in here? It's empty."

"It wasn't hard," Carter said, using his crutches to go down the hall toward the gym where she could hear bass from dance music she recognized from high school echoing through the hall. They walked toward the doors, which were closed, and opened them up, revealing not a gym, but a full, honest-to-God prom.

The fluorescent lights were off and replaced with strategic lighting and draped fabric hanging artfully from the ceiling like the kind she'd seen at expensive weddings on TV. All of the bleachers had been covered by the same sweeping fabric, illuminated in the school colors of blue and silver from lights on the floor. There was a DJ off to one side and two other people in uniform standing by with bottles of water like in the car.

She remembered their own prom, and while the decorations were pretty and had been placed by well-meaning volunteers and underpaid teachers, they had looked nothing like this.

"It's gorgeous," she said under her breath as they walked onto what would've been center court but sat underneath a temporary dance floor that had been installed. As they reached the center of the large, open room they stopped, and the music changed. Oh God, a slow dance, and not just any slow dance, but *the* song to dance to back in high school.

An awkward, nervous laugh bubbled up from her chest.

"I don't know if you're thoughtful or corny."

"Little of both." He smiled at her, making her stomach flip-flop right up into her throat. "Laura, how about a dance?" In the lighting, Carter looked more handsome than she had remembered. Being alone with him on the dance floor, with three people watching, brought back all of the insecurities she had carried with her through high school and then through her divorce. She tried to tell herself that she was a different woman now, one who didn't need the approval of the in-crowd, but she was still nervous. She took a deep breath and drew in some strength. It was funny how deep those insecurities ran. It was just her and Carter. That's all that mattered.

"I'd love to, but um…" She looked down at his crutches. As if on some invisible cue, the two uniformed servers came forward and took his crutches from him. Laura had no choice but to take his hands to help stabilize him. The cast on his leg could handle a lot of weight, and the healer in Laura took up his hands and tried to get him to let her bear some of his weight, but he resisted.

"Trying to heal me again?" he said when the two men were out of earshot as he started to dance with a coy smile.

"Not really," she said, looking over his shoulder so she wouldn't meet his eyes.

"You thought about it, didn't you? Didn't you?" he said, jiggling her hand until she looked at him.

Laura laughed. "Maybe a little."

"For the record, I think it's sexy as hell that you have a superpower."

"Pfft. I've never thought of it like that. I was always so scared someone would find out."

"I understand that, but it's cool. You're a super heroine, just like Catwoman."

"Wasn't she bad and also crazy? Are you calling me crazy?"

"No, but she was sexy as hell and you should take that as a compliment."

They danced a few more songs, and with each step, Laura felt her body relax. Even with his cast, Carter was a great dancer. It wasn't like they did anything fancy. There was no one to impress, so they just let their bodies move to the music while they chatted and laughed together.

The music brought back memory after memory, transporting her back to high school, reminding her of all of the sweet and gentle times she had in the beginning with Carter. One bad memory had blocked them out for a long time, but once she was able to look past it, the feeling of young love came back in full force.

They danced for a few more songs, all of them greatest hits from fifteen years ago. They sang the songs and laughed and shuffled around half-court, holding each other up.

"Carter...this has been—" She couldn't finish. Tears welled in her eyes, stopping her from going on. It was all too perfect. Surely something would happen and she'd wake up.

Carter ran a thumb under her eye, swiping away a single tear. "Hey, we're not done yet."

"What else can we do? This has been amazing."

Carter smiled and waved one hand to the men standing off to the side. On cue they brought the crutches forward, along with chilled water, and escorted them toward the back doors instead of the front.

"Isn't the car back that way?" Laura asked, threading her

arm through his when they reached the doors leading out to the football field.

"Yep."

"But?"

"Nope. Madam, your chariot awaits."

The two men opened the doors to reveal a black helicopter.

Laura's palms got sweaty. She had never been in one, and with every step, she was further out of her comfort zone than she ever had imagined she would be. She held on tighter to Carter and tried not to worry, overthink, or steal back control. She drew in a breath as the men opened the door and helped her and Carter get inside. The pilots fired up the engines, while Carter reached over in the dark cabin and fit the biggest set of headphones she had seen in her life on her head.

"Where are we going?" she asked, straining to make herself heard over the blades above them.

Carter's voice came through her headset like he was on a phone in a tornado, which wasn't untrue. "Not far. Have you been in one before?"

Her voice betrayed her fear. "No," she answered, a full octave higher than she had intended.

"Hang on, takeoff is the weirdest part."

She grabbed ahold of his hand and clung for dear life. With a gentle whoosh, they were up, leaving part of Laura's stomach behind at the old high school.

"It'll be dark, so we'll have a great view of the stars."

Carter was right, and about ten minutes later, Laura still hadn't released her death grip on his arm, but she'd relaxed just enough to enjoy herself while pointing out the constellations.

They touched down about twenty minutes later in a well-lit clearing near a lake halfway up what looked like a mountain or ridge. Laura's breath left her body, and while she refrained from kissing the ground, she sent a silent prayer of thanks up to the heavens that they were back on terra firma and she had worn black, which wouldn't show any panic sweating.

Behind them stood a gorgeous work of wood and glass. It was a mountain home that looked more like it belonged in the Swiss alps. The lighting beamed out from inside, showing a sumptuous interior decorated in warm woods and rich leathers. The stone path in front of them was lit along with the landscape around them, reflecting off what certainly was a remarkable garden. A trickle of water from a fountain she couldn't see mingled with the sounds of the creatures in the night under the Montana sky, speckled with stars.

"I wanted somewhere private where we could be alone."

Laura walked inside when Carter held open the door for her, trying to keep her jaw attached to her face. It was stunning. The rich textures, soft lighting, and delicate music all painted a homey and elegant picture that just begged even the most uptight person to relax. "Do you own this place?"

"Not yet. Would you like to?"

"Ummm, yeah," she answered before thinking. "Wait, you're joking, right?"

"Not at all." Carter grinned and headed toward the wall of windows at one side of the house. The view would be incredible in the morning, but right now, it was too dark to see anything. "Let's step outside before we turn in, shall we?"

Laura followed him out onto the deck and immediately looked up. Carter touched a pad on the wall, and the house behind them plunged into darkness. When Laura glanced up again, a starlight masterpiece was in the night sky.

"Oh my God."

"I know."

"Carter, this is breathtaking."

"So are you."

She met his eyes then. The moon was almost full, giving her enough light to make out his jaw and lopsided sexy smile.

"Do you remember when we used to look at the stars?"

Laura let her face turn toward the sky above them again, to drink in the sight of the constellations twinkling above her. "I do."

"I'm hoping you'll say that again."

"That we can look at the stars?"

"No."

Laura frowned and turned to study him just in time to see him reach into his pocket and get down on one knee.

CHAPTER 38

EIGHT MONTHS LATER

Laura walked into the Magic Kingdom holding Holden's hand in her own. Carter walked alongside them pushing the stroller carrying all of Holden's many things, stopping to crouch down and point out the statue of Walt Disney holding Mickey Mouse's hand to a stunned version of Holden, his eyes wide and searching everywhere.

"Mama! Loooooook!"

"I know!"

He let go of her hand and ran up to the statue with his little chubby legs marching with a sense of urgency, setting off the new light-up shoes Laura had picked out for him before they had left.

They had flown into Orlando last night. It had been Laura's first time in first class and Holden's first trip on a plane. Not only had Carter arranged for them to have private transportation to the airport, but when they had arrived at the airport, he had also asked the gate agent for wings for Holden and surprised them both when, after the welcome aboard message, the flight attendant announced to everyone it was a special little boy's first flight on his way to Disney. The whole plane had applauded while Holden sucked on a finger with a shy look and clutched Mickey for emotional support.

Everything had been exceptional. Carter had gotten off with a fine from the judge and was released from the travel restrictions. At first, he had offered to charter a flight, but Laura couldn't go that far. She had only convinced him to fly commercial because it was Holden's first flight, and he would be disappointed if they didn't see the X-ray machines after reading about them in board books about planes.

Carter had relented, with the trade-off being that they were staying in one of the most sumptuous suites she had ever seen. He had tried to press her for a final opinion on which of the seemingly countless resorts she wanted to stay at, but she refused to give an opinion, maintaining that anything was more than fine.

When Carter had first asked her about the idea of a honeymoon, Laura had been worried about leaving Holden. The only person she would consider leaving him with for that long was her mom, who, while making great progress, still had a long way to go and couldn't lift Holden yet. That's when Carter had mentioned he had always intended to bring Holden to Disney.

It was a dream come true. He had gotten a suite at the top of Animal Kingdom Lodge so Holden could have his own room, giving them some privacy, but also so Holden could watch all the animals from the balcony. Already the giraffes were a hit.

That morning he had promised them a special surprise, which was probably one of those meals with a stellar break-fast buffet and characters, which meant Holden was going to try to drown himself in syrup and lose his mind when a big fluffy character came around the bend. At least he would sleep well tonight.

"Oh my gosh! Mama! Look at that castle!"

"I know! That's Cinderella's castle," she said, trying to snap a picture of his face frozen in awe.

Holden turned up to face her in his Mickey hat with two big ears. The bill did nothing to shield his upturned face from the blazing morning sun. "Does Cinderella wear the blue dress?"

"Yep. She sure does."

"Does she live in there with the prince?"

"You remember! You have the best memory." Laura looked down at Holden and tickled his neck to make him smile, before he wriggled away and scrunched his face up even more. Carter caught her eyes and winked, holding his phone to catch the encounter on video.

"If the castle is that big, how big is the potty?"

Laura tried to stifle a giggle, while Carter had to bite his lower lip, still filming.

"I think they just have normal-sized potties."

Holden stopped and looked indignant as if Laura had just told him the grocery store was all out of Goldfish crackers.

"Cinderella can't have a normal potty, Mama! Her booty is too big."

Laura failed to hide her smile but quickly schooled her features. "Holden, that's not very nice to say. Where did you hear that?"

His head cocked to one side and he gave her his new I'm-just-pointing-out-the-obvious look. "Mama, that's why her dress is sooooo big," he said, and then added with a shrug, "so you know she needs a biiiiiiiig potty."

Laura and Carter broke out into laughter as they followed two steps behind Holden toward the castle. Carter slipped his hand into hers, snuck in a kiss, and fell in step, matching her pace.

"You look like you're thinking," he said.

"Is that bad?"

A trolley rolled up with an old-time barbershop quartet that started singing and dancing, leaving Holden fully enraptured and rooted to the spot.

Carter gave her that lopsided grin. "Never. I love watching you think. Penny for your thoughts?"

Laura blinked and turned to him. Before him, everything had been about survival. When John had left, she had fallen into the belief she could never rely on someone else again. Carter had crashed into her heart and shown her true love and support.

Not only had he moved his company back to Goldvein to help support the town and make sure she could stay near her mom and friends, but Carter had also encouraged her to enroll in a few classes next semester in full support of her dream to become a doctor. Everything with him had been perfect, right down to his newly mastered breakfast skills.

Laura smiled and kissed him back. "I'm just so happy."

"Is that just because we're in the happiest place on Earth?" he asked, wrapping his arm around her.

She loved the feel of his arm around her, cradling her close. "I think there's something else to it."

"Oh?" Carter glanced down at her and raised one perfect eyebrow above his shades that cost more than everything in her old closet. Being married to a billionaire had been an adjustment for sure, but she would've gladly fallen back into his arms even he if hadn't had a dime.

Laura looked up at him, feeling the love rain down like the Florida sunshine. "I guess dreams really do come true."

"Are we going to start talking in Disney quotes now, like we did on the plane?"

"Yes."

"Okay, I'll go first. I love you."

Laura laughed. "Cheap shot. That's in every movie. I love you more."

Carter pressed his lips to hers while Holden orbited around them, giggling, hugging their legs around the knees.

Carter pulled back from the kiss, just enough to speak. "I love you most."

Laura smiled again and kissed him one more time before she went in for the win with the quote she had been thinking of the whole way here.

"And they lived happily ever after."

CHAPTER 39

Ash sat and poured herself another cup of tea at her desk in the bullpen. Other cops liked coffee, and maybe she had been hanging around with Megan too long, but Ash liked taking care of her body.

A sergeant on the force, she had been a cop for almost ten years and could almost taste her next promotion to lieutenant. A lot of cops looked down on the patrol division, and Ash had considered moving over toward investigations, but she liked interacting with the people and seeing her two best friends, Megan and Laura, when she reported to crashes. From the moment she had met them, she knew they were something special.

Ash knew a lot of things. She always had.

Ever since she was a little girl, she had known when someone was lying. It wasn't that she had a feeling, rather she *knew*. She could smell it on them. No one else ever seemed to notice the change in the air, but she could almost taste it in her mind, it was so clear to her. It was like a change in aura if someone believed that sort of thing.

The first time she knew someone was lying was in

kindergarten, when some kid stole another's stuffed bunny. Ash tried to tell the teacher, but no one believed her until she said she needed to pee during recess, only to sneak back in and find the cuddly friend in the liar's desk, tucked behind his notebooks.

Giving the kid's bunny back to her friend and seeing the other student scolded was the first moment she felt the true power of justice. When a police officer had visited her school and held an assembly about catching bad guys, Ash knew exactly what she needed to do. Nothing had ever changed.

Well, until her mom started lying and her aura changed.

Ash shook off the memory and flicked her hair out of her face. She liked her hair short, except for the front where she parted it to sweep just across her eyes. She took a sip of her green tea and felt the warmth curl down through her ribs. In the summer, she made a point to brew tea and bring it in cold, but there was something about a hot drink in the afternoon slog of paperwork.

The door opened and Megan walked in, waving to the familiar faces who recognized her from calls and crashes they had all run together.

"Hey, ready for taco Tuesday?" Megan said, plopping into the chair next to Ash's desk.

"Yeah, I'm just checking this one thing."

"You just poured yourself a cup of tea. Is this matcha?"

Ash shook her head. "Nah, simple, and don't worry, I can take it with me. How's your afternoon look?"

"Eh, not too bad. Really, I'm done for today. Tomorrow, though, I'm heading to a ranch to approve a dry hydrant location request. You know the one where all the fires have popped up recently?"

"Yeah, it looked like arson. Did they ever confirm that?"

Megan shifted in the chair and shook her head. "No

cameras or anything like that. But those fires didn't start themselves, even if it was during a lightning storm."

Ash raised an eyebrow. "Oh yeah?"

"Yeah, we could tell. Something's going on, but we don't know for sure what. Either way, the new property owner wants a dry hydrant installed, in case it happens again. There's no water out there, but he has lakes and wants to protect the land."

"Seems like a good idea."

"Yeah. I'd love to live in the country someday." Megan stretched out her long, thin legs in her dark blue work pants that somehow were flattering on her. Even though the clunky black boots did nothing for anyone, somehow Megan managed to look approachable and feminine.

Ash pulled half a smile at her friend. "You would probably learn shit like how to garden and bake."

"Yeah, I'd love that," Megan said with a small, dreamy smile as if she was picturing herself there. She must have been staring off into space, because no one smiled like that while looking at the beat-up, stained carpet.

When she had met Laura and Megan, Ash had gotten a new scent or feeling—she never knew what to call it—but something about them drew her to them. From the outside looking in, they were all female and the same age, so it might be obvious that they would be friends, but it went deeper. Each were good at their jobs and didn't always fit in with the guys. There was an understanding, and then that feeling Ash got whenever she was around them, that had matured into the deepest form of friendship, moving more into sisterhood years ago.

Which was precisely why Ash had set up the search on Laura's missing husband. She hadn't been asked, but when you hurt her sister, you hurt her, and Ash didn't like being ghosted. When she thought of Holden being ghosted by his shit-for-brains bio dad, her blood boiled. It wasn't that Laura wanted him back. After all, she was in Disney with her new, super-hot husband, who, despite his DUI, Ash had known from the very first meeting was good people. Regarding Laura's ex, God knew it was a blessing when the garbage took itself out, but Ash had always had a funny feeling about it. She had to trust her feelings and firmly believed in knowing where your enemies were at all times. No body? No finale.

Megan pulled her hair up into a messy bun and then let it all fall while her hands dropped on her thighs with a slap. "Alright, come on. I'm starving."

Ash knew Megan was telling the truth just from her ability. "Yeah, okay. I'm ready. Are you driving or me?"

"Let's both go so I can leave from there. I've got to get home to feed my cats. Lincoln's on a special diet."

If it would've been anyone else, Ash would've rolled her eyes, but Megan was serious about her animals. "Okay, let me grab one thing off the printer, and I'll meet you outside."

"Sounds good," Megan said, gliding off through the bullpen, completely unaware that every warm-blooded male in the house tracked her fiery red hair out of the room.

Now Ash did roll her eyes and laughed to herself. Megan was so not interested in anyone, preferring to hang with Laura, Ash, or animals. Megan might be as fierce as the fire she fought, even if she doubted herself, but with men, she was a complete marshmallow.

Moving quickly and urging the Xerox on through sheer force of will, Ash waited for what seemed like an eternity of clunking and shifting from the machine as if it were trying to decide whether or not to give her the printout. With great pain and no haste whatsoever, the machine inched out her paper, which she snatched the second it was free so no one else would see.

Walking toward her desk to grab her keys and the now-warm tea in the disposable cup, Ash skimmed the results, feeling her pulse pick up. She hated being right, but it was the blessing and curse she had to bear.

Once again, she knew the truth.

Laura's husband wasn't missing after all.

ACKNOWLEDGMENTS

First, I need to thank my dear friend and writing buddy, Jenn, who writes with me every day, which helped me write the majority of this book in a month. I always look forward to chatting while we work on our projects.

Of course, a huge thank you to my husband, Kevin has supported and invested in me since the beginning. He is always cheering me on and giving me the space to pursue my dreams. I can never appreciate him or my son enough.

Another big thank you to Kate Studer, who took this new book and provided key insight into the series arc. Her comments were invaluable as always, and everything she suggested elevated the work and pushed me to set my sights higher for the character and their journeys.

Once again, Caroline Teagle Johnson created a stunning cover that took numerous edits and changes with the illustration. I am grateful to work with her. She has so much creativity and patience, especially as we revisited so many versions of the characters.

I am deeply grateful to have met Ann Suhz and Ann Riza in New York. Their keen eye for details has elevated this work and polished it to a shine.

Thank you to the Virginia Romance Writers and Ines Johnson for the craft workshops, especially when I was inspired and began drafting this story.

Lastly, thank you to all of the readers who have connected with me about my stories. I appreciate you more than you know.

ABOUT THE AUTHOR

Kathryn K. Murphy writes action-packed, small-town romance novels bursting with emotion.

If you want to know when Kathryn's next book will come out, please visit her website at www.kathrynkmurphy.com, where you can sign up to receive email updates.

www.ingramcontent.com/pod-product-compliance
Lightning Source LLC
Chambersburg PA
CBHW031620100726
47898CB00006B/1875